Mr. Monk
Is Cleaned Out

Mr. Monk Is Cleaned Out

Lee Goldberg

THORNDIKE
CHIVERS

This Large Print edition is published by Thorndike Press, Waterville, Maine, USA and by AudioGo Ltd, Bath, England.
Thorndike Press, a part of Gale, Cengage Learning.

LIBRARY OF CONGRESS CATALOGING-IN-PUBLICATION DATA

Goldberg, Lee, 1962–
   Mr. Monk is cleaned out / by Lee Goldberg.
     p. cm. — (Thorndike Press large print mystery)
   "Based on the USA Network television series created by Andy Breckman."
   ISBN-13: 978-1-4104-3137-0 (hardcover)
   ISBN-10: 1-4104-3137-1 (hardcover)
   1. Monk, Adrian (Fictitious character)—Fiction. 2. Private investigators—Fiction. 3. Eccentrics and eccentricities—Fiction. 4. Psychics—Fiction. 5. Large type books. I. Monk (Television program) II. Title.
PS3557.O3577M778 2010b
813'.54—dc22   2010027398

BRITISH LIBRARY CATALOGUING-IN-PUBLICATION DATA AVAILABLE
Published in 2010 in the U.S. by arrangement with NAL Signet, a member of Penguin Group (USA) Inc.
Published in 2011 in the U.K. by arrangement with Penguin Group (USA) Inc.

U.K. Hardcover: 978 1 408 49321 2 (Chivers Large Print)
U.K. Softcover: 978 1 408 49322 9 (Camden Large Print)

Printed and bound in Great Britain by the MPG Books Group
1 2 3 4 5 6 7 14 13 12 11 10

To Valerie & Madison

ACKNOWLEDGMENTS AND AUTHOR'S NOTE

This book takes place before the events in the final season of the *Monk* television series.

For many years on the TV series, and in all of my books except *Mr. Monk in Trouble,* Monk only drank Sierra Springs bottled water, a brand that really exists. The producers of the show abruptly changed Monk's water to Summit Creek without explanation or any acknowledgment that he ever drank anything else. I have done the same.

I am, as always, indebted to Dr. D. P. Lyle for his assistance on medical and forensic matters, to my friend Andy Breckman for entrusting me with his characters, to Kerry Donovan for her unwavering support and enthusiasm, and, finally, to the mysterious Dave, who gave me the title for this book in a comment on my blog.

I look forward to hearing from you at www .leegoldberg.com.

CHAPTER ONE:
MR. MONK AND THE ECONOMY

Some guys showed up the other day at the house next door, mowed the dead lawn, and spray-painted it green. The banks were doing that to a lot of the foreclosed homes in my neighborhood. I was current with my mortgage payments and my grass wasn't dead, but I was tempted to ask the guys to paint my lawn just so it would look as good from a distance as everybody else's.

The great detective Adrian Monk, my obsessive-compulsive employer, also liked the idea of spray-painting my lawn, but that was because he loves uniformity. It didn't matter to Monk that there was something inherently absurd about painting dead plants and that it might be a symptom of a much bigger problem than dying lawns.

For instance, Monk has an amazing eye for detail, but I'm sure he didn't notice that the gourmet cheese shop on Twenty-fourth Street had closed. The delightfully snooty *maître fromager affineur* told me that his business had plummeted because — with the exception of those individually wrapped, perfectly square slices of processed blandness that Monk liked so much — cheese had become a luxury in a world where people were having trouble affording the necessities.

It was a world that I, as a single mother raising a teenage daughter, had been living in for years. I'd never been able to afford gourmet cheese. But suddenly it seemed like everybody else was joining me. The state of California itself was now just like me — a free-spirited liberal with a mostly sunny disposition teetering on the edge of financial ruin.

But while everybody around me was losing their jobs and their homes, I took guilty comfort in the fact that as long as people kept killing one another, Monk would continue as a consultant to the San Francisco Police Department and I would remain gainfully employed as his assistant.

Monk was oblivious to the suffering, economic or otherwise, of those around him because he was totally preoccupied with his own. For him, suffering was a way of life, a vocation and an art form, something to wallow in with misery and, as odd as this may

10

sound, a certain amount of comfort. Suffering was as familiar and pleasurable to him as happiness is to the rest of us.

Even so, it was my job to ease his suffering as much as possible so that he could function in society and concentrate on solving murders.

It was up to me to make sure that the people around him, and the places he visited, met his incredibly arcane rules of order and cleanliness.

There was nothing scarier to Monk than change. For example, every day he wore the same thing: a brown sports coat over an off-white, one hundred percent cotton shirt buttoned up to the collar. The shirts all had eight buttons, of course. His tailored slacks had eight belt loops around the waist.

Monk aspired to a rigidly structured, symmetrical, and antiseptic life. I did my best to help him achieve that impossible and unappealing goal.

But as hard as Monk tried to exert absolute control over his environment, he still couldn't isolate himself from the global financial crisis, which he discovered for himself early one weekday morning at his neighborhood Safeway supermarket.

We went to replenish his supply of Summit Creek bottled water, the only beverage that he would drink. I'm not exaggerating — that's all he drank. No other liquid ever passed his lips. He even brushed his teeth with it.

So he was very unsettled to discover that there weren't any bottles of Summit Creek on the shelves. The space it usually held was occupied by bottles of Arrowhead and Evian.

He looked at me. "Where's my water?"

"I guess they sold out."

Monk cocked his head from side to side, studying the shelf the way he would a crime scene.

"No, that's not it. They've removed the product tag from the shelf."

"Maybe they aren't stocking it at this store anymore."

"Don't be ridiculous, Natalie. Summit Creek bottled water is a basic human necessity."

"For you, Mr. Monk."

"For all of mankind," he said. "Nobody can live without water."

I motioned to the dozens of other brands of bottled water. "There's plenty of other water for sale here."

"That swill is not water."

"It sure looks like water to me."

"That's exactly what they want you to think."

"They?" I asked. "Who are they?"

"Don't be fooled just because it's clear liquid. It could be anything. It could be spit."

"I don't think so."

"You are so naive," Monk said. "There are labor camps where starving slaves spend their miserable lives filling bottles with spit, which are then sold worldwide as counterfeit water to people like you."

"That doesn't make any sense."

"It's a cruel world," Monk said. "There's no end to the depravity."

"Think about it logically, Mr. Monk. Instead of going to the effort of enslaving people to spit in bottles, wouldn't it be a whole lot easier to just fill the bottles with tap water?"

"Tap water is treated sewage and sewage treatment plants cost hundreds of millions of dollars to build and operate," he said. "Do you really think they have treatment plants there?"

"Where?" I said. "Where is there? Who are they?"

"Grow up, Natalie." He shook his head and started marching down the aisle toward the back of the store.

I hurried after him. "Where are you going?"

"To find the manager and demand an explanation."

"Why don't we just try another supermarket?"

"This is my store," he said. "It's taken me years to get it properly organized."

"It has?"

"I come in late at night and arrange everything by product and expiration date. It's a job that's never done, but I enjoy it."

Of course he did. That wasn't a surprise. The revelation is that I knew nothing about this nocturnal pastime. I'd worked for Monk for years and yet there were still things I didn't know about him. It seemed that he had a secret life, one even duller and sadder than the one he lived in the open.

"They really let you do that?" I asked.

"I also scrub the scuff marks off the linoleum," Monk said. "Shopping carts are brutal on flooring when operated recklessly. People should be much more careful."

Now it made sense why the store employees let him rearrange the merchandise. It was a small price to pay for free cleaning services. They could spend their nights on permanent break.

We found the manager, a portly fellow in a red apron, stacking a display of cereal boxes at the end of one of the aisles. His name tag read *Arthur Upton.*

"Arthur," Monk said. "We need to talk."

The manager turned around with a weary sigh. "I've told you before, Mr. Monk, we aren't going to stop selling chewing gum just because some people spit it out on the street."

"What have you done with the Summit Creek bottled water?"

Arthur winced. "I thought you knew. We don't carry it anymore."

"You have to," Monk said.

"Nobody carries it anymore."

Monk shook his head and waved his hands in front of him, as if to dismiss the whole thing. "No, no, no, that's not allowed. You have to sell it."

"Summit Creek has gone out of business," Arthur said.

Monk kept shaking his head and waving his hands in frantic denial. "That's impossible. Unthinkable."

"Summit Creek borrowed millions of dollars to acquire an energy drink company a couple of years ago," he said. "The energy drink line bombed, driving Summit Creek even deeper into debt. They put the company up for sale, but nobody was interested in buying it. So they had to shut down."

"The government didn't step in to save them?" Monk asked.

"It's bottled water," Arthur said.

"It's the essence of life," Monk said.

"There's other bottled water. Hell, you could just turn on the tap and drink from there."

That remark was so offensive to Monk that it actually stopped his head shaking and hand waving. He looked Arthur in the eye.

"I would rather drink my own sweat but that won't be possible," Monk said, "because I will be dying of dehydration."

"Have juice," Arthur said. "Or milk."

"Milk? Do you know where milk comes from?"

"Cows," Arthur said.

"And you're honestly suggesting I should drink *that?*"

"Why not?"

"It's another animal's bodily fluids, Arthur. Maybe I should lap up some cow pee while I'm at it, too. Or some dog drool. How about a cool, delicious glass of pig mucus? Mmm, that sounds good."

"Milk is perfectly healthy," Arthur said.

"What you're suggesting is disgusting, unsanitary, perverted, and sick!"

"Okay, have a Coke. Or a Gatorade," Arthur said. "I really don't care."

"How can you deprive people of drinking water, tell them to drink bodily fluids, and call yourselves Safeway?" Monk yelled in exasperation. "That isn't the Safeway. That's the Deathway."

I took Monk firmly by the arm. "Let's go."

"Deathway!" he yelled, pointing his finger accusingly at the startled manager. "Deathway!"

I dragged Monk away. "Keep your voice down, Mr. Monk, or they will call the police."

"If they don't, we should, because a heinous crime is being committed here," Monk said, then screamed some more, "Deathway! Deathway!"

I pulled Monk into the relative privacy of the bottled water aisle and turned him around to face me.

"Calm down, Mr. Monk. It's not Safeway's fault that Summit Creek has gone out of business."

"It's a travesty," Monk said. "A crime against humanity."

"Maybe it is but there's nothing you can do about it. It's done. Summit Creek is gone."

He swallowed hard and looked at me as if

he might cry. When he spoke again, his voice was barely above a whisper.

"How will I survive? What am I supposed to drink?"

"I'm sure you can find another brand of bottled water that is every bit as good as Summit Creek."

"What do you know about Summit Creek?"

"It's water," I said. "In a bottle."

"It is much more than that," Monk said. "It is water of unmatched purity that pre-dates the existence of mankind. It is water that fell from the heavens more than twenty thousand years ago and has been sealed in limestone caverns deep below the Uinta Mountains ever since, unsullied, uninfected, and untouched."

"I'm surprised that you'd drink something so old," I said. "Didn't it pass its expiration date a long time ago?"

"There's nothing more pure on this earth than Summit Creek bottled water. It is water as God originally intended it. God's water, Natalie, that's what it is. And you would have me drink *this* instead?"

He waved dismissively at the bottles of water on either side of us.

"You don't have a choice, Mr. Monk."

"I don't accept that," Monk said. "There

18

must still be some Summit Creek on the black market."

"What black market?"

"It's where they sell scarce and illegal goods," Monk said. "We just have to find it."

"I know what a black market is, Mr. Monk. But I didn't know there was one for bottled water."

"There is now," Monk said.

I could see that I would have to employ preventative measures right away if I wanted to stop Monk from having a nervous break-down.

I hustled him out of the supermarket. He probably thought we were heading off in search of the mythical black market in bottled water. But I intended to take him straight to his shrink. Dr. Neven Bell could deal with Monk's problem while I relaxed in the waiting room with a hot tea and the latest issue of the *New Yorker.*

But my ingenious plan went awry the second my cell phone rang and I saw who was calling.

It was Death.

CHAPTER TWO:
MR. MONK AND THE
IMPOSSIBLE MURDER

Okay, maybe that last line was a bit melodramatic, but whenever Captain Leland Stottlemeyer called me, it was usually because he needed me to bring Monk to the scene of a murder.

The captain was careful to only summon Monk on those cases that he knew couldn't be solved quickly or easily, that were unusual in the circumstances of the crime, the complexity of the situation, or the crippling lack of evidence left behind.

But Monk would often show up uninvited at crime scenes and, more often than not, he'd solve the murder right on the spot to everyone's amazement. Stottlemeyer was impressed and grateful but I knew it also pissed him off. Those were cases that he and his detectives would have solved eventually without Monk's help. It wasn't necessary for Monk to show up and make them look like fools (not that Monk realized that was what he was doing).

It explained why Stottlemeyer wanted to use Monk as infrequently as possible. Each time Monk was called it was a tacit admission that there were some mysteries that the police couldn't solve without him. And that was almost worse for the department's image than not closing those cases at all.

But there was a far more compelling, personal reason that the captain didn't like calling him in.

Monk drove him absolutely crazy.

So I knew before we got to the crime scene at the intersection of Van Ness and Sutter that we were going to be faced with a puzzling mystery.

What I didn't know was whether Monk would be able to concentrate on homicide or if he'd only be thinking about where his next drink of water would be coming from.

The southbound lanes of Van Ness were closed off to traffic. The police were redirecting the cars to side streets, which caused a massive traffic jam. That's because Van Ness wasn't just a major boulevard; it was the link through the city between the northern end of the 101 Freeway, which tapered off near the Palace of Fine Arts, and the southern end, which picked up again at Mission and Twelfth streets and went straight down to Los Angeles.

I didn't have a siren or a bubble light for my car, even though I'd lobbied hard for them, so we would have been stuck in traffic with everybody else if I'd driven to the scene. But luckily for us, the Safeway was on Pine Street, just a few blocks north of Van Ness and Sutter, so we left my car there and walked to the crime scene.

The center of attention was a four-door BMW sedan with tinted windows that was parked behind the crosswalk in the lane closest to the grassy median.

The driver's-side door of the BMW was open, the window shattered. Crime scene investigators in white jumpsuits were all over the car, taking pictures and dusting for prints.

An unmarked Ford Crown Victoria sedan from the police fleet was parked right behind the BMW. A U.S. Mail truck and a Toyota Prius were in the next lane and were also being closely examined by the CSIs.

Captain Stottlemeyer leaned against the driver's-side door of the Crown Vic, his arms crossed over his chest, irritably chewing on a toothpick and glowering at everything and everyone, including Lieutenant Randy Disher, who was talking to some people on the sidewalk and taking notes with his usual eager intensity.

The captain saw us just as Monk spotted the BevMo liquor store on the corner. Monk abruptly turned and went into the store, surprising me and Stottlemeyer, who tossed his toothpick into the street and started marching angrily our way.

I hurried into the store after Monk, who was approaching the young woman behind the register.

"Do you carry Summit Creek bottled water?" he asked.

"I'm sorry, sir. We don't," she said with a big smile. "I'm afraid they're no longer in business."

"Of course you're afraid — any rational person would be. So how come you're smiling?"

"Because it's a pleasure to serve you."

"But you haven't," Monk said. "And now we're going to die."

Her eyes widened and her smile faltered. "Die?"

"He means from your kindness," I said to her and her smile perked back up. I grabbed Monk by the arm and yanked him out the door. "Harassing cashiers isn't going to change anything. You're just making things worse."

"They can't get any worse. Didn't anyone

see this coming? Didn't anyone realize the severity of the situation?"

"I know that Summit Creek was your favorite, and it's a shame that it's gone, but it's not like there's no more drinking water left on Earth."

"That's exactly what it's like," Monk said. "Open your eyes, woman. The apocalypse is nigh."

"Nigh?" I said. "Are we suddenly living in the Middle Ages?"

"Now you're beginning to understand the gravity of the situation."

Stottlemeyer walked up to us. "Is there something in that liquor store I should know about?"

"They don't carry Summit Creek bottled water," Monk said. "Nobody does. You have to do something."

"As serious as that is," Stottlemeyer said, "I think a murder takes priority."

"It is a murder," Monk said.

"Whose?" the captain asked.

"Mine," Monk said.

"Since you're still breathing, let's investigate this murder first," Stottlemeyer said. "We'll get to yours next."

"What does it matter?" Monk said. "We're all going to die anyway."

"That's the spirit," Stottlemeyer said.

"Look at the bright side."

The captain wasn't being sarcastic. For Monk, that was as bright as things got.

"What happened here?" I asked the captain.

"I have no idea and it happened right in front of me."

The captain started walking back toward his car and we followed, though I still had to drag Monk along to get him to move.

"I don't understand," I said. "You witnessed the murder?"

"We did and we didn't," he said. "Mike Clasker, the former CFO of Big Country Mortgage, was on his way to testify in court and Randy and I were following as his escort. He insisted on driving himself because he was afraid that if he arrived in a police car, or accompanied by cops, that he'd be seen as a criminal."

"Because he is one," I said.

"Clasker was given immunity in return for testifying against his boss," Stottlemeyer said.

"That doesn't make Clasker any less guilty," I said. "It just means he's getting away with it."

"Getting away with what?" Monk asked.

We both looked at him.

"Don't you read the newspaper or watch

25

the news?" Stottlemeyer asked.

Monk shook his head. "It's too scary and depressing. I'm already scared and depressed. I don't need more reasons to feel that way."

"But you are aware of the subprime loan debacle, the collapse of the U.S. housing market, and the resulting global economic crisis," Stottlemeyer said.

"No," Monk said.

"How can you not know about those events?" Stottlemeyer said. "Don't you go out into the world? Don't you talk to people?"

"I try to avoid it," Monk said. "You should, too."

Stottlemeyer sighed, stopped beside his car, and rubbed his temples.

"Okay, Monk, here it is in a nutshell. Big Country Mortgage gave very low, adjustable-rate loans to people so they could buy homes that they actually couldn't afford. Many of those people then borrowed against the equity in those homes to buy even more things they couldn't afford."

"Were they insane?" Monk asked.

"They were deceived," Stottlemeyer said. "Big Country convinced them that there was no risk and that the loans were within their means. But then interest rates went up, property values fell, and people ended up owing Big Country more money than their homes were worth. Hundreds of thousands of people are losing their homes, their savings, everything."

"I could have been one of them," I said. "I nearly fell for one of those subprime loans myself."

Monk looked at me with surprise. "How could you?"

"Because I'm paid a pittance and I thought that I could tap into the equity in my house for some quick cash."

"What do you need more money for?"

"Oh, I don't know," I said. "Frivolous stuff like food, clothing, and electricity."

"What do you do with all the money I give you?"

"I pay my mortgage," I said.

"And what do you do with what's left over?"

"There is nothing left over," I said.

"You obviously don't know how to handle money," Monk said. "Maybe if you ironed your cash, you'd learn to appreciate it more."

"I took out one of those loans, Monk," Stottlemeyer said, coming to my rescue. "It was the only way I could afford an apartment after my divorce."

"You don't iron your money, either," Monk said.

"Nobody does," Stottlemeyer said. "Only you do."

"Maybe that's why everybody else is losing their homes, their savings, and their jobs and I'm not."

"You're a sensitive guy, Monk."

"How are you holding up, Captain?" I asked.

"I'm barely holding on, especially now that the city is forcing detectives to take three weeks off without pay to cut costs. But I'll manage," Stottlemeyer said with a sigh, then turned back to Monk. "Getting back to Big Country, the guy who ran the company, Jack Moggridge, knew how toxic those loans were, but he lied to investors and regulators, and cashed out all of his company stock right before the market collapsed."

"That's fraud and insider trading," Monk said. "It's also cheating."

"Yes, it is," Stottlemeyer said. "Clasker was going to help us put Moggridge away."

"And in return, Clasker got to walk free with his millions and his Pacific Heights home," I said. "That infuriated a lot of the people who were swindled by Big Country."

"That's why we were following him from

his house to the court, to protect him," the captain said. "Everything was fine until we hit the red light at this intersection. When the light turned green, he didn't move. People started honking their horns. So we got out to see what was wrong."

The captain turned to look at the BMW and so did we. The tinted windows were so dark that it was impossible to see inside the BMW from where Stottlemeyer's car was parked.

"I couldn't see anything until my face was practically pressed against his driver's-side window," he continued. "That's when I saw what had happened. There was blood all over. The door was locked, so I had to break the window with the butt of my gun to get inside."

"How was Clasker killed?" Monk asked.

"He was strangled with piano wire."

"Was there anybody else in the car?" I asked.

"He was all alone," the captain said. "We walked him from his house to his car, so I know there was nobody in it then. We didn't see anybody enter or leave the vehicle from the moment we left the house until now. And we haven't moved from this spot since it happened."

Monk stepped up behind the BMW and

crouched down to look underneath it.

"The car isn't parked over a manhole, if that's what you're thinking," Stottlemeyer said. "It was the first thing that I checked."

"I was looking for this." Monk picked something up and then turned to show it to Stottlemeyer. It was the toothpick that the captain had tossed earlier.

"That's mine," the captain said.

"I know," Monk said, motioning to me. I took a Baggie out of my purse and held it open for him. "Littering is a crime. You are setting a very bad example for your men."

"Sorry," the captain said.

"Littering is just the beginning. Then the rot sets in. The next thing you know, you're planting evidence, soliciting bribes, and drinking hard liquor."

Monk dropped the toothpick in the Baggie, which I stuck back into my purse to throw out later. I have a very large purse to accommodate the disinfectant wipes, Baggies, antiseptic ointment, rubber gloves, bottled water, Windex, rattlesnake antivenin, and everything else that Monk has me carry around. If my purse was any larger, it would need wheels.

A short, pudgy forensic technician wearing a white jumpsuit, white bags over his shoes, and a white shower cap climbed out of the backseat. He looked like the Pillsbury Doughboy. I wanted to poke him in the tummy to see if he'd giggle.

"There's no hidden exit in the floor, Captain," Pillsbury said, peeling off a pair of white garden gloves. "The only way in or out of that car is through the four doors or the skylight."

"I want this car towed back to the lab and completely dismantled anyway, Pete," the captain said. "The answer is in there somewhere."

"Yes, sir," Pillsbury Pete said and walked back to the forensics van to confer with the other techs. I suddenly had a craving for slice-and-bake cookies.

Monk walked around to the driver's side and peered inside. Clasker's body was gone but the seat, dashboard, and windshield were still covered with his blood spatter. It was a gruesome sight. I lost my craving.

"This is probably a stupid question," I said. "But could it have been suicide?"

"He was practically decapitated by that piano wire," Stottlemeyer said. "Even if you could do that to yourself, which I doubt, there are easier, far less painful ways to kill yourself."

"So you're saying that somebody garroted Clasker in a locked car on a busy street in broad daylight right in front of two police officers and got away unseen."

"That about sums it up," Stottlemeyer said.

"You know what you're saying is impossible."

"I do," Stottlemeyer said. "That's why I called Monk."

CHAPTER THREE:
MR. MONK AND
THE BLACK MARKET

Monk circled the car several times, holding his hands up in front of him, framing what he saw.

Stottlemeyer and I stood together, watching him. We'd seen Monk's little Zen dance a thousand times but it was still oddly mesmerizing. Or maybe we simply found it reassuring in a very basic way. After all, we knew that eventually Monk would find the answers that eluded us. This was just the first step.

If only Monk could solve the really big mysteries in our lives and his own with the same certainty.

Disher joined us and regarded Monk for a moment himself before speaking up.

"None of the pedestrians saw anything, sir."

"I'm not surprised," Stottlemeyer said. "We're two trained law enforcement professionals. We were staring right at the car and we didn't see anything."

"It's a locked-room mystery," Disher said. "Only in a locked car."

"I suppose it is," Stottlemeyer said.

"Maybe the killer was a monkey," Disher said.

Stottlemeyer turned and glared at him. "Why would you think it was a monkey?"

"Because the classic locked-room mystery of all time is Edgar Allan Poe's 'The Murders in the Rue Morgue,' " Disher said. "And a monkey did that."

"Thanks for ruining it for me," I said.

"Were you planning on reading it?" Disher asked.

"No," I said. "But if I ever wanted to, now I can't."

"We were behind Clasker's car the whole time, Randy," Stottlemeyer said. "Did you see any monkeys?"

"No, but they didn't see any monkeys in the Rue Morgue, either. They found out about the monkeys later. Maybe we will, too."

"I don't think so," Stottlemeyer said.

"We should keep an open mind," Disher said.

Stottlemeyer glanced at Monk, who was making his fourth or fifth walk around the car. "What do you think?"

Monk stopped, sighed, and looked up at the sky with a frown. "I have thirty bottles of Summit Creek left. If I eat a lot of fruit and drink only a few teaspoons of water a day, maybe I could make them last for two months."

"I was asking about the murder," Stottlemeyer said.

Something across the street caught Monk's eye. I followed his gaze and saw three homeless men standing on the corner, watching the activity.

"What is it?" I asked.

"Those hobos over there," Monk said. "I need to talk to them."

"I already did," Disher said. "They don't know anything."

But Monk wasn't listening; he was already on his way across the street. I was about to go after him when Stottlemeyer gently tugged on my sleeve.

"This is important, Natalie. Clasker got killed right in front of two cops. The press is going to make us look like morons. We have to solve this fast. Please try to get Monk to focus."

"I'll do my best," I said.

He let go of me and I went after Monk, who was waiting for me on the sidewalk and eyeing the three men. "They hold the se-cret."

"To what?"

"The black market," Monk said. "It's where they do all their shopping. Watch and learn."

Monk rolled his shoulders, unbuttoned his collar, and strode over to the three men, snapping his fingers as he went.

"Hey, dudes," he said. "What's up?"

They stared at him.

"Far out," he said, snapping his fingers some more. "Do you know where I can score some primo water?"

They walked away.

"Groovy," Monk said, waving at them. "Keep on truckin'."

"That was educational," I said. "What did I learn?"

"They saw us with the captain," Monk said. "They thought we were fuzz. We need to put some distance between us and the Man."

Monk headed east on Sutter and right into the heart of the Tenderloin, which had a long history of being one of the most violent, crime-ridden areas in the city, even though it was tucked between the Civic Center and the opulence and excess of Union Square. Supposedly the neighborhood got its colorful nickname because the police were given "battle pay" to work there and, if they managed to survive, could afford to eat tenderloin instead of chuck steaks.

I don't know if I believe that story, but it certainly fits San Francisco's character.

The Tenderloin was dense with the homeless and the crazy, along with prostitutes and drug dealers. But if you moved quickly and didn't look for trouble, you'd be fine. But Monk wasn't following those simple rules.

"You don't want to be here, Mr. Monk." The truth was that I didn't want to be there, at least not with him doing what he was doing.

"Loosen up, Natalie, or you're going to blow my cover. Follow my lead so you don't draw attention to yourself."

"You mean like this?"

I started snapping my fingers, taking long strides, and bobbing my head like a rooster, just like Monk, only more exaggerated and ridiculous. I looked like I was trying to imitate Steve Martin and Dan Aykroyd as those two "wild and crazy guys."

Monk nodded at me approvingly. "That's more like it. Now we're fitting in."

There was no satisfaction in making fun

of Monk because he never got the joke. He was incapable of seeing himself as others saw him. But I did it anyway because it made me feel better.

Monk approached an older man at the mouth of an alley. The man was in filthy, ragged clothes, wearing a ski cap and drinking from a bottle in a paper bag. His hair was matted and his whiskers looked like a Brillo pad that hadn't been rinsed after cleaning dishes. He smelled like a urinal.

"Whatcha drinking, man?" Monk said.

"What's it to you?" Brillo growled.

"I need the 411 on the H_2O," he said. "I like to drink the clean stuff."

"What are you talking about?"

"It's cool. I'm not Smokey. I'm just a thirsty hobo bum like you, hanging ten."

"You get near me and I'll stick you." Brillo yanked a shiv out of his pocket with his free hand and clutched his bottle close to his chest with the other. "This bottle is mine."

Monk immediately backed away, holding up his hands. "I dig you, man. It's copacetic and antiseptic."

Brillo glared at us and dragged himself into the alley, settling down in a nest of blankets and cardboard behind a Dumpster.

"Mr. Monk, this is pointless," I said.

"Street people don't drink Summit Creek."

"Because it's too valuable," Monk said, spotting a lanky black man in a long leather jacket and leather pants strutting by across the street. "And he knows that."

"Who's he?"

"The Huggy Bear." Monk hurried after him and then, as he got near, slowed down and began snapping his fingers again, getting the man's attention.

I groaned and caught up with Monk just as he approached Huggy Bear.

"Hey, my man, what's the score?" Monk asked.

Huggy Bear turned around. "You want to score?"

"Right on. This hip cat is ready to boogie."

The man reached into his overcoat and pulled out a Baggie full of multicolored pills.

"Those are narcotics," Monk said. "Neato."

"I got all the candy you and your lady need," Huggy Bear said, grinning at me. "Just name your flavor."

"Out of sight," Monk said. "But what have you got to wash them down with?"

"Huh?" Huggy Bear said.

Monk leaned close and whispered, "I'm

looking for something very special. God's water."

The man looked confused. "You mean like a golden shower?"

"Yes," Monk said. "A golden shower."

I spoke up quickly, shaking my head and stepping in front of Monk. "No, no, no, he's not interested in a golden shower."

"Yes, I am," Monk said.

"No, you're not," I said.

"I desperately want it."

"No, you don't."

"Excuse us a moment," Monk said to Huggy Bear and then pulled me aside, lowering his voice to a whisper. "What are you doing? You're going to blow the deal."

"Do you know what a golden shower is?"

"It's obviously street code for Summit Creek, water that's as valuable as gold."

"It's pee."

"Summit Creek is not p-p-p —" Monk's expression hardened with anger. "It's not that."

"What you're asking for is," I said. "A golden shower is when someone pees on you."

Monk opened his mouth to speak, struggled to find the words, but he clearly just couldn't get his mind around the horrific concept. It was too terrible to contemplate.

His eyes rolled back in his head and he started to collapse. I caught him and lowered him, and myself, slowly to the ground until I was sitting with his head cradled in my lap.

Huggy Bear hurried off, which was fine with me. I took a disinfectant wipe from my purse and dabbed Monk's forehead with it. Nothing soothed him quite as much as disinfectant.

"It's okay, Mr. Monk, you're fine," I said. "Nothing happened."

"It has in my head," Monk said. "It's an image that will haunt me for the rest of my life, which is about sixty days, give or take."

"You're in the Tenderloin, Mr. Monk. That's the kind of thing people sell here," I said. "Not bottled water."

"We need to arrest that man."

"He's gone, Mr. Monk."

"Huggy Bear is a sicko," he said.

"Yes, he is." I dabbed Monk's forehead some more.

"A pee-peddling, drug-dealing sicko," Monk said. "I bet he hasn't washed his hands all day."

"You need to calm down, Mr. Monk."

"What about my water?"

41

"We'll find you new water to drink," I said. "But until then, you need to pull yourself together."

"I've never had anything else to drink."

"Think of it as an adventure," I said.

"I hate adventure," Monk said.

"Think of it as a new experience."

"And I hate new experiences."

"Don't think at all," I said.

"All I do is think. It's a blessing and a curse."

We sat there in silence. Across the street, the Pillsbury CSI technician walked up to a parked Chevy Malibu. He yanked a parking ticket out from under a windshield wiper, crumpled it up, and tossed it in the street before driving off.

That seemed to snap Monk out of his malaise. It gave him a sense of purpose. He stood and snapped his fingers at me for a wipe. I gave him one.

Monk marched across the street to the discarded ticket and picked it up with the wipe. I already had a Baggie out for it when he returned.

"Pete littered," Monk said. "And it's not just any scrap of paper. It's a parking citation, an official police document. That shows a blatant disrespect for the law."

"Yes, it does." I held out the open Baggie.

Monk dropped the wipe and the crumpled ticket inside.

"He's a law enforcement professional. This is what happens when a leader sets a bad example," Monk said. "I wish Captain Stottlemeyer could see what his toothpick has wrought."

"I'll keep the Baggie for him," I said.

"The captain is going to be so ashamed."

That thought, and the certainty that he'd been proved right, perked Monk up. Balance had been restored. He rolled his shoulders and we started walking back toward Van Ness.

"We were sitting on the sidewalk," Monk said, moving briskly. "Weren't we?"

"Yes, we were."

"We're going to have to burn the clothes that I'm wearing when I get home."

"You could wash them instead."

"Would you wash clothes that had been irradiated?"

"Your clothes aren't radioactive."

"I wish they were," Monk said. "It might kill some of the germs. You should burn what you're wearing, too."

"I can't afford to burn my clothes," I said. "Unless you'd like to give me a raise."

"Let's compromise," he said.

"Okay, what do you have in mind?"

"You burn your clothes and I don't give you a raise."

"How is that a compromise?"

"You're meeting me halfway."

"And what are you doing?"

"I'm already there," he said.

I had to smile. As exasperating as he was, he was himself again, at least until he got thirsty.

Chapter Four:
Mr. Monk in Therapy

Dr. Neven Bell's office in North Beach was all dark wood and leather furniture and was more masculine than a jock strap. I felt like I was sitting in the parlor of a private, and very snooty, men's club.

But the decor was a sharp contrast to the man who actually occupied the office. Dr. Bell was gray-haired and balding, wore lots of sweaters and tweeds, and exuded so much confidence and warmth that you couldn't help feeling safe and comfortable around him. Whatever your problem might be, he looked like the man who had the answer.

I'd only been sitting in the waiting area for a few minutes, barely enough time to read half of the cartoons in the *New Yorker,* when Dr. Bell slipped out of his office, closed the door behind him, and came to me.

"Adrian and I are going to need the rest

of the afternoon," he said.

"What about your other patients?"

"Fortunately, my day is clear."

That was a surprise — not that Monk needed more attention, but that Dr. Bell had the time to give it to him on such short notice. Usually the shrink was so booked up that he wouldn't indulge Monk for even an extra minute once a session was over. Apparently, even shrinks were feeling the pinch of the bad economy.

"That's good, because he's lost his grip," I said. "His reaction to this water thing is way, way over the top, even for him."

"It's not about the water, Natalie." Dr. Bell sat down on the edge of the coffee table. "It's about what it represents."

"Of course you'd say that," I said. "You're a shrink."

"It's a bottle of water to you and me, but for Adrian it's a profound loss that requires a fundamental adjustment for him emotionally and psychologically."

"All he has to do is switch brands," I said. "I'm sure there are other waters that are just as old and pure."

"You don't understand. This is an attack on his carefully ordered and maintained life. He's losing one of his last remaining ties to his mother, to his past, to a way of life."

"A dysfunctional way of life," I said. "A lot of his problems are his creepy mother's fault."

"Now who is sounding like a shrink?" Dr. Bell said with a smile.

"There's a reason Monk is obsessive-compulsive and his brother, Ambrose, won't leave the house."

"Even so, losing the water he loves means facing, at least to some degree, his inability to control his world," Dr. Bell said. "He needs to accept the loss and then confront the uncertainty and necessity of change."

"He still has to drink something."

"Don't worry. Adrian won't die of thirst. He'll get through this and come out of it a stronger person."

"Will two hours be enough time for you today?" I said.

"I think so," Dr. Bell said, getting up again. "Convincing Adrian, however, might be more difficult."

I was in the mood for a latte at Starbucks but my sense of fiscal responsibility prevailed and I went to McDonald's for coffee instead, using the money I'd saved to buy a small order of fries and a copy of the *San Francisco Chronicle*.

I took my coffee, fries, and newspaper and

walked up to Washington Park so I could enjoy the fresh air and the cloudless blue sky.

I was lucky and found VIP seating — a bench that was perfectly positioned to give me fabulous, postcard-perfect views wherever I turned my head.

In front of me, Coit Tower rose above the trees and the rooftops on Stockton Street. To my right, south on Columbus Avenue, I could see the top of the Transamerica Pyramid. And to my left, I could see St. Peter and Paul Church, white as a wedding cake, on Filbert Street.

But instead of appreciating those views, I couldn't take my eyes off my newspaper. It was like looking at a train wreck, a plane crash, and a naked celebrity all at once.

Almost all the stories were connected to the economy in some way, which would ordinarily be a big bore. But not in these dark days.

There was a big piece on Jack Moggridge, the ongoing criminal trial, and the tens of millions of dollars he'd taken from Big Country. That wasn't news. The big development was the discovery of what he'd done with all of his profits.

Moggridge invested almost every penny he had with Bob Sebes and his Reinier

Investment Fund, which six months ago undoubtedly seemed like a very smart move. Sebes was regarded as a financial genius in the banking industry and his $2 billion fund delivered consistent returns for his investors regardless of the ups and downs of the world economy.

But this time, the economy had gotten so bad that many of Sebes' investors, in deep financial troubles, were cashing out of the fund because they needed money. The problem was, Sebes didn't have the cash to cover the withdrawals and a few weeks ago he was forced to make a terrible confession.

His fund was a fraud, a massive Ponzi scheme, and the $2 billion was all gone. Where it had gone, he wasn't saying.

So that meant Moggridge was broke.

And while that was sweet, poetic justice for his criminal actions, it was hard to savor knowing that his victims would never be compensated for what they'd lost because of him.

Meanwhile Sebes, responsible for one of the biggest financial frauds in history, had been placed under house arrest in his Pacific Heights mansion pending his trial. The news today was that a judge, despite the public outcry, had upheld the house arrest, arguing that Sebes had surrendered his passport, was wearing a GPS tracking device on his ankle, and, as one of the most reviled men on Earth right now, there was nowhere for him to run.

I could understand the judge's ruling, but it still pissed me off.

If I mugged a guy in Washington Park for the hundred dollars in his wallet, I'd go to jail. But Bob Sebes had defrauded banks, pension plans, charities, and thousands of individuals out of billions of dollars and he got to stay at home, eating caviar and drinking champagne all day in his satin pajamas.

Why did he get locked up at home instead of in a jail cell? Was it because he was rich? Because he was once a highly respected figure on Wall Street? Because he hobnobbed with movie stars, famous athletes, and world leaders?

Of course that was why.

What made it harder for me to accept was the fact that even if he was eventually sentenced to prison, it wouldn't be the same one that I'd have to go to for mugging somebody. I'd be sent to some godforsaken hellhole and have to share a tiny windowless cell with some drooling child molester. But Sebes would get sent to a Ritz-Carlton prison with individual suites instead of cells, four-hundred-ply bedsheets, satellite TV, and espresso machines.

There was a file photo accompanying the article of Sebes and his wife, Anna, a former concert violinist, relaxing on their yacht in Marin. She was his college sweetheart and, like many long-married couples, they'd grown to look like fraternal twins. Or maybe they just shared the same plastic surgeon.

They both looked tanned, healthy, and comfortable, and far younger than their fifty-plus years. They also looked pretty pleased with themselves, which is probably why the editor chose the picture for the story. But to be fair to the Sebeses, I'd probably look vibrantly youthful and smugly self-satisfied if I had a few billion dollars in the bank, vacation homes in France and Hawaii, a yacht, his-and-hers personal trainers, and a full-time chef.

The rest of the stories on the front page were just as cheery and upbeat. I read about the state's $30 billion budget shortfall, the demise of a historic restaurant that had survived such calamities as the 1903 earthquake, and the possible closure of the *Chronicle* itself, which would leave the city without a single newspaper.

I crumpled up the paper and tossed it in the trash. I was so angry and depressed that I was tempted to ask Dr. Bell if he had a couple of hours for me, too.

No wonder Monk didn't bother keeping up on the news. I considered following his example and living in blissful ignorance, only in his case it was blissless.

On my way back to Dr. Bell's, I stopped at a grocery store and picked up an assortment of bottled waters for Monk to choose from to replace Summit Creek. I didn't expect him to pick one right away, but at least it would be a start.

Monk was waiting for me outside of Dr. Bell's office when I drove up. He didn't look as content as he'd been when he found the crumpled parking ticket, but he wasn't as overwrought as he'd been when we'd arrived at the crime scene. He got inside the car, buckled up, and let out a long, mournful sigh.

"Was Dr. Bell helpful?" I asked as we drove off.

Monk shrugged. "When you know that a blazing meteor is heading straight toward Earth and will completely eradicate the human race, how helpful can a visit to your psychiatrist really be?"

"Don't you think you're exaggerating just a tiny bit?"

Monk nodded. "A tiny bit."

"It's a bottle of water, Mr. Monk."

"It's a meteor. The thing is, it's already hit Earth. We just haven't died yet."

At his apartment, Monk set every bottle of Summit Creek water that he had left on the dining room table for inspection and counted them several times. He wrote the number down on a piece of paper. And then he counted them again.

"The number hasn't changed, Mr. Monk. It won't change until you drink a bottle."

"This is serious business, Natalie. I need to be exact and vigilant. My survival depends on it."

I set out the bottles of water that I'd bought on the other side of the table.

"You should start sampling some of the other bottled water that's available," I said, motioning to the samples I'd laid out.

"You can't replace Summit Creek," he said.

"You don't have a choice," I said. "Unless you'd prefer to die a slow, miserable death."

"I've been doing that since birth."

I picked up a bottle of Arrowhead water. "What about Arrowhead? It comes from a spring in the San Bernardino Mountains."

"Those are dirty mountains," he said.

"Dirty mountains?"

"I've seen them and they are caked with dirt."

"All mountains are covered with dirt," I said.

"Those mountains are dirtier," he said.

"Okay," I said, picking up another bottle. "How about Hawaiian Springs water? It's fresh rainwater from the lush peaks of Mauna Loa that's percolated through thirteen thousand feet of porous lava."

"Only thirty days pass between when that water drops from the sky, falling through thick layers of airborne pollutants, and when it's bottled," he said. "I don't want to drink smog, airplane exhaust, and bird gas."

"Bird gas?"

"Birds have disgusting dietary habits," he said. "They'll eat anything."

I set the bottle aside and picked up another one.

"How about Crystal Geyser? The water comes from springs at Mount Shasta in California, the Cherokee National Forest in Tennessee, and the Blue Ridge Mountains in South Carolina. You get the best water from across the entire nation in one bottle."

"You want me to drink mixed water? What are you thinking? That's like drinking mixed nuts."

He was right. I should have known better

than to suggest that one to him, not that his reasoning made any sense.

I picked up the last bottle.

"You can't go wrong with Evian. It is gourmet water derived from rain and melting snow on the highest, most pristine peaks of the majestic French Alps." I was laying it on thick but I wanted to make the sale. I was the Billy Mays of bottled water. "It takes fifteen years for the water to filter through deep aquifers of glacial sand before it's bottled."

"Fifteen years? Don't make me laugh." Monk picked up a bottle of Summit Creek. "This is pristine water from the Ice Age, before the dawn of man. There's simply no comparison."

He'd shot down all four brands. But I wasn't discouraged. That was just round one and the game was rigged in my favor. There were a lot of bottled waters out there and I knew that Monk would have to pick one of them eventually.

He licked his lips and let out a dry, wheezy cough. All of this talking about water had obviously made him thirsty. He took his bottle to the kitchen, found a teaspoon, and carefully poured some water into it.

Monk slowly sipped the teaspoon of water, his eyes closed, savoring the taste of prehistoric Earth.

"What's our next move on the case?" I asked.

"What case?" he said, opening his eyes and licking the spoon.

"The murder of Mike Clasker."

"Who?"

"The man who was strangled with piano wire in a locked car in a busy intersection on Van Ness Boulevard in broad daylight right in front of Captain Stottlemeyer and Lieutenant Disher."

"Did they see who did it?"

"No, they didn't," I said, practically screaming at him by this point. "Didn't you listen to anything you were told at the crime scene?"

"Bits and pieces," he said. "I can't concentrate when I'm dehydrated."

"You had a drink of water ninety minutes before we went to the crime scene."

"It was a long, brutal walk in the blazing sun from the grocery store to that intersection."

"It was a few blocks," I said. "It was hardly the Bataan Death March."

"I dry out quickly."

"Captain Stottlemeyer is counting on you, Mr. Monk. You need to focus on this case."

"I'll get right on it," he said. "After we burn my clothes."

CHAPTER FIVE:
MR. MONK AND
THE PERFECT BALANCE

My daughter, Julie, was curled up on the living room couch, texting on her iPhone, when I came into the house lugging a large plastic trash bag.

Julie was taller than me, more of a woman than a little girl now, and that troubled me. Only when she smiled did I see the child in her again. But the smiles weren't as frequent as they used to be.

She was at that sullen, moody, hormonal stage of teenage life when everything I did was irrational, unfair, capricious, outrageous, dictatorial, immoral, unethical, and inconvenient. She had so many adjectives to describe how wrong I was about everything that I wondered if she consulted a thesaurus before our arguments. Then again, that would have required her to crack open a book, which I rarely saw her do anymore. Most of the time, she was at her computer, communicating with her friends or surfing the Web.

Julie barely looked up when I came in. "What have you got there?"

"Four bottles of water and the clothes Mr. Monk was wearing today."

"Why do you have his clothes?"

"He wanted me to burn them but he doesn't have an incinerator."

"Neither do we," she said. It came out sounding more like a warning than a statement of fact.

"No, but we can build a bonfire in the backyard or burn them in our fireplace."

"You aren't going to, are you?"

"Why not?" I said, just to needle her.

"Because it's crazy and someone might see you," she said. "I have to live in this neighborhood."

"Of course I'm not going to burn his clothes." I dropped the bag near the front door and took out the bottles of water, lugging them over to the couch. "What made you think that I would?"

"Because you do a lot of crazy things for him and it's embarrassing."

"For me, maybe, but not for you."

I put the bottles on the coffee table, sat down next to her, and opened up the Hawaiian Springs water for myself.

"What about the first-aid kit he gave me

that I had to take to school every day?" she asked. "Or the lunches with everything cut into squares?"

I took a big sip of the water. I couldn't taste Hawaii in it, or any pollutants or bird gas, but the water did feel crisper and lighter on my tongue than what came out of my kitchen sink.

"It's not unusual for sandwiches to be square," I said.

"It is for cookies and potato chips," she said. "People thought I was the nut who sat with a pair of scissors cutting my potato chips into squares."

"The fact that Mr. Monk took so much time and effort on your behalf shows how much he cares for you."

"That's not what it shows," she said. "So what are you going to do with his clothes?"

"I'll drop them off at Goodwill on my way to work in the morning."

"I need you to take my bike in to be repaired, too. Something is wrong with the gears."

We were having a conversation but she hadn't looked up at me and was texting the entire time. I didn't know how she could have two conversations at once, even if one was verbal and the other one was not.

"Why don't you take it to the bike shop

yourself?"

"Because it's, like, miles away."

"You're on summer vacation," I said. "What else do you have to do?"

"Why should I walk it all the way there when it's much quicker and easier for you to just drop it off?"

"Because I am not your slave. What if I get a stain on my pants? I'll have to come back home and change my clothes or Mr. Monk will insist on setting fire to them when he sees me."

"You wouldn't have to run errands for me if I had a car," Julie said.

Our arguments often came back to her constant nagging for a car. She hated being seen in mine, a Buick sedan, and felt that being "dropped off by her mother" everywhere was humiliating.

"So buy one," I said.

"I don't have the money."

"Get a job," I said.

That got her attention. She looked at me as if I'd just told her to run naked down the street singing show tunes.

"It's summer," she said. "I've just come off of a long, hard year of school. I need to recharge. Like bears need hibernation in the winter."

"So where do you think this car is going

to come from?"

"You could buy me one."

"With what?"

"Don't you have some money set aside?"

"We can't afford an aside."

"What about for emergencies?"

"We can't afford emergencies, either."

Julie sighed with the full weight of her teenage angst and frustration. It was quite a sigh, truly Monkian in its exaggerated theatricality. I was tempted to applaud.

"You could ask for a raise," she said.

I laughed. "From Adrian Monk?"

"Why not?"

"You have met the man, haven't you? He's not just a tightwad — his wallet is hermetically sealed. And I mean that literally."

"You could ask your parents for the money."

"They are not an ATM and you have to stop treating them that way."

"You could get a loan against the equity in our house."

"You're just full of ideas of things that I can do to generate cash," I said. "What about things that *you* can do?"

"You're the parent. I'm the child. It's your job to support me and give me the resources I need to thrive in the world."

"Suddenly when money is involved, you're

a child. But when it comes to staying out on Friday night, you want to be treated as an adult. Do you see the contradiction there? The hypocrisy?"

"Not really," she said.

"Now you're just playing dumb," I said, getting up. "I'll get your bike fixed. That way we don't have to have this car conversation again."

"I'm going to need a car someday," she called after me as I walked away.

"I'm sure you will. And when that day comes, I hope you have some money set aside to buy one."

I didn't tell her that my parents bought me a car when I was her age and I wasn't going to volunteer the information anytime soon, either. There was no benefit right now in her knowing that hypocrisy was a family trait.

In the morning, I folded the backseat down and we wrestled the bike into my car through the trunk. One of the tires brushed against my pants in the struggle, leaving a tiny smudge that I couldn't wipe off. If I wasn't seeing Monk, I would have ignored the mark and gone about my business. But it was a workday, and Monk expected me at his door promptly at ten a.m.

I was tempted to yank the bike out of the car and make Julie take it to the shop herself, but I'm not that vindictive. At least not when I'm in a hurry.

So I ran back into the house and changed my pants, which only left me enough time to drop off Monk's dirty clothes at Goodwill before going to his house. The bike repair would have to wait until the end of the day.

Monk was lying on his couch, licking his lips and gasping for each breath, when I came in.

"Captain Stottlemeyer called," Monk wheezed. "He wants us to come down to the station."

"Has there been a break in the case?"

"I don't know. But I can't go."

"Why not?"

"Can't you see?" Monk said. "I'm a desiccated corpse."

"You're not a corpse yet."

"I feel dead. Are you sure I'm not dead?"

"Corpses don't whine."

"But I'm desiccated," he said. "I'll be nothing but bleached bones soon."

"How are your bones going to get bleached in a dark apartment?"

"I'm going to leave a can of bleach here beside the couch and detailed instructions for you when you find my bones."

"I'm not bleaching your bones, Mr. Monk."

"Some assistant you are," he said. "What do I pay you for?"

"Come to think of it, you haven't paid me this month," I said. "Thanks for reminding me."

He groaned. And wheezed. And gasped.

I ignored his death throes and went to his desk, took out his checkbook, and brought it over to him.

"Can't you see I'm withering away? How can you take money from me while I'm withering?"

I handed him a pen. "Because I've earned it."

"Maybe tomorrow," he said. "If I feel more moist."

"If you don't write that check, get off that couch, and go down to see the captain, I am going to take a sip from one of your last bottles of Summit Creek."

"You wouldn't dare," he said.

"I happen to have a bottle right here," I said, reaching into my purse for it.

"Okay, okay, relax. Don't do anything that I'll regret." Monk sat right up and filled out the check. "You realize that putting a gun to a person's head and forcing him to sign a document against his will nullifies it."

"I'm not putting a gun to your head," I said. "It's a bottle of water."

"It's the same thing." He tore off the check and handed it to me.

"Have a teaspoon of water and let's go," I said. "You have a murderer to catch."

I managed to get him on his feet, hydrated, and out to the car within a few minutes. I had bills to pay that night so we made a quick stop at the bank to deposit my check, and then we headed downtown. Monk glanced over his shoulder at the bike in the backseat and frowned.

"What's that doing in here?"

"There's something wrong with the gears. I'm going to take it to the bike shop on my way home tonight."

"Did you wash the bicycle before putting it in the car?"

"No."

"Do you know where those tires have been?"

"On the road. On bike trails. Maybe a few sidewalks."

Monk nodded, took a handkerchief from his pocket, and covered his nose and mouth. "Those wheels are caked in decay, disease, and death."

"All the big Ds," I said.

"You'll have to get the car fumigated."

"I'm not fumigating the car because of a bike."

"It's not the bicycle itself that's the problem. I love bicycles. It's the wheels. They are unsanitary."

"No one is asking you to eat off them," I said. "I didn't know you loved bikes."

"Riding a bicycle is one of the few times in life when it's possible to experience perfect balance."

"Then how come I've never seen you ride one?"

He sighed and slumped sadly in his seat. "It wasn't meant to be. I had a traumatic experience on a bicycle before I finished learning how to ride."

"Everything for you is a traumatic experience," I said. "What made this one any worse?"

"The kids ridiculed me for using training wheels."

"Everyone uses training wheels at first," I said. "That's not unusual at all."

"That's what I thought, but kids can be so heartless and cruel," Monk said. "Every time I tried to ride my bike, they'd point at both sets and hurl nasty insults at me."

"Both sets?"

"Of training wheels," he said. "Front and back."

"You had training wheels on the front of your bike?"

"Of course I did. It wouldn't be symmetrical or safe otherwise. Anything else would be suicidal."

"Didn't you notice that the other kids only had training wheels on the back?"

"They're lucky they survived," Monk said. "They're probably all dead now, unless they gave up the risky lifestyles they had as children."

I could see why the kids made fun of him. If I was a kid on his street, I probably would have ridiculed him, too.

"It's never too late to learn to ride a bike, Mr. Monk."

"It is for me," he said. "I'm too late for everything worthwhile in life."

There was no point in arguing about it with him, though that was true of all of our disagreements. Monk had his set view of things and nothing was going to change it, particularly if doing so would detract from his wallowing in sweet misery. Charlie Brown was a happy-go-lucky guy compared to Adrian Monk.

CHAPTER SIX:
MR. MONK AND THE RERUN

Disher was at his desk outside of Stottlemeyer's glass-walled office in the Homicide unit when we came in. The blinds were closed on the captain's windows, which usually meant he was taking a nap, sneaking a cigar, or talking to his ex-wife.

"What's the captain up to?" I asked.

"I don't know," Disher said. "He's been locked up in there since he got in this morning."

Monk licked his lips. "My throat is so dry."

"Have something to drink," Disher said.

"Don't taunt me," Monk said. "It's cruel."

"I mean it. Have a drink." Disher motioned to the watercooler. "It's Alhambra."

"It's distilled water," Monk said.

"Isn't that clean and healthy?" Disher asked.

"It's tap water that's been vaporized into steam, cooled, and recondensed into water again."

"So it works on the same theory as a transporter beam," Disher said. "Only with water instead of a landing party from the *Enterprise*."

"I have no idea what you're talking about," Monk said. "The point I'm making is that it's still tap water. You might as well offer me a refreshing glass of battery acid."

Disher walked over to the watercooler and filled a paper cup with water. He sipped it. "I had no idea this was *Star Trek* water. It actually tastes like the future."

"Did the forensics report come in on Clasker's car?" I asked.

"Yeah," Disher said, returning to his desk with his paper cup of water. "No hidden compartments or secret mechanisms, but we found lots of fingerprints. Most of 'em are from Clasker and his family, or from people we can't ID, but we got two interesting hits. Some of the prints belonged to Moggridge, the man Clasker was supposed to testify against."

"Where was Moggridge at the time of the murder?" Monk asked.

"Sitting in the courtroom waiting for Clasker to show up," Disher said. "But you've broken better alibis than that."

"Moggridge could have taken a ride with Clasker in his car months ago," Monk said.

"Or maybe this proves that Moggridge cased Clasker's car for the guy he hired to do the killing," Disher said.

"You still have to find the killer," I said.

"I think we have," Disher said. "One of the prints we found belongs to Armando Alvarez, who is wanted in Mexico for carrying out dozens of executions for the Juarez drug cartel. We just arrested him."

"How did you find him?" Monk asked.

"Some of the other prints in the car belong to guys at a car wash a few blocks from where Clasker was killed. I sent some officers to see if they could match some of the other unidentified prints to workers there. When the officers showed up, one of car wash guys bolted. The officers tackled him. It was Alvarez. He got sloppy and left a fingerprint behind when he murdered Clasker."

"Or maybe that's where Clasker went to get his car washed," Monk said. "And it's a coincidence that one of the workers is a wanted fugitive."

"Or maybe Alvarez picked that place because it was close to Van Ness and Sutter," Disher said. "He could slip away, murder Clasker, and be back on the line without anybody noticing. The car wash was his alibi."

"How did he get in and out of Clasker's car without anybody seeing him?" I asked.

"I don't know. But Alvarez is the guy. We just have to figure out how he did it." Disher studied his cup of water. "Maybe he found a way to distill himself in and out of the car."

Stottlemeyer opened the door to his office. He looked like he'd been up all night and it hadn't been much fun. "Come in, I want to talk with you."

Disher started to get up, but Stottlemeyer held up his hand in a halting gesture. "Just Monk and Natalie. This is a private matter."

"Oh, I get it," Disher said, grinning. "This is about my birthday, isn't it?"

"You got a birthday coming up?" Stottlemeyer asked Disher as Monk and I walked into the dark office. "When?"

"As if you didn't know," Disher said. "I've never had a surprise party, so this will be a real surprise."

Stottlemeyer gave Disher a long, dead-eyed stare, then closed the door and turned to me. "Do you know when his birthday is?"

"In two days."

"Oh, hell. I guess I'd better get him something. What does he like?"

"How should I know?" I said.

"Women always know these kinds of things," Stottlemeyer said.

"You've worked with the man for years and you don't know what he likes?"

"We're coworkers. We aren't dating."

I sighed. For a man who detected for a living, it was amazing to me how clueless he could be sometimes. "What did you want to talk to us about, Captain?"

"You mean it's not about Randy's surprise party?" Monk said.

"No, Monk, it's not." The captain sat on the edge of his desk and faced us. "I'm afraid I've got some very bad news."

"It can't be worse than the news I got yesterday," Monk said. Then his eyes went wide. "Oh my God. Have they stopped making Wet Ones? Or Windex? Or Lysol? Maybe I should just kill myself now and get it all over with."

"Relax, Mr. Monk. Whatever the news is, it's not that bad," I said.

"I'm not so sure about that, Natalie." The captain took a deep breath. "This isn't easy for me to say and I hate that I have to do it, but these are hard times. You're fired, Monk, effective immediately."

"What did I do?" Monk asked.

"You didn't do anything. You're great. It's got nothing to do with you and everything

73

to do with the economy. The department can't afford consultants. They can't even afford me."

I was suffering a bad case of déjà vu. We'd played this same scene before, only a few months ago. Monk was fired by Stottlemeyer, ostensibly by the department to save money and score political points with the surly rank and file. But I thought it had more to do with the captain's feelings of inadequacy following a public flaying at a police convention over his heavy reliance on Monk to help solve crimes. I didn't know what the firing was really about this time but I wasn't going to accept it.

"Captain, have you already forgotten what happened the last time you fired Monk? It was a disaster. You know you'll regret this."

"I already do, but this came down from upstairs, not me. The city has no money, so the department has to make brutal cuts. I'll give you an example. We're reducing the number of patrol cars on the streets by twenty percent because we don't have the money for the gasoline, the automotive maintenance, or the officers."

"But the streets are going to be a lot less safe and more crooks are going to get away with their crimes," Monk said.

"I know that, but there's no way around

it, Monk. We just don't have the money to do the job we're supposed to do."

This was a bad rerun of an episode I didn't like the first time I saw it.

"You said that before, Captain, and then you came crawling back to him."

"This time it's different, Natalie. You know it is. All you have to do is look out the window. Have you seen all the stores going out of business? All the people losing their homes? The tax dollars have dried up. Every city, county, and state agency is being gutted. Education, social services, you name it. We're all going to feel the pain in one way or another."

I knew he was right but it didn't make it any easier to accept. If Monk was out of a job, so was I. I couldn't just give up without a fight.

"Mr. Monk can solve more crimes single-handedly than all the detectives in that squad room combined," I said. "You know that, Captain."

"So what do you want me to do? Fire them to save Monk? I'll tell you what, Natalie, you can go out there and pick the guys who should lose their jobs so an outside consultant can keep his. How about Randy? Or me?"

"All I'm saying is that Mr. Monk is cost-effective. Isn't that what this is all about, saving money? Or are you saying it's something else?"

"The captain is right," Monk said. "No police officer should lose his job because of me."

"You are the best detective in this city, Mr. Monk. If they have to make cuts, shouldn't they keep the best?"

"They're cops," Monk said. "I'm not."

"This isn't fair," I said.

"Welcome to my life," Monk said and then turned to the captain. "You know you can call on me for help with a case anytime, whether I get paid or not. I'll be there."

"I know," he said.

"Can I be there even if you don't call?"

"No," Stottlemeyer said. "Are you going to be all right?"

"I'm never all right," Monk said and went to the door, pausing for a moment before he opened it. "Q-tips."

"Excuse me?" Stottlemeyer said.

"Get Randy a box of Q-tips," Monk said. "It's always the perfect gift."

Disher grinned at us from his desk as we came out of Stottlemeyer's office. He didn't seem to pick up on my sudden depression or Monk's sadness. But I gave Disher the benefit of the doubt on Monk, who always wore a sad expression. Only someone who spent as much time as I did with Monk could notice the subtle changes in the intensity of his sadness.

"If you're wondering what to get me, your troubles are over," Disher said. "I've opened a wedding registry at Nordstrom."

"But you aren't getting married," I said.

"Nordstrom doesn't have to know that," he said.

As Monk and I headed out of the squad room, I pulled the Baggies containing the toothpick and the parking ticket out of my purse and dropped them into a garbage can.

"We won't need these now," I said.

Monk stopped midstride. He rolled his shoulders, tipped his head from side to side, and then held out his hand to me, snapping his fingers.

"Wipe, wipe," he said.

I gave him two. He took one in each hand, reached into the garbage can, and retrieved the two Baggies, which he held up and examined for a moment.

"You're not thinking about lecturing the captain about littering and setting a bad example now, are you?" I said. "This is not the right time."

When he lowered his arms, there was a strange smile on his face.

The smile wasn't actually strange. What was strange was that he could find anything to smile about two minutes after getting fired.

But it was a smile I knew well. There was no question about what it meant.

He'd just solved a murder.

"I need to see Clasker's car," Monk said.

CHAPTER SEVEN:
MR. MONK AND
THE MAGIC TRICK

Captain Stottlemeyer tried to explain to Monk that he'd just been fired, and that he was no longer involved in the investigation, and that he had no business asking to go to the crime lab to examine Clasker's car.

But Stottlemeyer didn't try very hard. It was a halfhearted protest at best because the captain's pressing need to solve a seemingly impossible high-profile murder was far greater than his concern about taking advantage of his friend's compulsions.

I didn't protest too much, either, because I knew Monk couldn't stop himself from pursuing the case to the end, regardless of whether he got paid or the department appreciated his efforts.

I also knew that anyone who has evidence that could help solve a murder has an obligation to share it with the police, regardless of whether the police have just fired you and your comely assistant.

Stottlemeyer, Disher, Monk, and I headed downstairs to the crime lab's garage, which was located in a building on the other side of the parking lot.

If this was an episode of *CSI,* the garage would have been a neon-lit cavern of brushed stainless steel, where buxom women and buff men in Versace lab coats moved sensually around the sleek curves of the car with their high-tech equipment to the pulsating beat of hip-hop.

The reality was a lot less cool and sexy. The walls of the garage were unpainted cinder blocks, the floors were concrete, and panels of fluorescent lights hung on chains from the exposed rafters. Clasker's BMW sedan was parked on a white tarp in the middle of the room. The equipment was an ordinary assortment of mechanic's tools on a rolling cart, a cordless mini-vacuum, some flashlights, lots of evidence Baggies, and a nice digital camera.

The car doors had been removed and the hood and trunk were open.

Pillsbury Pete was on his knees, wearing rubber gloves and a white jumpsuit, and plucking bugs and things from the front grille with tweezers and sticking them in Baggies.

"What do you think that stuff is going to

tell you, Pete?" the captain asked.

"Where the car has been and when it was there," Pete said. "The information might prove helpful to your investigation."

"It won't." Monk went up to the left rear passenger side of the car and peered inside.

"I just collect the evidence," Pete said. "It's up to you guys how to use it. Or not."

"Let's say I wanted to take a broken bicycle with filthy, disgusting wheels to the shop for repair in this car but it wouldn't fit in the trunk," Monk said. "Could I fold down the seats?"

"Of course you could," Pete said. "It's a common sixty-forty split seat, so you could still fit in a passenger, too, if you wanted."

Pete reached past Monk, pressed a release button, and lowered the larger portion of the backseat.

"What does a dirty bike have to do with anything?" the captain asked.

"I didn't know you could fold down the backseat of a sedan until Natalie put Julie's broken bicycle in her car this morning."

Disher looked at Monk with disbelief. "How could you not know that?"

"I don't own a car and I'm usually not in one when people are transporting large, dirt-caked items from one place to another."

"But you are part of the modern world we

81

live in," Disher said.

"Have you forgotten who you're talking to?" Stottlemeyer asked Disher. "The only person who leads a more sheltered life than Monk is his brother."

Monk pointed to the opening into the trunk. "There's your secret compartment."

Pete stepped aside and Stottlemeyer stepped forward.

"You're saying the killer hid in the trunk?" the captain asked.

"He got inside the night before," Monk said. "When the car stopped at the intersection, he dropped the backseat down, burst out, and strangled Clasker."

Stottlemeyer turned to Pete. "Did you find any evidence that there was a guy in the trunk?"

"We've found some strands of hair, but they could have come from suitcases, clothes, golf clubs, beach chairs, or any number of things belonging to the victim and his family. We won't know until we run the DNA, but that will take some time."

Stottlemeyer sighed and faced Monk. "Even if I buy that the killer was in the trunk, it doesn't explain how he got away. We were standing next to the car right up until the medical examiner and the crime scene techs arrived. And in all that time, I never saw anybody get out of that car."

"Yes, you did," Monk said.

"No, I didn't," Stottlemeyer said.

"Yes, you did," Monk said. "We all did."

"You couldn't have," Stottlemeyer said. "By the time you got to the scene, the body had been removed and the forensic investigators were crawling all over the car."

"And that's exactly when the killer made his daring escape."

I'm sure Monk wasn't aware of it, but he'd dropped all pretense of dehydration. He was too caught up in his summation to pander to his own fears and phobias, to wallow in his present, expected, or imagined misery.

"Then he must have been wearing an invisibility cloak," Disher said.

Monk shook his head. "We were looking right at him."

"How is that possible?" I asked.

"It's no different than a magician performing his act in front of a live audience," Monk said. "And like any good magician, the killer pulled off his trick using a clever, but subtle, distraction."

"What did he do?" Stottlemeyer asked.

"He got out of the car," Monk said.

"Yes, we know that," Stottlemeyer said wearily. "What we don't know is *how.*"

"He opened the back door, stepped out of

the car, and told us all about his predicament." Monk turned to Pete. "You said the only way out of the car was through the doors or the skylight. You forgot to mention the trunk."

"My mistake," Pete said. "But I still don't see who the killer is."

"Look in the mirror," Monk said. "It was you."

We all stared at Pete in disbelief. Monk had made an outrageous accusation. But the outrageousness was tempered by the fact that he'd never been wrong before. He knew that he was right. I could see it in his stance and in the forceful way he spoke. All the tentativeness, worry, and misery that usually colored his actions were gone.

It was during these summations, when he pulled a case together, when he corrected the imbalance created by the murder and the mystery, that he was the most in control of himself and everything around him.

I loved those moments because it was one of the rare times that Adrian Monk was truly happy. I only wished it could last, which is why I never begrudged him the pleasure of drawing out his summations for as long as he possibly could, even if it could become unbearably irritating for everybody else.

"That's absurd," Pete said. "I'm the lead forensic investigator. I didn't arrive at the scene until after the captain's call came in."

"You didn't ride from here to the crime scene with the rest of the forensic investigation team," Monk said. "Did you?"

"No, I didn't. I got the call when I was on my way into work, so I drove to the scene in my own car. There's nothing unusual about that. It happens all the time." Pete turned to Stottlemeyer. "You know how it is."

Stottlemeyer nodded. "I've lost count of how many times I've had to get out of bed in the middle of the night to go look at a corpse."

"There you go." Pete looked at Monk. "You might as well accuse the captain and Lieutenant Disher of murder while you're at it. They were behind Clasker's car the whole way. How do you know they didn't do it and are lying to us about the locked car?"

"I'm not saying a word without my lawyer and union rep present," Disher said.

"He's not accusing us of anything," Stottlemeyer said. "He's making a point."

"He's not making any points with me," Disher said. "He's losing them."

"I'm illustrating that this whole line of

85

speculation is utterly ridiculous," Pete said. "If we follow Monk's twisted reasoning, then you two are far more likely suspects than me or anybody else."

I spoke up. "But they were right behind Clasker's car the whole time. There are other drivers who can attest to that. And if they got out of their car and strangled Clasker, there would have been dozens of witnesses. It makes no sense."

"Neither does Monk's accusation," Pete said.

"You were in Clasker's car," Monk said. "And then you got out."

"I was in the car because I'm the lead forensic investigator. I collect evidence at crime scenes. That's my job. You have seen me do it a thousand times before. I got out of the car to give you my preliminary observations."

"That's what you wanted us to think," Monk said.

"My God, this is truly Kafkaesque." Pete looked imploringly at Stottlemeyer. "Are we really going to stand here and listen to this nonsense?"

"Yes, we are," Stottlemeyer said.

"He's saying I'm the killer because I was doing my job," Pete said. "It's insane."

"Here's what happened," Monk said. "You

knew the route Clasker would take to court from his house. So you parked midway there, a few blocks off of Van Ness, and walked to Clasker's house. You put on your clean suit and slipped into the trunk of his BMW. The clean suit served two purposes: it protected you from unintentionally leaving behind forensic evidence or any of it sticking to yourself. It also allowed you to be seen in the car *after* the murder without attracting suspicion. You waited until the right moment, sometime after the forensic crew arrived, to creep into the backseat again. Anyone who saw you crawling around inside the car at that point naturally assumed you were there to collect evidence, not that you had been there all along."

"That's an outrageous theory without a single shred of evidence to back it up," Pete said. "And I say that as an expert on evidence."

"He's got a point, Monk," Stottlemeyer said.

"It won't be hard to prove that his mortgage is with Big Country," Monk said. "And that he's losing his house."

"Me and tens of thousands of other people," Pete said, "including half of the officers in the police department."

"It gives you a motive," Monk said.

"Is that all you've got?" Pete said. "Because if it is, it's laughable."

"I notice that you're wearing rubber gloves now," Monk said.

"Of course I am," Pete said, speaking in an intentionally patronizing tone of voice, making it clear he felt like he was dealing with a complete idiot. "It's so investigators like me don't contaminate the crime scene with our own fingerprints while we are doing our jobs."

"But you weren't wearing rubber gloves at the crime scene," Monk said. "You were wearing work gloves. That's because rubber gloves are too thin. You were afraid the piano wire would slice through the gloves and into your fingers while you were garroting Clasker."

"No, I wore them because I didn't want to cut myself on any unforeseen sharp objects or edges while I was reaching under seats," Pete said, his patience gone and his every word dripping with irritation. "The other reason we professional crime scene investigators wear gloves is protection. If my gloves are the so-called evidence for your inept theory, I think it's time that you concluded this farce and moved on to more credible lines of inquiry."

But I knew Monk was just building up to

his "ah-ha" clue and I was sure that Stottle-meyer and Disher did, too.

"Oh, there's more. Do you recognize this?" Monk took a Baggie out of his pocket and held it up to Pete.

"It looks like a toothpick to me," he said.

"It's not just any toothpick," Monk said. "It's the one that the captain threw on the street in an act of wanton lawlessness."

"We were nowhere near Chinatown," Disher said.

"He's talking about a different kind of wanton, Randy," Stottlemeyer said, "though I have no idea why."

"I am completely lost," Disher said. "Can we please start over from the beginning?"

Monk glared at Pete. "Why was your car parked three blocks away from the scene?"

"Because there was horrible traffic and I don't have a siren," Pete replied. "I had to take a roundabout route to the scene and grabbed the first open parking spot I found."

"You parked illegally, didn't you?"

"I didn't pay attention to the parking restrictions because I am exempt from them when I am on official police business."

"When you got back to your car, you found a parking ticket under your wind-shield wiper," Monk said. "You crumpled up the ticket and threw it on the street. You littered. I saw it with my own eyes."

"I was tired and irritable. I shouldn't have thrown the ticket away, even if I didn't have to pay it, but that doesn't make me a killer. It makes me a litterbug."

"You should have looked at it first before you threw it away. Overnight parking is illegal on the street without a permit. You were cited at four forty-two a.m., several hours *before* you say that you arrived at the scene." Monk took the other Baggie out of his pocket and showed him the parking ticket inside. "If you'd kept this, instead of following the captain's shameful example and throwing it on the street, I might never have suspected that you were the murderer."

Pete lowered his head. He was caught and he knew it. His demeanor changed.

"I'm losing everything. My home, my car, my savings. Even my wife left me," Pete said. "Clasker ruined a lot of lives but he gets to keep everything in his life that I lost in mine. I couldn't live with that."

"But you can live with murdering the guy," Stottlemeyer said.

"I don't see it as murder," Pete said.

"Maybe you don't," Stottlemeyer said. "But I do. And I'm betting a jury will, too. Get him out of here, Randy."

Disher stepped forward, handcuffed Pete, and read him his rights as he led him away.

"That will teach him to litter," Monk said.

"I think the bigger crime here was murder," Stottlemeyer said, taking the two Baggies from Monk.

"One leads to the other," Monk said.

"Technically, he littered *after* he committed the murder," Stottlemeyer said. "So my tossing the toothpick on the street had nothing to do with anything."

"Of course it did," Monk said. "Your criminal act was still fresh in his mind when he saw that ticket on his car. He might have thought twice about littering if not for your recent example. It was that carelessness that did him in."

"Okay, I'll buy that," Stottlemeyer said. "So you should thank me."

"For admitting you were wrong?"

"For my wanton lawlessness. If it wasn't for my littering, you wouldn't have caught him," Stottlemeyer said. "But forget it. I don't mind. What matters is that you closed the case. You did good work, Monk. In fact, it was incredible. I feel like a bigger fool than usual for letting this one slip past me."

"Does this mean I get my job back?" Monk asked.

"If it was up to me, it would, but it's not,"

Stottlemeyer said. "I'm sorry."

The captain clapped Monk on the back and walked away.

Monk watched him go. All the joy of solving the case was gone. The sadness was back. And so was something else. He slumped his shoulders, licked his lips, and wheezed.

"My throat is so dry," he said.

CHAPTER EIGHT:
MR. MONK CUTS BACK

In the space of just twenty-four hours, Monk had lost his drinking water and his income. I was worried that he might be on the verge of a complete nervous breakdown. So I called Dr. Bell and got Monk an emergency appointment just to be on the safe side.

While Monk was in with his shrink, I started calling other law enforcement agencies, from local police departments to the California Department of Fish and Game, to see if they were interested in his consulting services. Ordinarily they would be, they told me, but now they were all in as bad as or worse financial shape than the SFPD.

So I started approaching private security firms.

The last time Monk got fired, he immediately snagged a cushy position at Intertect, a slick high-tech detective agency. He even got a liberal expense account, a company car, and full medical coverage.

Unfortunately, Intertect went out of business and the other agencies in the Bay Area were making desperate efforts to cut their costs. I tried to convince them that one Adrian Monk was worth fifty Sam Spades, but nobody was buying my pitch.

So when Dr. Bell emerged from his office for a break after two hours of counseling Monk, I was nearly as distraught as his patient and told him so.

Dr. Bell sat down in the chair across from me. "Of course you're feeling some anxiety, Natalie. It's not just Adrian's livelihood that's at stake. It's yours, too."

"How is Mr. Monk doing?"

"He's much better now," Dr. Bell said. "He's curled up in the fetal position on my couch, clutching a bottle of Summit Creek to his chest and sobbing tearlessly."

"*That's* an improvement?"

"I came out here to see if you had a line on a few job openings yet to give him some hope."

"He doesn't believe in hope."

"He says he doesn't but really he does. Hope is what has kept him going through all the adversity he's faced over the years, whether he admits it or not."

"Unfortunately, Doctor, I don't have any

hope to give him. There are no jobs available for out-of-work detectives, no matter how brilliant they are."

"You'll find something for him. But you might have to widen your search outside of his comfort zone," Dr. Bell said.

"Anything outside of his front door is outside his comfort zone. I'm not even sure he *has* a comfort zone. You should know that better than anybody."

"I'm confident that there's a job out there that's right for a man of his considerable skills and that you will find it. In the meantime, he's going to be relying on you more now than ever before."

"I don't know if I'm up to it, Doctor."

"All you have to do is be there. Everything is changing around him. But he knows you're the one thing he can always count on."

"He said that?"

"He doesn't have to," Dr. Bell said. "And I suspect you feel the same way about him."

"Don't start psychoanalyzing me. I can't afford it. Let's concentrate on Mr. Monk."

"Fair enough. This crisis could ultimately turn out to be a very positive experience for him. He can learn that change often is another word for opportunity."

"That sounds nice on a fortune cookie

but I'm not sure it's true, at least not in my life."

Monk emerged from the office, still clutching the bottle of water. "I think it would be a good idea if I spent the night here. Perhaps the entire week."

"I have other patients, Adrian."

"They won't mind," Monk said.

"Yes, they will," Dr. Bell said.

"Then it's too bad for them," Monk said. "I'm more important to you than they are."

"I care equally about all of my patients."

"But me more equally."

"I also have a life of my own," Dr. Bell said.

"You can go on with it," Monk said. "You won't even notice I'm there."

"You don't need me now, Adrian." Dr. Bell stood up. "I'm confident that you can handle this on your own until our next appointment."

"You're probably right," Monk said. "I can hold on until five."

"Our next appointment is the day after tomorrow."

Monk made a little squeaking sound. Dr. Bell walked to the front door and held it open for us.

"Think of this as an investigation," Dr. Bell said. "But instead of solving a crime

96

and looking for the perpetrator, you'll be looking for new opportunities and, ultimately, finding yourself."

We walked outside onto the street. We stood side by side for a moment in silence. Then Monk looked at me.

"Did that make any sense to you?"

"None at all," I replied.

"It's nice to know I'm not alone on that."

"You're definitely not alone, Mr. Monk." I slipped my arm around his and we walked to my car.

As soon as we got back to Monk's house, he immediately started cleaning. He scrubbed the floors and countertops, dusted every shelf, washed every window, disinfected all the doorknobs, shined the lightbulbs, and vacuumed the ceilings. It was how he handled stress. He found all the cleaning very calming.

While he occupied himself with that, I called anybody I could think of who did any kind of investigating, from insurance companies to home inspection services. I called the city editor at the *San Francisco Chronicle* and told them that they ought to put Monk on the Sebes case, but they weren't interested in his services.

Nobody was.

So I followed Dr. Bell's advice and widened my job search outside of detectives. I called the folks at Diaper Genie and urged them to hire Monk, their biggest fan, to market their innovative product. He was, after all, the one who nominated the inventor of the diaper disposal unit for a Nobel Prize.

As much as the Diaper Genie people appreciated Monk's enthusiasm, and his fervent belief that their dirty-diaper-bagging gizmo should be used for disposing of all household trash, they just didn't have a position for him.

By the time I finished that call, it was already six p.m. and, with no murders to investigate, my workday was over.

Monk joined me at the dining room table carrying two teaspoons of water and offered me one.

"No, thanks," I said.

He sipped from one spoon and then the other. "Have you found us any work?"

"I'm afraid not."

"Well, you can stop now. I've come up with a plan of action."

"What is it?"

"I'm going to volunteer to consult for the police for free until they can afford me again."

"We talked about that the last time they fired you," I said. "What's their incentive for paying you if they know you'll do it for nothing?"

"I'll take that chance. I have some money saved up."

"It could be a long time before they can afford outside consultants again," I said. "For all we know, it could even be a year or more. Do you have that much money set aside to support yourself and me?"

"Hell no," he said. "That's why you're going to have to take a significant pay cut."

"How significant?"

"You'll be assisting me pro bono."

"I see," I said, trying not to lose my temper. "And how am I supposed to pay my bills?"

"I suppose you'll have to work nights at a part-time job."

"I need a full-job."

"I *am* a full-job."

"You certainly are," I said. "But you aren't going to pay me."

"Don't be so selfish and materialistic. There are more important things in life than money."

"Like assisting you, for instance."

"Yes," he said. "It's like a higher calling."

"What about my obligations as a mother

to support and care for my daughter?"

"Julie is not a child anymore. She's nearly eighteen. It's time she got a job, enjoyed some independence, and learned the skills she's going to need to live on her own. You've coddled her for too long."

Monk was right about Julie, not that he knew anything about raising a kid or even living on his own. And, as much as I hated to admit it, even to myself, he was right about me.

I was a widow, Julie was my only child, and I liked having her near me. I didn't want to let her go. I'd been spoiling her and keeping her too close, limiting her independence out of my own neediness.

And Julie, being a very smart kid, probably knew that and, as much as she chafed against my overprotectiveness, found ways to use it to her advantage. The conversation we had last night proved that to me.

I had to agree with Monk. It was time for Julie to get a job, if for no other reason than to gain some work experience and learn that money isn't easy to come by.

But that didn't mean I accepted Monk's argument and was ready to work a graveyard shift in some menial job just so I could devote my days to doting on him.

I knew how much Monk needed me,

especially now, but I had to put my family first. If he couldn't afford to pay me, I would have to find a new job, regardless of the consequences for him.

But I didn't want to deal with it right at that moment. It had been a long day for both of us. Putting off a decision for another day or two, until I saw how things were shaking out, wouldn't make a difference.

"Let's talk about this tomorrow," I said. "I've got to get going before the bike shop closes."

"Okay, but my mind is made up," he said.

"It usually is," I said.

I left Monk's place, dropped off Julie's bike, and stopped at Mama Petrocelli's to pick up a pizza on my way home.

I could never walk into the place without Warren Horowitz, the fortysomething owner, flirting with me and begging me to work for him again. I'd waited tables there fifteen years ago right after he bought the place from the Petrocellis. Warren still used their recipes, though he'd added a "Matzorella Pizza" to the menu just to make the place his own.

"If you won't work for me," Warren said, "the least you could do is marry me."

"It's tempting," I said. "But I think I'll take a salami pizza to go instead."

"Hebrew National or Italian?"

"Italian," I said.

"You're breaking my heart, Natalie," he said.

"I'm making a sacrifice so you'll marry a nice Jewish girl."

"Have you been talking to my mother?"

I left without getting engaged, set the pizza out on the kitchen table when I got home, and found Julie in her room, video-chatting with three of her friends at once on her Mac.

She and her friends were sharing video clips and watching them together from afar. Well, not that far. Two of the three girls Julie was iChatting with lived right around the corner.

I would have preferred that she hung out with her friends in person rather than sitting at her computer looking at their faces on a screen. Video-chatting seemed emotionally distant and totally unnecessary when it was possible to actually meet in person without much effort. She didn't agree. I know because we'd argued about it a dozen times.

"Dinner is ready," I said, standing in the doorway to her room.

"Can I eat in here?" she asked without looking away from her screen.

"We need to talk. In person. Face-to-face, the way it was done in the olden days."

"Can't we talk later? I'm busy."

"Now," I said. Call me old-fashioned, but I liked to eat dinner together whenever possible.

She dragged herself into the kitchen as if she was facing a root canal. Her attitude only made what I intended to say to her that much easier.

"Thanks for embarrassing me in front of my friends," Julie said, dropping into her seat at the table. She looked at the pizza in front of her like it was a plate of dog poop.

"Were they in the room? I didn't see them there." I took a bite out of my pizza. I wasn't going to let her ruin the meal for me.

"That's not funny," she said. "You know they were on the computer. They could see and hear everything. You need to be aware of that when you enter my room."

"You do. I don't," I said. "If you saw them in person instead of on the computer, I could say whatever I wanted in your room without any risk of embarrassing you."

"You could just stay out of my room," she said. "That would solve the problem."

I could still remember how sweet and loving my daughter used to be before her hormones started kicking in. She still could be sweet but it was a rare event. I found myself having to assert my authority more and more and I hated it.

"Don't talk to me like that," I said. "I'm your mother. I could solve the problem by taking that computer away from you."

"It's mine," she said.

"But I pay for the electricity it runs on and the Internet connection that allows you to chat with your friends," I said. "Your computer isn't going to be much use to you if I shut that stuff off, is it? This brings me to what I wanted to talk with you about. We're going to have to cut back on our spending around here."

"We don't spend anything as it is," she said.

"It may mean doing without some things," I said. "The police department is in a budget crunch, so they had to let Mr. Monk go."

"That's great," she said. Suddenly even the pizza looked good to her. She picked up her slice and started eating.

I found her reaction perplexing.

"How do you figure that?" I asked.

"Last time he got fired you got a Lexus as a company car."

Ah, so that was it.

Julie saw this as a chance to get my crappy Buick.

She thought Monk's firing meant he'd get a better-paying job with a big detective agency like last time and that her car problems would be solved.

She was so wrong, and she deserved the disappointment she was about to experience for being so self-centered. All she was thinking about was her own needs. What about our needs as a family? What about Monk's needs?

It occurred to me that teenagers are a lot like Monk. They think the whole world revolves around them, their troubles, and their needs.

Julie was in for a wake-up call from life tonight.

"This time it's different," I said. "There's no job waiting for him anywhere. He's out of work and so am I. All we've got to live on is my last paycheck."

"So you're fired, too."

"That's right. No new car. No new anything. Because there's no money."

She set down her pizza and looked at me. I saw some genuine concern in her eyes. For a moment, the sullen, insolent, and hormonal Julie was gone and my loving daughter was back.

"This is the longest you've ever held one job," she said.

"It's also been the most interesting, exciting, surprising, challenging, frustrating, exhausting, and aggravating one I've ever had."

"And the most dangerous," Julie said.

"And the lowest paying," I said.

"What are you going to do?"

"Look for something else."

"What about Mr. Monk?"

"I'm going to try to find a job for him that we can do together," I said. "And if I can't, then he's on his own and so am I."

"Can he even function without you?"

"I'll never abandon him entirely. He will always be a part of our lives, no matter what happens."

"Whether we like it or not," she said.

"I like it," I said, surprising myself as much as Julie with the admission. "I don't think I would have stayed with him this long if I didn't. I like who I am when I am with him. In fact, it wasn't until I started working for him that I even knew who that was."

"You're not making any sense at all," Julie said. Sullen, disapproving, hormonal Julie was back. It was like my daughter had a split personality disorder.

"What all of this means for you," I said,

"is that you are going to get a job."

"Excuse me?" she said.

"You're going to work this summer. Things are tight around here and you're expensive to maintain. So you're going to start paying some of the costs. I'll pay for food, utilities, medical care, all of the essentials. But if you want to go to the movies, or buy new clothes that you don't really need, or send twenty-five hundred texts on your cell phone, or download some songs from iTunes, you're going to pay for it."

"With what?"

"The money you earn," I said. "Working."

She stood up, her face reddening with anger. "You can't do that."

"Why not?"

"It's summer," she said.

"That's when kids work," I said. "That's why they are called summer jobs."

"Maybe that was true in the Dark Ages, but not now."

"These are the Dark Ages for us," I said. "That's what I am trying to tell you."

"You can't put children to work."

"Why not?"

"It's wrong — that's why," she said. "There are laws against it. They're called child labor laws."

"You aren't a child and, up until now, you

haven't done any labor," I said. "Tomorrow morning you're going to start looking for work. This isn't open to debate. It's an edict."

"What if someone sees me working?" she said. "They'll think we're poor."

"We are," I said. "That's what I've been trying to tell you."

She pointed her finger at me like it was a weapon.

"This is all your fault. You've failed and now I have to suffer for it."

"You don't know anything about suffering," I said. "But you're about to learn some things about sacrifice and hard work and what it really means to be an independent adult, which you keep telling me is how you want to be treated. Well, congratulations, sweetheart, your wish just came true."

"You are the worst mother ever," Julie declared.

She was lashing out, desperately trying to hurt me. She'd have to raise her game to do that.

"I've been wearing that crown for a while now," I said.

"You're out of work, we're broke, and you can't support us, so now I've got to get a job so we can eat," she said. "What would Dad think of you right now?"

Julie stormed out of the kitchen, and it's a good thing that she did. Because if she'd been near me, I would have slapped her right across the face and earned my crown.

CHAPTER NINE:
MR. MONK IS CLEANED OUT

Julie didn't show up for breakfast the next morning. I knew she was up, though, because I could hear her moving around in her room behind her closed door.

I didn't know whether she was sulking over having to find work or avoiding me because she regretted the hurtful things that she'd said.

Either way, I was content just to eat my Grape-Nuts cereal, drink my Trader Joe's instant coffee, and read the *Chronicle* without any confrontations or icy silences.

I opened the paper expecting the lead story to be all about the police closing the Clasker murder case, a clipping I'd hoped to use to get Monk some work. The story was there, but it was buried at the bottom of the page and no reference was made to Monk's role in solving the case. Stottlemeyer would be hearing from me about that.

The big story on the front page, and most

of the others, was about Bob Sebes and a financial scandal that was being compared to the Bernie Madoff case.

While Bob was locked up in his mansion, his wife, Anna, ventured out every day, not the least bit intimidated by the paparazzi on the street. She strolled past them to her black Mercedes like a supermodel showcasing the latest designer fashions, which, in fact, she unabashedly was doing, too.

Anna Sebes looked positively elegant in an old-fashioned, movie star kind of way, evoking Bette Davis or Joan Crawford at their peak. She wore a scarf or a hat, huge dark sunglasses, and her signature gloves, which hid her arthritis-gnarled hands.

"My husband is under arrest," she said to reporters. "Not me. Why should I stay locked up in that dreary house? I'm not accused of any wrongdoing."

Maybe so, but prosecutors were moving fast to freeze her assets, claiming they were the spoils of her husband's swindles. In fact, their yacht was put in her name and $10 million had been transferred to her personal account only days before the Ponzi scheme was revealed.

Along with the news stories, there was a profile of Bob and Anna Sebes' long marriage, their active roles in local charities, and his recent near-death experience from an allergic reaction to alcohol while partying on his yacht on the high seas, hundreds of miles from a hospital.

I guess that story was meant to humanize the Sebeses, but it didn't stir any sympathy for them with me and I'm sure it didn't with anybody else.

My hunger for salacious gossip and scandal now sated, I finished my breakfast, left the Classifieds section open to the jobs page for Julie, and headed to Monk's place. I brought my laptop along with me so I could search the Internet for a job for us.

I was walking up to Monk's door when my cell phone rang. It was Ted Drysdale, the manager of my bank.

Teddy and I had dated briefly a few years back and he was very sweet, but we just didn't click as a couple. Neither one of us was hurt in the breakup and he'd sort of watched over me ever since, turning a blind eye if I occasionally had overdrafts and waiving the late fees if my mortgage payments were tardy.

After a few pleasantries, he said, "I'm sorry to call you so early, but I wanted you to know that there's a problem with your checking account."

"Don't worry about the low balance,

Teddy. There won't be any overdrafts. I deposited my paycheck yesterday."

"That's what I'm calling about. It bounced."

"My check from Adrian Monk? Are you sure?"

"Of course I am. He has the only checks I've ever seen where all the numbers are even, including the check number, the account number, and the payment amount. So don't write any checks, use your credit card."

I already owed so much on my credit card that the interest charges alone had long since surpassed the principal debt.

"Thanks, Teddy. I appreciate it," I said. "I owe you coffee at McDonald's."

"Did Starbucks close?"

"No, I just can't afford it anymore."

I hung up and took a few deep breaths to calm myself before seeing Monk. I didn't want to march in angry and say something I might regret. It might not be his fault. There could be a perfectly innocent, reasonable explanation for Monk writing me a bad check. But if there wasn't, he wouldn't have to worry about dying from dehydration. I'd kill him with my bare hands.

I opened the door and walked in, announcing myself as I always did.

"It's me, Mr. Monk," I said.

Monk was in the kitchen cleaning his toothbrush with boiling water, part of his morning ritual, but he was mewling while he did it.

"What's wrong?" I asked.

"I had to use four teaspoons of Summit Creek to clean my toothbrush," he said. "That puts me four teaspoons closer to death."

"Before you die, I'd like you to pay me for last month's work."

"I did," Monk said. "On my deathbed."

"You were on the couch."

"Aha!" he said, pointing his finger at me accusingly, as if I was a murderer he'd just caught in an incriminating slip of the lip. "So you know I already wrote a check. You are trying to take advantage of my dehydration to double dip. That's a betrayal of my trust and tantamount to embezzlement. Natalie, I am surprised at you."

I could play the guilt game, too.

"And I'm hurt that you'd even think for a millisecond that I would take advantage of you that way," I said. "How could you after all these years and everything we've been through together? You should be ashamed of yourself."

114

"Then why do you want me to pay you twice?"

"Because the check you wrote me yesterday bounced."

"How could it bounce?"

"Either you called the bank and canceled payment" — which was what I suspected he did — "or you don't have enough funds in your account to cover the check."

"I didn't call the bank and I have plenty of money in my account," he said. Then he caught himself. "By plenty, I mean barely enough to survive."

"Then there's a problem," I said. "And we're going to the bank right now to solve it."

Carly Tran frowned at her computer.

She was a young, very energetic woman who'd introduced herself to us as our personal banking officer. Monk explained to her that a check that he'd written had bounced even though there was an adequate, if not sizable, amount of money in his account. She gave us a big smile and said it would be her pleasure to take care of the matter.

Now she was frowning. I took that as a bad sign.

"I'm afraid that your current account balance is zero," she said, turning the screen around in case Monk didn't take her word for it.

"How can that be?" he asked.

"On the first even-numbered business day of each month for the last several years, you received a regular transfer from your investment manager into your checking account," she said. "That transfer didn't occur for the last three months, so your funds were depleted."

I turned to Monk. "You have an investment manager?"

"Yes," Monk said. "He also pays some of my recurring bills for me, like my rent, utilities, that sort of thing."

"You never told me that."

"I don't discuss my personal finances with my underlings."

"We need to talk to this guy," I said. "Who is he?"

"His name is Bob Sebes," Monk said.

Carly Tran stared at him in shock. So did I. Monk looked between us both and smiled.

"Impressed, aren't you?" Monk said, clearly pleased with himself. "You didn't think I moved in those rarified circles. Not everyone is invited to participate in the Reinier Fund. Just special people like me."

Carly and I shared a look and then I faced Monk.

"You honestly don't know?" I said.

"Don't know what?" Monk said.

"That Bob Sebes was arrested for orchestrating one of the largest frauds in American history."

"You must be mistaking him for someone else," Monk said. "Bob Sebes is a highly respected member of the financial community and an absolute genius with numbers. He's delivered a consistent twelve percent return with his Reinier Fund for years."

"It was a lie. There were no investments," I said. "It was a massive Ponzi scheme. He used the money from new investors to pay dividends to his earlier ones. It all fell apart when the economy tanked and people started withdrawing their money. There's two billion dollars missing."

"Pyramid schemes always fail — it's inevitable. Bob Sebes is far too smart for that." Monk shook his head and glanced at Carly. "You're a financial professional — you tell her."

"She's right, Mr. Monk. It's been all over the news. Private individuals, charities, universities, and banks all over the world were swindled by him, including ours,"

Carly said. "Have you been in seclusion somewhere?"

"No more than usual," Monk said.

"How much of your money did he have?" I asked.

"All of it," Monk replied.

Carly cleared her throat. "Obviously, you shouldn't write any more checks until you have replenished your checking account. But under the circumstances, I'm afraid we will have to put a ten-day hold on any deposits you make to this account for the time being." She smiled again. "Is there anything else I can do to serve you today?"

"No, thank you," I said.

I don't know what I was thanking her for. She'd only given us bad news and placed new restrictions on his account.

"Please feel free to stay here as long as you like." She got up from her desk and walked away to give us some privacy.

Monk shook his head. "There must be some kind of mistake. Bob Sebes would never do something like this to me."

"Why did you give him your money?"

"For all the right reasons. I was impressed by the Reinier Fund's steady, even returns and I trusted his good name."

"His good name? What do you know about high finance and hedge funds?"

"Nothing," Monk said.

"So why did his name mean anything to you?"

And then it hit me. He didn't know anything about Sebes' reputation. "Oh my God. You mean his 'good name' literally, don't you? I can't believe it. You invested with him because his name and the name of his fund are palindromes, the same spelling forward and backward."

"It's a very good indication of trustworthiness," Monk said. "Did you know his wife is named Anna?"

"It doesn't mean a thing."

"I also looked at his client list. It included major institutions and very wealthy individuals."

"He wiped them all out," I said.

"I'm sure this is all a big misunderstanding." Monk stood up. "I want to see him."

"He's under house arrest, Mr. Monk, and there's a mob of reporters and angry investors camped outside his door. He won't see you."

"He will," Monk said and walked away.

It took me a moment to get to my feet. I was feeling a little weak-kneed. It might as well have been me who'd invested my life savings with Bob Sebes. Because if Monk was broke, then it meant I was, too.

CHAPTER TEN:
MR. MONK VISITS HIS MONEY

There was a line of satellite trucks, news vans, and motor homes parked along the street outside of Sebes' Pacific Heights mansion. Reporters, cameramen, and photographers sat around on folding camp chairs and chaise longues. They were waiting for Bob Sebes to emerge and, in the meantime, using the house as a backdrop for their daily live news updates on the scandal.

Sebes had come out only once since being released on bail with a GPS tracker strapped to his ankle, and that was to attend another court hearing. He'd barely made it to his Mercedes before the pack surrounded his car, trying to get a picture or a sound bite from the unrepentant swindler.

But Anna left the house almost every day. The press followed her around at first, on the off chance they could catch her making some lavish purchase or that she'd slip up and say something stupid to them. She was too smart for that, so they soon lost interest in her.

There were lots of uniformed police officers, sheriff's deputies, and even a couple of FBI agents outside the house, too, just in case Sebes tried to make a break for it or his victims decided to form a lynch mob.

No one paid any attention to us as we walked up to the house. Bob Sebes' Tudor-style mansion had become a tourist attraction. People came from all over to pose for pictures in front of the big iron gate with his initials written in gold lettering in the center.

Since the scandal broke, the golden B.S. had taken on an entirely new meaning.

I was surprised to see two familiar faces on the other side of the gate, walking up the front path to the door. And they were equally surprised to see me.

Stottlemeyer and Disher turned around and came back to the gate.

"What are the two of you doing here?" Stottlemeyer asked.

"I've come to see Bob Sebes," Monk replied.

"Sebes isn't going to talk to you."

"He will."

"Why would he want to do that?" Stottlemeyer asked.

"Because the bank says that he took all of my money," Monk replied. "And I want an explanation."

Stottlemeyer stared in shock at Monk. "*You* invested with Sebes?"

Monk nodded.

"He's been cleaned out," I said.

"Oh my God," the captain said.

"I don't know what's worse," Monk said. "Swindling people out of their money or besmirching a sacred word like *cleaned.*"

"I do," I said.

"This is terrible news," Disher said. "Which I hope you received after you bought my birthday gift."

"Show a little sensitivity, Randy," I said.

"You're right. That was a terrible thing to say. I'm so sorry," Disher said. "I want you to know that you can exchange whatever you bought for me from my Nordstrom registry for something less expensive on the list. It will be our secret." He motioned to me and the captain. "And theirs, too. But the surprise party is still on, right?"

Stottlemeyer rubbed his forehead and sighed. "I think what Randy is trying to say is that we both feel awful about this, Monk. I know it couldn't come at a worse time for you."

"There's never a good time to lose everything," I said.

"The timing doesn't matter, Natalie," Monk said. "It's always the worst time for me. It has been since birth, which is a horrible way to enter the world. I still haven't gotten over it."

He grimaced with disgust and shivered from head to toe.

"I don't understand why you invested with Sebes," Stottlemeyer said. "You're not the kind of guy who takes risks with his money. Or with anything."

"I had faith in his good name," Monk said.

"It's a palindrome," I said.

Stottlemeyer nodded. So did Disher.

"That was a great movie," Disher said. "I wonder why Tina Turner didn't act again after that."

"Palindrome," Stottlemeyer said. "Not *Thunderdome*."

Disher nodded again. "Is that also a huge cage where you fight to the death with chainsaws?"

"A palindrome is something that reads the same forward as it does backward," Stottlemeyer said. "Like the word *level*."

"That's not nearly as exciting as a Thunderdome," Disher said. "I'm not surprised that they didn't make a movie about it."

Stottlemeyer turned to Monk. "You gave the guy everything you had because you liked his name?"

"When something is level, it inspires confidence and security," Monk said. "Everything about Bob and Anna Sebes and the Reinier Fund was level."

"Apparently not," Disher said.

"That's why I need to talk to him," Monk said.

"You and a few thousand other people," Stottlemeyer said. "But he's not talking to anyone."

"He'll talk to me," Monk said.

"I can't think of a reason why he would," Stottlemeyer said.

"Because I'll be going in with you, and you're here to talk with him about a murder," Monk said. "And I will prove he did it."

Stottlemeyer looked around to make sure nobody heard Monk, then stepped close to the bars, speaking in a very low, conspiratorial voice.

"We're investigating a suspicious death. We don't know yet whether it was an accident or a murder. But one thing we do know, without question, is that Bob Sebes didn't do it, though it could have some connection to his fraud case, which is why the

Tiburon police brought us into it."

"Who was killed?" I asked.

"Russell Haxby, Reinier's chief compliance officer," Disher replied. "He was electrocuted in his hot tub last night at his home in Tiburon. His gardener found him this morning. The press hasn't picked up the story yet but it won't stay a secret for long."

"How was he electrocuted?"

"The bug zapper on his overhang fell into the water," Disher said. "And he got zapped."

"If Haxby was the compliance officer, he was in a good position to testify against Sebes," Monk said. "That's a strong motive for murder."

"Yes, it is," Stottlemeyer said. "But if it was a murder, Sebes could not have done it."

"You can't rule anyone out," Monk said.

"Haxby was killed in Tiburon at around eight p.m. and Sebes was right here in his house across the bay."

"How do you know?"

"Because Sebes is wearing a tamperproof ankle bracelet with a built-in GPS tracking system that is constantly monitored. On top of that, his house is surrounded, and under twenty-four-hour surveillance by the police, the FBI, the sheriff, and the national news media."

Monk rolled his shoulders and cocked his head from side to side.

"He's the guy," Monk said.

"We don't even know it was murder," Stottlemeyer said, the veins in his neck bulging as he tried to control both his exasperation and his voice from rising.

"He's the guy," Monk said.

"Sebes has an airtight, ironclad, irrefutable alibi."

"That proves he's the guy," Monk said.

"Because he couldn't be the guy," I said.

"Exactly," Monk said. "Plus he took all of my money and besmirched the word *clean* for eternity."

Stottlemeyer got so close to the gate that his face was practically up against the bars, his nose poking through the space between the slats.

"You're not a consultant with the police anymore, you're not here to investigate a murder, and you're crippled by a staggering conflict of interest that makes you incapable of being objective about any of this. But I'm going to let you in to see him anyway."

"You are?" Disher said. "Why?"

"Because Monk is my friend and this son of a bitch took all of his money. Monk deserves the chance to confront him."

"Thank you, Leland," Monk said.

"Just don't make me regret it," the captain said, opening the gate and ushering us in.

"You will," I said as I passed him.

"I know," he replied with a sorrowful nod, and we trooped up to Bob Sebes' front door.

Anna Sebes greeted us at the door. She was expecting Captain Stottlemeyer, but she still asked to see his badge as a formality. She didn't ask the rest of us who we were and motioned us inside with a sweep of her gloved hands.

The marbled entry hall was ringed by two grand curving staircases that framed a massive crystal chandelier hanging from the ceiling over a sculpture of a generously endowed naked man on a pedestal.

Monk shielded his eyes from the sculpture as we followed Anna into the great room, which was filled with paintings, sculptures, and knickknacks that I'm sure were all hugely expensive masterpieces.

A massive window framed a spectacular view of the Golden Gate Bridge, making it appear as if the span and the bay were just two more works of art in Sebes' possession.

Bob Sebes was standing in front of the window, his back to us as he admired his view. He was wearing a Tommy Bahama aloha shirt, long shorts, and leather flip-flops.

"Smile, everybody," he said. "I'm sure there's some jerk with a telephoto lens on a boat out there, taking pictures of us right now for some sleazy Web site. But I don't care. The view is the only thing that makes me feel free."

I groaned. "Oh, boo-hoo. You're lucky you're not living in a homeless shelter like some of the retirees that you've left penniless."

Bob Sebes turned around and looked at me. "Who are you?"

"I'm the woman who is going to vomit all over your hundred-thousand-dollar rug if I hear you whine any more about how rough life is for you now that your Ponzi scheme has collapsed."

"It's a nine-hundred-thousand-dollar rug and I'm as victimized as any of my investors, perhaps more so, because I have been abused by the courts and demonized by the media."

"Careful, Bob. I feel breakfast coming up," I said.

Stottlemeyer gave me a sharp look. "That's enough, Natalie." He turned to Bob. "We're here to ask you a few questions about Russell Haxby."

"Finally. He's the man who should be wearing this." Bob pointed to the ankle bracelet on his right leg. It looked like a laptop power adaptor attached to a tiny dog collar. "He's one of the key players who orchestrated the fraud, exploited my trust, and ruined the lives of so many people."

"You should have two," Monk said, still using his hands like visors, hiding most of his face.

"Two of what?" Bob asked him.

"Ankle bracelets. One for each leg."

"One is enough," Disher said.

"Only if you have one leg," Monk said. "But even then the right thing to do would be to get an artificial leg and put a GPS ankle bracelet around that, too, so you would still need two."

"Adrian?" Bob cocked his head and stepped toward us. "Is that you?"

I nudged Monk. "You can lower your hands now. We're past the naked man."

"He's got blisters," Monk said.

"The naked man?" I asked.

"Bob. On his heels. He's also got rampaging *tinea pedis* between his toes."

"You mean athlete's foot?"

"It's hideous," Monk said.

Bob stepped up close, peered at Monk,

129

and broke into a big grin.

"It *is* you," Bob said. "Adrian Monk! I am so glad to see you."

"You disgust me," Monk said, turning away.

"I didn't take your money, Adrian. You have to believe me. I'd hire you to prove it, but these jackals have frozen my assets. I'm telling you, I'm innocent."

"You have oozing blisters and virulent fungus on your feet," Monk said with disgust. "You've lost your innocence."

Stottlemeyer cleared his throat to direct everyone's attention back to him. I suppose it was more polite than shooting his gun in the air.

"If you didn't rip off everyone, Sebes, who did?"

"Russell Haxby was the ringleader of the scheme, but I'm sure there were others involved. There had to be. It's too big for one man to have pulled off on his own."

"No one believes that there aren't other people in your office who are guilty, too," Stottlemeyer said. "But they were taking orders from you. It was your fund. You were running it."

"Yes, I was the visionary, the big-picture guy. But I worked at the macro level of the business, not the micro level, not on the sales and trading floors. I wasn't the one who dealt with regulators or the accountants. I left those day-to-day details to Russell and others. I thought my directives were being carried out, but they weren't. They were ripping everybody off, me included. Isn't that why you're here?"

Stottlemeyer shook his head. "Russell Haxby is dead. He was electrocuted in his hot tub last night."

"Oh, God, no," Anna gasped, holding a gloved hand to her mouth. Bob went to her and they held each other for a long moment.

"You seem pretty broken up over a guy you just accused of masterminding the scheme to rip off your investors and frame you for the crime," Stottlemeyer said.

"That's because he's one of the few people who could have proved my innocence," Bob said, breaking away from his wife, but taking her hand.

"Haxby was cooperating with the prosecutors," Stottlemeyer said. "He was going to plead guilty to conspiracy this week and agree to testify against you in exchange for a lesser sentence."

"Of course he was," Anna hissed, "to focus attention away from himself and heap all the blame on poor Bob. Now that Russell is dead, we're screwed."

"Or saved," I said. "Depending on how you look at it."

"Did you come here to accuse us of something?" Bob said. "If so, get it over with already."

"You're filth," Monk yelled, stabbing a finger at Bob. "Putrid, disgusting, horrific primordial slime that isn't fit to walk among civilized men. You're a blight on humanity, Bob Sebes."

I'd seen Monk confront a hundred murderers but I'd never seen anything approaching this level of moral outrage from him. He was shaking. Then again, nobody had ever stripped him of every penny he had to his name. I didn't blame him for losing control.

"I didn't take your money," Bob said.

"Forget about the money," Monk said. "It doesn't matter anymore."

"It doesn't?" I said.

"Look at yourself, Bob. Your feet are being devoured by a parasitic fungus," Monk said. "They look like Chia Pets. In the name of all that's holy, wash your disgusting feet before the fungus spreads and the entire city is infested with your wanton pestilence."

We all stared at Monk for a long moment.

"Okay," Bob said softly, carefully. "I'll

soak my feet in some baking soda."

"Acid would be better," Monk said. "Or amputation."

"We didn't come here to criticize his personal hygiene," Stottlemeyer said to Monk.

"Perhaps if somebody did a long time ago, he wouldn't have committed his heinous crimes," Monk said. "The fungus has probably gone to his brain and rotted it away. He's got fungal foot brain. That's what happens when you engage in wanton pestilence!"

There it was again, *wanton pestilence.* Monk really liked that phrase. I was waiting for him to throw the word *feculence,* another of his favorites, into the discussion, too.

"Thanks a lot, Monk," Disher said. "You've just handed Bob Sebes his entire defense strategy on a silver platter."

Stottlemeyer turned to Disher. "What's he going to say? 'I'm innocent, Your Honor. I had athlete's foot'?"

"It's the fungal-foot brain defense," Disher said.

"It's absurd," Stottlemeyer said.

"Oh, really?" Disher said. "Thirty years ago, Dan White assassinated the mayor of San Francisco and a city supervisor and his defense was that he ate too many Twinkies.

That got him off with voluntary manslaughter instead of premeditated murder."

"You've got a point," Stottlemeyer said. "I stand corrected."

Bob looked at Monk. "Could athlete's foot fungus really spread to the brain?"

"It can spread everywhere," Monk replied. "It's probably creeping toward us right now."

Monk took a big step back. So did Disher.

Stottlemeyer rubbed his temples. "Let's forget about the foot fungus for a moment and talk instead about Russell Haxby. Can you think of anyone who might have wanted him dead?"

"Are you saying he was murdered?" Anna asked.

"I'm saying it's a possibility. It looks like he died in an accident, but until we're sure, we're treating it as a homicide."

"Any of his coconspirators in the fraud could have done it," Bob said. "Or any of the victims of his crime."

"Or you," Disher said.

"I couldn't have killed Haxby. Maybe you haven't noticed, Detective, but I can't even go outside and pick up my morning newspaper without it being broadcast live on CNN. Besides, even if I could leave the house, this ankle bracelet tracks my every move. You can probably tell me the last time I walked from the kitchen to my bedroom. So how could I possibly have killed anyone?"

"You could have hired someone to do it for you," Disher said.

"I needed Haxby alive," Bob said. "But even if I wanted him dead, I don't know any hit men and I don't have any money to hire one if I did, do I?"

"You tell me, Bob," Stottlemeyer said. "Perhaps you've got some money stashed away in an offshore account somewhere. Or your wife does. If you do, you know we're going to find it and any recent withdrawals either of you might have made."

"We're broke," Bob said.

"That makes three of us," I said.

"But at least we aren't being consumed by a flesh-eating fungus," Monk said. "I guess that proves there really is some justice in this world."

Chapter Eleven:
Mr. Monk and the Zapper

As soon as we stepped outside of Sebes' house, Monk took about a dozen wipes from me and rubbed them on his hands, his face, and his neck.

"Once that man is in prison," Monk said, "this house has to be burned to the ground and the ashes launched into outer space."

"Just because he has athlete's foot?" Disher asked.

"Any athlete with a foot like that would cut it off." Monk shoved the dirty wipes into a plastic Baggie, sealed it, and handed it to me for later disposal.

"Then he wouldn't be much of an athlete anymore," Stottlemeyer said. "Unless his sport was arm wrestling."

"Or hot dog eating," Disher said.

"Bob Sebes is the killer," Monk said. "There's no question about it."

"You're just saying that because he stole all your money, sullied the word *clean,* and has foot fungus," the captain said.

"Of course I am," Monk said. "What more evidence do you need?"

"We usually like to start with a murder."

"Take me to the crime scene and I'll prove it's a homicide."

"Have you forgotten that the captain fired you?" I said. "You are no longer employed as a consultant to the police department. You aren't employed at all. You're broke."

"So you're saying that I have plenty of time on my hands to spend at the crime scene."

"No, that's *not* what I am saying." I looked to Stottlemeyer for some support. "You tell him."

The captain shrugged. "What could it hurt? A drive out to Tiburon might take his mind off his troubles."

"Oh, now I get it," I said, feeling my face flushing with anger. "You didn't let Mr. Monk in to see Sebes out of sympathy for his plight. You did it because you knew he'd get hooked on this case. You took advantage of him."

"I want to do this," Monk said.

"Of course you do, and the captain knew you would." I glowered at Stottlemeyer. "You should be ashamed of yourself."

I would have slapped him but I didn't

137

want to make a scene in front of the press and get myself arrested for assaulting a police officer. I'd have a hard enough time finding work without a recent, and very public, arrest hanging over my head.

So I glowered at him some more and marched away.

I didn't speak to Monk as we followed Stottlemeyer over the Golden Gate Bridge to Tiburon. I was too angry at Monk and at the captain to speak without saying something I'd regret. I was also terrified about where my next paycheck was going to come from. It certainly wouldn't be coming from Monk now.

What kind of job could I find that would take me and Monk as a package deal?

And how long could I afford to keep looking for that elusive job before I had to abandon him and find something just for myself?

But even if I was freed of Monk, what job could I hope to find in this troubled economy? I didn't have qualifications for much of anything. As a matter of fact, I wasn't even qualified to be Monk's assistant when he hired me.

I felt a twinge of anxiety in my stomach. That's where I felt all my twinges, good and bad. It wasn't a pain or a cramp; it was more like a quiver, the strumming of a taut guitar string. I had so many worries building up in me that it felt like someone was doing an anxiety guitar solo in my stomach.

We followed Stottlemeyer to a house high in the densely wooded hills above Tiburon. The picturesque village still looked a lot like it did a hundred years ago. Many of the original buildings were still intact, while others were refurbished houseboats that were brought ashore when the lagoon was filled in back in the 1940s. Tiburon had a lot of charm.

Haxby's house was covered with cedar shingles and looked like four different houses of different heights that had been crammed together. The gabled and flat roofs intersected at odd angles, creating a collision of geometric shapes. Errant beams seemed to jut out like broken bones and the windows looked like enormous glass shards.

The house was an intentional rebuke of architectural symmetry and Monk regarded it like it was Bob Sebes' feet.

And yet, I liked it. Despite all the bizarre angles, and the extraneous structural elements that looked as if someone forgot to saw them off, the sprawling house blended naturally into the wooded surroundings.

There were houses just like Haxby's all over Marin County and the California coast. But since Monk didn't get around much, he hadn't been exposed to what architects would call the New Shingle or Shed Modern style. I called it Rich Hippie Chic. Monk had a different name for it.

"That house is an abomination. It should be demolished."

"The crime scene is around back," Stottlemeyer said, ignoring Monk's architectural review.

We followed the captain, our feet crunching and crackling on the loose gravel and pine needles. Monk grimaced, trying and failing to find a clean path.

"This is like walking on hot coals, except that I would prefer the coals."

"They'd burn your feet off," Disher said.

"And any germs along with them. Walking on pine needles is deadlier than walking on used syringes. One poke and you're dead."

We reached the backyard and Monk jumped on the wooden patio as if it was a life raft. From where he stood, we could survey the yard.

Thick bushes had been planted to create a green border around the backyard that didn't obstruct the view of the bay. It could be seen between the trees from the first-floor windows of the house or from the hot tub, which looked like a large wooden barrel that had been cut in half and set into the patio. Just outside of the bushes, at the far end of the property, was a cedar-shingled tool shed that matched the style of the house but had a half-moon cutout in the door.

The hot tub was empty now and cordoned off with yellow crime scene tape that was tied around two deck chairs and two of the posts of the wooden overhang that shaded the patio.

"The zapper was hanging from a hook on one of these two-by-fours." Stottlemeyer pointed to one of the slats that made up the top of the overhang. "The hook was old and rusty. Maybe a gust of wind came up and knocked the zapper into the hot tub."

"If the zapper was plugged into a ground fault circuit interrupter outlet, Haxby would have survived," Monk said.

"But it wasn't," Stottlemeyer said. "The house was built in the 1960s and I guess Haxby never got around to upgrading his outlets."

Monk squatted and examined the electric plug against the house.

"This is a new outlet," he said.

"How can you tell?" I asked.

"The screws are all shiny." Monk walked around and examined the other outlets. "These are all new outlets. Why would someone replace the outdoor outlets and not upgrade them to National Electrical Code standards?"

"Because he was an idiot, or lazy, or cheap," Stottlemeyer said. "Maybe he hired an unlicensed electrician who didn't know what the hell he was doing. Violating the National Electrical Code isn't evidence of a murder."

Monk approached the hot tub, his head cocked to one side, his hands framing the scene in front of him.

"Did Haxby live here alone?" Monk asked.

"Yes, but he often had guests," Disher said. "Of the single-female variety."

"How often did he use the hot tub?"

"His neighbors say they could hear it going every night," Disher said. "Sometimes he was alone, and sometimes he had little parties in there with several guests of the single-female variety at one time."

"So, in other words, a variety of single females of the single-female variety," Stottlemeyer said.

"I guess so," Disher said.

"That's a lot of variety," Stottlemeyer said, almost wistfully.

Disher glanced at the big house, the view, and the empty hot tub that Monk was circling. "Some guys have it all, Captain."

"And some guys get parboiled in their Jacuzzi and then don't have anything but a tombstone," Stottlemeyer said. "It's all a matter of perspective."

Disher brightened up immediately. "So that means we win."

"It's not a competition," Stottlemeyer said.

"Of course it is," Disher said. "I'm having a birthday and he's not. So who needs women and money?"

Stottlemeyer and Disher shared a look, as if to say, *Who are we kidding?*

"I don't," Monk said.

"That's not entirely true," I said. "You need me."

"Not in the same way," Monk said, stepping gingerly behind the nearest border of shrubs. "And you're not a woman."

"I'm pretty sure that I am."

"Not to me," he said.

"Then what is she, Monk?" Stottlemeyer asked.

"A Natalie."

Disher smiled at me. "You're still a woman to me."

"Don't get fresh, birthday boy," I said and

turned to Monk. "You also need money."

"Not in the same way," Monk said, crouching behind the shrubs so all we saw was the top of his head. "I don't need it to support an extravagant lifestyle."

"I think that having a full-time assistant doing every little thing for you is a pretty big extravagance," Stottlemeyer said.

"Is that what I am?" Disher said. "An extravagance?"

Stottlemeyer gave him a look. "You're not my full-time assistant."

"Since you got divorced, you're at the office eighteen hours a day. So am I. The only time I am not at your beck and call is when you're asleep, and even then I'm often doing every little thing for you."

"It's not the same at all," Stottlemeyer said, lowering his voice. "Monk can't function without Natalie."

"You can't function without me, either," Disher said.

"Of course I can," Stottlemeyer said.

Monk popped up from behind the shrubs like a jack-in-the-box.

"There's a rectangular impression in the dirt back here," he said. "And the dirt has been raked from here all the way back to the tool shed."

Stottlemeyer frowned. "What's your point,

144

Monk?"

"It's just an observation." Monk headed for the tool shed and we all followed after him.

"Your work for me doesn't extend beyond official police business," Stottlemeyer said to Disher.

"How is going to the drugstore to buy you Metamucil official police business?"

Monk opened the tool shed door and leaned his head inside.

"If I'm not regular I can't think clearly and it takes longer to solve the thorny crimes," Stottlemeyer whispered.

It was a good thing Monk didn't hear that. I wished that I hadn't, either.

"Besides, the city is paying you and I'm not, so it's not an extravagance — it's chain of command," the captain said. "End of discussion."

"Thank God," I said.

Monk leaned his head out of the tool shed. "It was definitely murder."

"How do you know?" the captain asked.

Monk took a handkerchief out of his pocket, reached into the tool shed, and picked up a foam rubber mat, the kind you use to cushion your knees while you're gardening.

"This rubber mat fits the rectangular

impression in the dirt beside the hedge," Monk said.

"The gardener could have used it," Disher said. "He could have raked the dirt, too."

"True, but that doesn't explain this." Monk put the mat back in the shed and pulled out a rake. "There are charred bugs between the tines of this rake. Here's what happened. At some point, either on the night of the murder or over a period of time before, the murderer replaced the outdoor electrical outlets with non-GFI ones. Last night, the killer crept behind the hedge, rested his knees on this rubber mat, and waited for Haxby to get into the hot tub. Once Haxby was in the water, the killer used the rake to lift the zapper off the hook and drop it into the hot tub."

"Wouldn't the killer have been electrocuted when the rake touched the live wires on the zapper?" Disher asked.

Monk shook his head. "The rubber mat protected him from that. After the murder, he raked his footprints, put everything back in the shed, and slipped away."

Stottlemeyer nodded. "It's a murder."

"I want to be there when you arrest Sebes," Monk said.

"He couldn't have done it," Stottlemeyer said.

"What about his wife?" Monk said. "Was she out last night?"

"Yes, she was," Disher said.

"Ah-ha," Monk said. "Does she have an alibi?"

Disher shook his head. "She took a long drive."

"To Tiburon to kill Russell Haxby and prevent him from testifying against her husband," Monk said. "Case closed."

"She couldn't have done it, Mr. Monk," I said.

He looked at me with astonishment. "How would you know?"

"Anna Sebes has arthritis in her hands," I said. "It's what ruined her career as a concert violinist and it's why she wears gloves. She couldn't have used a screwdriver to replace the outlets or lifted that rake, snagged the bug zapper, and dropped it into the hot tub."

"I'm telling you Sebes did this," Monk said. "He could have hired a hit man."

Stottlemeyer sighed wearily. "We've already been over this. His money is frozen, his phones are tapped, and he's wearing a GPS ankle bracelet. How could he contact a hit man?"

"Through his wife," Monk said.

"You don't find hit men in the yellow

pages, Monk. And even if you could, they don't work without being paid. It's much more likely that a pissed-off investor, unable to take his revenge out on Sebes, took his anger out on Haxby instead. The killer could be any of a thousand people."

"It could be one of your crime scene investigators, for example," I said.

Stottlemeyer gave me a nasty look. "Or the murder could have nothing to do with Sebes at all. Maybe it's a female of the single variety who didn't appreciate him entertaining other females of the single variety in his hot tub."

Monk shook his head. "No, it was Sebes."

"I appreciate the help you've given us today, Monk, especially after what Sebes has done to you. But that's another reason why you can't be involved in this case."

"That didn't stop you from dragging him out here and using him," I said.

"You can't be objective," Stottlemeyer continued, ignoring my remark. "Your judgment is clouded."

"I can be perfectly objective about that thieving, lying, soulless beast of wanton pestilence."

"There you go," Stottlemeyer said. "You just proved my point."

"That was a purely objective assessment,"

Monk said. "Haven't you met the man?"

"I don't want to see you anywhere near this case," Stottlemeyer said. "Or I'll arrest you for obstruction of justice, impersonating a police officer, and anything else I can think of."

"He's the guy. I am never wrong about this."

"He might be responsible in some way for Haxby's murder, and if he is, I'll find the evidence to prove it. But you're dehydrated, jobless, and broke. You can't possibly be thinking straight."

"I was born thinking straight."

"You're done here." Stottlemeyer put his arm around Monk, who, surprisingly, didn't flinch. "But if there is anything I can do to help you through this ordeal, you call me. Day or night, it doesn't matter. I want to help."

"I appreciate that, Leland," Monk said. "As a matter of fact, there is something you can do for me."

"Name it," he said.

"Arrest Bob Sebes for murder."

Chapter Twelve:
Mr. Monk Gets a Job

Monk was quiet on the drive back into the city. I was quiet as well. We both had a lot to think about and none of it was very pleasant.

It was only the late afternoon but I was ready to quit for the day and I didn't think Monk would object — not that he really had any right at this point. Since he wasn't paying me, I was no longer his employee.

We pulled up in front of his apartment building.

"Are you going to be okay tonight?" I asked.

He nodded and got out. "Ordinarily, I would drown my sorrows in Summit Creek water, but that would be suicide, considering how few bottles remain in existence. So I think I'll go to Safeway later and clean the scuff marks off of the floor, look for expired items, and organize the canned goods alphabetically and by food group."

I suddenly had an inspiration. "You can't go there."

"It's okay, Natalie. I've forgiven them for not carrying Summit Creek. It's not entirely their fault."

"I'm not talking about that."

"Oh, you're worried about Arthur. I'm sure that after hours of deep contemplation and careful reflection, he's realized that I was totally in the right. He's probably deeply ashamed and eager to make amends before I die of dehydration, a penniless pauper."

"I'm not talking about that, either."

"Then what are you babbling about?"

"They've been taking advantage of you for years, Mr. Monk, letting you clean and straighten up for nothing. It's time they started paying you for all the work that you do for them."

"It's not work," he said.

"It is for everybody but you."

"But I like doing it."

"There's nothing wrong with being paid to do something that you like so much that you'd do it for free. In fact, that's the definition of the dream job."

"So it's like your situation working for me."

It was a no-win situation. If I said no, I

would offend him. If I said yes, he would use that as an argument for me to continue working for him for no salary.

So I took the cowardly way out. I smiled, said nothing, and sped off in my car without even a good-bye, leaving him standing there at the curb, looking perplexed.

I drove over to Safeway, where I found Arthur stocking some granola bars on the shelves. I apologized profusely for Monk's bad behavior the other day. Arthur said that he understood, or maybe he was just being polite to a customer. Emboldened, I talked up how much the store meant to Monk, and said that he demonstrated that devotion by keeping the place organized and spiffy for years, on his own time, often in the wee hours of the night.

"Mr. Monk takes real pride in the store, that's for sure," Arthur conceded. "He can be irritating, but he does more to keep the store clean, and the shelves orderly, than any of the people who work here. He's also a lot more loyal, punctual, and dependable than they are."

Arthur had fallen right into my trap.

"Then you should hire him," I said. "And me, too."

I touted my past experience as a bartender and blackjack dealer to prove that I was adept at handling both money and difficult customers, and I promised that I'd keep Monk in line so Arthur wouldn't have to.

Fifteen minutes later, I walked out with two bags of groceries that I'd purchased with my new employee discount. Monk and I were to report for work the next morning as cashiers and stock persons.

I called Monk with the good news as soon as I got in the car. He wanted to start immediately, but I made him promise not to go to the store until morning. He could scrub the sidewalk outside of his house if he had an irresistible urge to clean something.

The news seemed to lift his spirits and I was pretty pleased with myself, too. Our new jobs weren't glamorous, or intellectually stimulating, but at least we'd be getting paychecks.

As happy as I was about getting us new jobs so fast, I knew that I wouldn't be earning nearly enough to make my mortgage payment, much less pay all of my other bills. The truth was, I was still in very deep trouble.

But I decided not to dwell on the scary stuff and to bask in my achievement for a while.

The basking ended the moment that I walked in the front door of my house and saw Julie sitting at the kitchen table, her shoulders slumped, a frown on her face.

Julie was still in a funk over yesterday's bad news and I dreaded telling her that things had gotten much worse. Somehow, I didn't think she'd be happy to learn her mom was now a cashier at Safeway.

I was right. She was mortified.

Julie's first reaction was to ask me to hide if anyone we knew ever came into the store.

"That's not very likely," I said. "The store isn't in our neighborhood."

"You shop there, don't you?"

"Because it's close to where I work," I said and then immediately corrected myself. *"Worked."*

"I'm sure other people we know work on that side of town. They could wander into the store to pick up some groceries on their way home. You might not have a chance to hide. So you should wear glasses, and a wig, and use a different name on your name tag, like Charlene, Roxi, or Ethel."

"Why Charlene, Roxi, or Ethel?"

"Those are good cashier names," she said. "Very working class."

"When did you become such a snob?"

"Do you realize what would happen to me if word got out about you at school?"

"I'm a cashier at Safeway," I said. "Not a

drug dealer or a hooker."

"They wouldn't be as bad."

"Are you suggesting I try those instead?"

"You know what I mean. You're being sarcastic but this is my life we're talking about."

"We aren't the only ones facing a financial crisis. There are plenty of people worse off than us. Look around at all the bank foreclosures on our block. I'm sure there are kids in your school whose parents have lost their homes."

"And those kids are gone," she said. "They've moved. They don't have to live with the shame."

"Of course they do. They're just doing it somewhere else."

"Where nobody knows them," she said. "That's a big difference."

"I'm not going to hide and I'm not going to wear a disguise. I'm not ashamed of working to support my family and you shouldn't be, either. In fact, now it's even more important that you find a job and earn your keep. We need every cent we can get."

She looked at me glumly. "Is it really that bad?"

"Yes, it is."

"Maybe we should move," she said. "And take the equity we have out of the house and live on it."

My teenage daughter was talking to me about our equity. I was struck by how childish and mature she could be at the same time.

"I bought this house with your father," I said. "I feel him in every room. It's one of the few things I still have that we both shared. That's the equity that matters most to me. It's worth making sacrifices for. I will not move just because you can't bear the thought of somebody seeing me in a Safeway uniform."

There was a long silence. Evoking her father's memory seemed to have knocked the wind out of her. She nodded somberly and her eyes began to tear up. It made me feel a little guilty for bringing Mitch into it.

"I'm sorry about what I said to you last night," she said. "*Really* sorry. I know Dad is proud of you. We both are. I didn't mean it."

"I know you didn't," I said, giving her a kiss on the cheek and stroking her hair. "It's okay."

"After last night, I thought things couldn't get any worse."

"If you and I support each other, and keep a positive attitude, we'll get through this. We might even come out of it better off than we were before."

"I don't see how we're going to end up rich with you working at Safeway."

"I don't mean better off financially. I mean as people. You're going to learn some things about yourself, and what you're capable of, that will surprise you."

She wiped her eyes with the back of her hand and sniffled. "There's a 'help wanted' sign down at the car wash. The pay is probably lousy, but it has the benefit of being walking distance from here."

"And you'll impress Mr. Monk," I said. "You'll be doing God's work."

"I guess it's better than joining a convent."

"The pay is certainly better," I said.

"On the other hand, if I went to a convent, there's not much chance that my friends would see me."

"I'm all for the convent," I said. "I can think of a lot of good reasons for you to go there, including the money it would save us on clothes, food, and broadband."

"I think I'd rather help God out by scrubbing bird poop off of Hondas," she said.

"It's your decision," I said. "But it's going to take you a lot longer to reach sainthood that way."

"I've already blown my shot at that," she said, smiling slyly at me, and headed to her room before I dared to ask her how she'd done that.

Russell Haxby's murder, seen as a severe blow to the prosecution's case against Bob Sebes, was front-page news in the *San Francisco Chronicle* that morning.

The article was illustrated with a grainy photograph of Bob Sebes, standing at his picture window, staring sadly out at the bay. The picture must have been taken just before we arrived, and I couldn't shake the feeling that Sebes was posing for the cameras that he knew were watching him.

The article noted that Haxby was Sebes' chief compliance officer and was killed after agreeing to testify against his former employer.

But the implication that Sebes might have been behind the murder was squashed by Captain Stottlemeyer, who was quoted as saying that Sebes was not a suspect in the murder and had been under "constant surveillance" by law enforcement, both by virtue of the monitoring device on his ankle and the round-the-clock police presence outside of his home. The captain told reporters that Sebes was questioned as part of a routine effort to learn more about Haxby's professional and personal relationships.

Bob Sebes' lawyer released a statement saying that Haxby's murder was a "devastating blow" to his client's efforts to prove his innocence but that he was confident "the truth will prevail and Bob Sebes will be cleared of all the charges against him."

There was no mention of Monk's presence at the questioning of Bob Sebes or at the scene of Haxby's murder. I went to pick Monk up and found him already waiting for me outside of his apartment. He was wearing a long-sleeved, white button-down shirt (buttoned at the collar), black pants, and black dress shoes that were shinier than Dorothy's ruby slippers.

"You don't have to interview for the job, Mr. Monk. You already have it."

"This is the standard Safeway apparel for a clerk," Monk said as he got into the car.

"It is? Arthur didn't tell me," I said. "How did you know what it was?"

"Because I'm not blind and I pay attention to the world around me," Monk said. "It's also what I wear when I go in at night to straighten things up."

"You masqueraded as an employee?"

"No, I was simply showing respect by conforming to the store's employee dress code."

I was wearing jeans and a V-neck sweater.

159

I guess I was already off to a bad start. But when I got to the store, Arthur was cool about it. He gave me a white Safeway polo shirt and said there were some spare women's black slacks in the employee locker room that I could borrow for the day and bring back cleaned tomorrow.

When Arthur gave us our black Safeway aprons emblazoned with the store logo, a white *S* against a red background, Monk reacted as if the president of the United States was awarding us the Medal of Honor.

"I can honestly say that I've lived my life trying to embody the values inherent in the name of this store," Monk said, standing at attention. "I promise to be a credit to the apron and to Safeway."

"That's great," Arthur said. "You can start by unpacking the new shipment of breakfast cereals onto the shelves on aisle twelve."

I thought Monk might salute, but he simply nodded and hurried off to do the task that he'd been assigned.

Arthur turned to me, watching me warily as I put on the apron and tied it around my waist.

"You're not going to give me an acceptance speech or swear an oath?" he asked.

I touched the Safeway logo on my apron.

"I feel like the Supergirl of groceries with this on my chest. Do you have a cape to go with this?"

"I'm afraid not," he said. "You're on register three this morning, Supergirl. Charlene is out sick."

"Charlene?" I said.

"Do you know her?" Arthur asked.

"No," I said, trying to remember if Julie had ever visited this store with me. "It's just a pretty name."

"Common, too," Arthur said. "We've got two Charlenes in the store."

"How about Roxi?"

"She retired last year," Arthur said and went back to the office.

The morning went by surprisingly fast. The job kept me busy, but it didn't take much concentration. I scanned the grocery items over a bar-code reader, so there wasn't much ringing up to do, unless the customer bought fruit or vegetables. I didn't even have to think about how much change to give, since the register did that for me, too. Most of my work involved bagging items, putting on a cheerful face, and engaging in polite small talk with the customers.

I tried to occupy my mind by imagining what my customers' lives were like based on the things they were buying. I had no idea if I was right or wrong, of course, but I was able to amuse myself. It distracted me from my troubles.

Monk was doing much the same thing, only in his own way. He unpacked the breakfast cereals, but then he took it upon himself to arrange all the products on the aisle by brand, by alphabetical order, and by expiration date, with the oldest boxes in back.

When Monk finished, he proudly showed off his work to Arthur, who appreciated the orderliness but wasn't very pleased that the newest boxes of cereal were out in front.

"We want to sell the products that expire sooner first," Arthur said. "But people won't buy them if they are hidden in the back."

"Don't you want to sell customers the freshest possible products?"

"These products are still fresh and tasty," Arthur said. "But they will go bad if we sell the newer products first. To meet demand, we get new shipments in all the time, even while there are still some unexpired packages of those same products on our shelves."

"Wouldn't you want to buy the freshest possible product?"

"It's not about what I want to buy," Arthur said. "It's about what we need to sell."

"That doesn't make any sense."

"You have to start thinking like a grocer instead of a customer. If we did it your way, we'd never sell anything and we'd waste a lot of perfectly fresh, healthy, and delicious products." That's when Arthur noticed two grocery carts full of cereal boxes at the end of the aisle. He cocked his head, curious. "Are all of those expired products?"

"No, those are damaged and defective goods."

"They don't look torn, dented, or opened to me."

"They're odd," Monk said.

Arthur walked over to the cart and picked up one of the boxes. "This package of Cap'n Crunch doesn't expire until November seventeenth. That's four months from now. What's odd about that?"

"The expiration date is the seventeenth day of the eleventh month," Monk said. "The box might as well be contaminated with rat poison."

Arthur shushed him, looking around to make sure that no one but me had overheard. Luckily, there was hardly anybody in the store.

"Do you want to create a panic?" Arthur said. "Never mention the word *contaminated* in a grocery store."

163

"Not only is the expiration date wrong," Monk continued, lowering his voice, "but 'Captain' is misspelled, there are three pieces of cereal in Crunch's spoon and five tassels on his epaulets. What kind of quality control is that? The Quakers should be ashamed of themselves."

"What Quakers?"

"The Quakers at Quaker Oats," Monk said, pointing to the manufacturer's logo, which depicted a man in old-fashioned Quaker garb. "William Penn would be outraged if he saw this box. You should write them a very stern letter."

"Forget about cereal," Arthur said, rubbing his temples in a way that immediately reminded me of Captain Stottlemeyer. "Why don't you take your break?"

"This has been a break for me. I'm completely relaxed. You've really taken my mind off my troubles."

"Maybe you don't need a break, but I do," Arthur said. "From you. I'm going to my office for a cup of coffee."

"Take your time," Monk said. "We'll mind the store until you get back."

Chapter Thirteen:
Mr. Monk Rounds Up

Before Arthur left the floor on his break, he assigned Monk to the cash register next to mine. It seemed, at the time, like the safest place to put him.

The first thing Monk did was put on a pair of surgical gloves, the kind he often put on at crime scenes.

"Why are you doing that?" I asked.

"Because I don't want to become a drug addict."

"You can't become a drug addict from handling money," I said.

"I beg to differ. According to a 2009 study presented at the two hundred thirty-eighth National Meeting of the American Chemical Society, there are traces of cocaine on more than ninety percent of the paper money in circulation."

"You're kidding," I said.

"I wish that I was, Natalie. All it takes is one sniff of your unprotected hands after handling the wrong ten-dollar bill, and bang, you're a crack whore."

"Okay, I can see the leap to junkie, but why would I become a prostitute?"

"How are you going to afford crack on what you make here?"

"Good point," I said.

"And the banknotes that aren't coated in coke are infected with countless diseases, including, but not limited to, swine flu, E. coli, and flesh-eating Ebola."

"Was that in the study, too?"

"It's just common sense. The dirtiest thing in the world is money. You have no idea where it has been or how many hands have touched it."

Monk went to his register and, after thoroughly cleaning the counters and cash register with Lysol, began ringing up customers.

He removed his gloves after each customer, cleaned his hands with a disinfectant wipe, then put on a fresh pair before handling the next transaction.

Monk insisted on putting each item in an individual plastic bag before putting them all together in the larger grocery bags, which he packed by food groups and household products.

He carefully wrapped apples and other

easily bruised fruit and vegetables in paper towels, taped them securely, and bagged them as if they were Ming vases he was preparing to ship overseas.

The customers didn't seem to appreciate all the extra attention he was giving to their purchases, or the slow, methodical pace at which he moved.

But I was too busy with my customers to try to speed him along. That's because things were moving so glacially at his register that everyone was coming to mine.

Eventually, my line finally ebbed and I was able to take a little break and watch as Monk rang up his last customer, a tight-faced old lady with collagen fish lips, hip-hop hair extensions, and tattooed, arched eyebrows over the ones that had been tweezed into extinction.

"That will be twenty-four dollars," Monk said with a smile.

"But the amount on the register says twenty-three fifty-seven," she said, pointing a ruby-bejeweled finger at his register screen.

"It's wrong."

"Are you saying my purchases don't add up to twenty-three fifty-seven?"

"I rounded up."

"Why the hell did you do that?"

167

"Because it's the right thing to do," Monk said. "You're old enough to know that."

Her eyes went wide. "Did you just call me old?"

"Pulling your brow up over the back of your head doesn't change the fact that you're sixty-seven."

"I am not," she said.

Monk sighed wearily. "You were born in San Francisco between December 1943 and January 1944. It's obvious from the ruby birthstone ring that you're wearing, which is from B. Barer and Sons, Nob Hill jewelers who designed a new setting every year that they were in business, from 1909 to 1982, when they sold out to a national chain."

"It was my mother's," she said.

"No, it wasn't."

"Are you calling me a liar?"

"An old one," Monk said. "But you're still not very good at it. Your wallet is open and I can see the birth date on your driver's license."

Her face turned so red it looked as if she'd been standing on her head for their conversation. "If you knew my birthday, then why did you go into all that rigmarole about my ring?"

"I didn't want to embarrass you."

What he was doing was showing off his observational skills, his prodigious memory for irrelevant facts, and his total lack of social graces. I'm sure that it made him feel good, too, proving to himself that his skills were every bit as sharp as they'd always been, not that anybody doubted it, except perhaps himself. Being fired, and losing your life savings, can make a guy insecure, especially about the things he is certain of.

I've felt that way myself, which is why I didn't step in and take away Monk's moment.

The old lady stammered and huffed and puffed before finally speaking again, her voice dripping with moral indignation.

"My age doesn't change the fact that you're rude and you're overcharging me by forty-three cents."

"It's a pittance," Monk said.

"It's a rip-off and I won't stand for it, regardless of how small the amount happens to be. It's the principle that matters."

"Indeed it is," Monk said. "Pay me the twenty-three fifty-seven and I'll make up the difference myself."

"But there is no difference," she said.

Monk reached into his pocket and took out two quarters, which he slapped on the counter. "Now, if you'll give me your money, please, I would appreciate it. You're holding up the line with this nonsense."

She looked behind her. There was no one there.

"You're a crazy person," she said, put her cash on the counter, and left.

"Thank you for shopping at Safeway," Monk called after her. "Come again soon."

Monk swept the money into his palm, put it into the register, then looked over at me as he peeled off his gloves. "Can you believe that woman? Some people have no manners."

"You can't round out the totals, Mr. Monk."

"I have no choice. Nobody has come up with a cash register that will do it automatically. How hard could it be?"

"Nobody is going to pay more than what it says on the register."

"I do," he said, wiping his hands with a disinfectant wipe. "But you make a convincing argument."

"I do? You're convinced?"

"I am," he said.

"Unbelievable," I said.

"Why should the customers be penalized for the store's mistake?" Monk said. "So I'll just have to round down when the totals are uneven."

"Then the store will lose money."

"Maybe that will be an incentive for them to fix their registers."

"More likely it will be an incentive for them to fire you," I said. "They are in the business of making money. If you insist on rounding out the totals, you will have to make up the difference out of your own pocket every time."

"I can live with that."

"No, you can't, because then it will cost you money to work here. How are you going to pay your bills if you give away your salary to your customers?"

"It will all even out."

"How do you know?"

"Because everything always does," Monk said, putting on a fresh pair of gloves. "It's the natural law of the universe."

I realized this was an argument I couldn't win. I would just have to convince Arthur not to let Monk work the registers. Or stick price tags on items, because he'd round those numbers off, too.

I could see that this job wasn't going to be any easier on me than assisting Monk on homicide investigations. In fact, it might even be harder, because in addition to doing my own job, I would have to simultaneously try to anticipate any problems

Monk would face with his tasks and attempt to mitigate them before he caused too much trouble.

I was still thinking about this when Monk's next customer came in and so did mine. Since Monk took ten times as long to handle a customer as I did, my line soon grew.

I tried to keep one ear and one eye on Monk while I helped my customers, but it wasn't easy, especially when things began to get out of hand.

The following account is what I overheard, what I saw, and what I reconstructed after the fact.

Monk was ringing up groceries for a married couple in their forties. I guessed their ages and assumed they were married by their wedding rings and general body language.

The man was fashionably unshaven, his hair fashionably mussed, his shirt fashionably wrinkled. His wife was unfashionably wearing no makeup, her hair was unfashionably messy, and her blouse was unfashionably baggy on her thin frame.

It's funny, and truly unfair, how what can look so good on men can look so awful on women. But I'm sure Monk didn't like the look of either one of them.

The woman seemed to be holding on to the grocery cart for support, as if it was her walker.

"Are you all right?" Monk asked her.

"She would be feeling better if you'd hurry up with our groceries," the man said tightly.

"It's okay, Ted. He's just being considerate and conscientious about his work, and that is rare these days. We shouldn't stomp on it."

Monk smiled. "Thank you for noticing."

"I'm sorry," Ted said. "Kimberley has been feeling lousy and I'd just like to get her home."

Monk glanced at the groceries in front of him. Windex, aluminum foil, flour, sugar, butter, chocolate, antifreeze, a huge bag of apples, pie tins, aspirin, cassava beans, cherries, peaches, powdered sugar, whole and sliced almonds, apples, a box of cupcake cups, vanilla extract, paper towels, rhubarb, strawberries, Grape-Nuts cereal, a T-bone steak, sixteen cans of Campbell's soup, Mylanta, Taster's Choice Instant Coffee, and *People* magazine.

"You're making her cupcakes," Monk said.

"With extra buttercream frosting," Ted said, giving his wife a smile. "She loves frosting. And I'm making apple tarts, almond cookies, almond brownies, strawberry-rhubarb pie, chocolate cake —"

"He's trying to fatten me up," she said with a grin.

"I just want you to eat," he said. "So I'm blatantly tempting you with all of your favorite sweets."

"You haven't had much of an appetite?" Monk asked her as he began bagging the items.

"I'm nauseous all the time. I practically have to force myself to eat."

"You won't have to force yourself to eat cupcakes with triple frosting," Ted said. "You won't be able to resist, I promise."

"My back hurts, my head aches, and my hands and feet won't stop tingling, so I'm not getting much sleep, either," she confided in Monk.

Ted turned to his wife. "You don't have to give him your entire medical history. He's a cashier, not a doctor." He looked back at Monk. "Could you please cut the chitchat and hurry this up, buddy? We've been standing here for fifteen minutes already."

"It sounds like you're fighting an infection of some kind," Monk said.

"That's what the doctor says," Kimberley said. "He just doesn't know what kind."

"I do," Monk said.

And that was when I noticed something very strange: Monk hadn't taken a step back. Usually, if someone sneezes, he'll dive for cover, as if the room was being sprayed with automatic weapon fire.

But there he was, talking to a woman with a raging unidentified infection that made her look like a reanimated corpse, and he wasn't even reaching for a disinfectant wipe.

I felt a tingle along the back of my neck. It was my unconscious mind alerting me to something that my conscious self was too stupid to notice. Why couldn't my unconscious and my conscious learn to communicate better?

"I think I've read about people like you," Kimberley said. "Are you one of those immigrants who was a respected doctor in his homeland but your degree isn't recognized here, so you're stuck doing a menial job you're overqualified for?"

"No," Monk said. "I'm one of those former homicide detectives who was thrown off the police force on psychological grounds, was hired back on as a consultant, but then was let go when the economy took a nosedive, property tax income tanked, and local government was forced to slash expenses."

They both stared at him.

"So, in other words, you don't know anything about medicine," Ted said.

"But I know a lot about murder," Monk said.

That was when a dozen uniformed police officers suddenly appeared from every direction, their guns drawn, totally surrounding us.

"Nobody move," the lead cop yelled. "It's all over now."

CHAPTER FOURTEEN:
MR. MONK CASHES OUT

"Drop your weapons and raise your hands," the lead cop said.

Everyone raised their hands, but there were no weapons in sight besides the ones the cops were holding.

"Lock down the store," the cop said.

The officers fanned out, moving all around us, patting down me, Monk, and the handful of customers in the place for weapons.

Arthur came rushing up from the back of the store and nearly got himself shot. The lead cop spun around and aimed his gun squarely at him.

"I'm the store manager," Arthur said, raising his hands. "What's going on here?"

"A robbery," the lead cop said. "One of the cashiers tripped the silent alarm."

"That was me," Monk said, waving his hand.

"So where are the robbers?" the cop asked, his face as craggy as the Grand

Canyon, his eyes as flinty as, well, flint. There was something overwhelmingly stony about the guy.

"There was no robbery," Monk said.

The stony cop holstered his weapon with an angry scowl. "Then why did you set off the alarm?"

"To stop a murder," Monk said.

"Whose?" the cop asked.

"Hers." Monk motioned to Kimberley, the woman in front of him.

"What are you talking about?" she said, clearly stunned by Monk's declaration. "No one is trying to kill me."

"Your husband is," Monk said. "He's been killing you for weeks."

"Are you insane? I love my wife," Ted said, putting his arm protectively around her waist. "I'm doing everything I can to nurse her back to health."

"He is," Kimberley said.

"The evidence says otherwise," Monk said.

The cop stepped up beside Monk. I was able to read his name tag now. His name was Travis Morgan. "What evidence?"

"It's right here in front of you," Monk said.

Morgan glanced at the groceries. "Cake mix? Fruit? Almonds? These aren't exactly lethal weapons."

"He's killing me with kindness," Kimberley said, looking lovingly at her husband.

"That's true," Monk said.

"You hit the silent alarm because a customer was baking cupcakes for his wife?" Arthur said, looking at Monk incredulously.

Monk nodded. "With triple buttercream frosting."

"Oh my God," Arthur said, covering his face with his hands. "What have I done?"

Morgan motioned to another officer. "Call headquarters. Tell them we need to get someone down here for a psych evaluation pronto."

I cleared my throat and stepped out from behind my counter. "Excuse me, Officer Morgan. There is something you should know about this man."

"He's nuts," Ted said. "That's obvious to everyone."

"His name is Adrian Monk," I said. "And until yesterday, he was a consultant to the Homicide Department, working directly with Captain Leland Stottlemeyer."

Morgan nodded, regarding Monk in a new light. "I've heard of this guy."

"What have you heard?" Monk asked.

"That you're nuts," the cop said.

"If Mr. Monk says that this man is killing

his wife, then he is," I said.

"And you are?" Morgan asked.

"Natalie Teeger, Mr. Monk's assistant."

"And you're working as a cashier, too?"

"It's a long story," I said.

"Everybody stay right where you are. Don't move. Don't touch anything. I'll be right back. I've got to make some calls."

"We can't wait around here while you deal with this lunatic," Ted said. "My wife isn't feeling well. She needs to get home to bed."

"He's right," Monk said. "Your first call should be to the paramedics. This woman needs to get to a hospital right away."

"We just got back from the doctor," Kimberley said. "He gave me some antibiotics and said all I needed was plenty of bed rest."

"That's because it didn't occur to your doctor that there might be nefarious forces at work," Monk said.

"Nefarious forces?" Ted said.

"I'm talking about you," Monk said.

"Enough," Morgan said. "Save it for the detectives."

"I am a detective," Monk said.

"I'm talking about the real ones," the cop said. "You know, the ones with badges instead of aprons."

The paramedics arrived first, laid Kimberley down on a gurney, and put her on an IV, but they didn't take her away. The police had instructed them to wait, unless her health was in immediate danger.

Her husband, Ted, stood beside her, holding her hand and glaring hatefully at Monk.

Ted wasn't the only one. Arthur paced in front of the aisles, looking up every so often to glower at Monk, who didn't seem bothered at all by the nasty looks he was getting. In fact, he appeared positively chipper.

His spirits rose even more when he spotted Captain Stottlemeyer coming in. The captain huddled for a moment with Officer Morgan, sighed wearily as he listened, then ambled over to Monk.

"I didn't know you were working at Safeway now," the captain said.

"It's our first day," Monk said. "But I think it's going really well."

I glanced over at Arthur and, from the expression on his face, it was clear that he didn't agree with Monk's assessment. The captain, who'd worked with Monk for a very long time, didn't need to look at Arthur to know Monk's point of view wasn't shared by his employer.

"Aren't you a little overqualified for the job?" Stottlemeyer asked.

"These are desperate times," I replied.

"We can't be picky about where our next paycheck comes from as long as we get one."

"It wasn't meant as a criticism, Natalie. I'm just laying the groundwork for my theory."

"What theory?" I asked.

"I think Monk is so bored intellectually by this job that his mind is working overtime, finding crimes where none exist."

"The crime is right here," Monk said, motioning to the groceries in front of him.

"You want to arrest the guy for encouraging an unhealthy diet?"

"It's fatal, Captain."

"This is nothing," Stottlemeyer said. "You should see what I buy at the grocery store."

"His wife is suffering from chronic poisoning," Monk said. "Her next meal at home is likely to be her last if we don't do something."

"How they eat is their choice, Monk. It's not a police matter."

"She told me about her symptoms: her loss of appetite, her nausea, the tingling in her hands and feet. Those are all classic symptoms of arsenic poisoning."

"And the same symptoms can come from divorce, filing your income taxes, and listening to Rush Limbaugh," the captain said.

"She also suffers from back pain, dizziness, and headaches."

"So do I," Stottlemeyer said. "It's called stress, Monk."

"But those are also typical signs of poisoning by ethylene glycol," Monk said, hefting the canister of antifreeze. "Which is found in antifreeze."

"Her problems could come from lots of things," Stottlemeyer said. "I called her doctor on my way down here and he says she's got an infection."

"That's because he didn't see her husband's grocery list. Ethylene glycol tastes sweet — that's why he's making fruit pies and all those cakes with triple frosting. It's so she won't detect the poison in her food. Cherry pits, peach pits, cassava beans, hydrangea flowers all contain cyanide, which tastes like almonds. That's why he's making so many almond desserts. Now he's adding arsenic to the mix." Monk hefted the big bag of apples to illustrate his point. "Apple seeds are rich in arsenic."

"Oh, for God's sake, I've listened to enough of this crap," Ted said, stepping forward. "Those apples are for apple pie, you idiot. All the ingredients you think are poison are common, ordinary foods we eat every day. You could look at anybody's groceries and make the same outrageous accusations. Are you going to call the police every time somebody buys the ingredients to bake a cake? Or when somebody buys bug spray, rat poison, and Ding Dongs?"

"He's got a point, Monk," Stottlemeyer said.

"It's easy to prove chronic poisoning once you know what to look for. His wife can have her blood and hair tested for arsenic and cyanide or she can have a biopsy done of her kidney to determine if she has oxalate crystals. The results will speak for themselves."

"I am not going to stick needles in my wife and put her under a knife just to satisfy the paranoid delusions of a crazy stranger," Ted said. "All we want to do is go home and put this miserable day behind us."

"It's my decision," Kimberley said, sitting up on her gurney. "Not yours."

Ted turned around in surprise. "You don't actually believe him, do you?"

"Do you have a big life insurance policy?" Monk asked her.

"One million dollars," she said.

"Has there been any change in your financial situation?"

She studied her husband suspiciously. "We both lost our jobs and have had to downsize."

"How can you look at me that way? How can you even think for one second that I could hurt you?" Ted said. "You know how much I love you."

"You cried when we had to sell your Porsche," she said.

"Of course I did. Any man would," Ted said, looking to Stottlemeyer for support.

"I've never had a Porsche," Stottlemeyer said.

"But if you did, wouldn't you cry if you had to give it up?"

"I'm not a big crier," the captain said.

"I also didn't start feeling sick until you insisted on taking over the cooking," she said.

"I wanted to help out more around the house, that's all, especially after we had to let the cleaning lady go," Ted said. "And how do you thank me? By accusing me of attempted murder? I'm shocked and deeply hurt. I'm going to assume it's your infection talking, not you."

"What do we have to lose by taking the tests?" she asked.

"Our deductible, maybe even the entire cost of the tests. You know how little money we have now. We shouldn't throw any of it away to appease a lunatic Safeway cashier."

She nodded and turned to the paramedics.

"Take me to the hospital. I want those tests."

The paramedic wheeled the gurney out the door, Ted following after them, a definite, sorrowful drag to his step.

Stottlemeyer motioned one of the officers over. "Follow him to the hospital. I'll be there shortly."

The officer nodded and headed out.

"He's guilty," Monk said.

"I know and so does she," Stottlemeyer said.

"You've saved her life, Mr. Monk," I said.

Stottlemeyer waved Officer Morgan over. "Gather up all these groceries. It's evidence."

Arthur approached us. "Shouldn't the couple pay for all of that before they leave?"

"We'll give you a receipt for it," Stottlemeyer said.

"It's not the same as cash," Arthur said. "Or credit."

"No, it's not," Stottlemeyer said, shifting his gaze to us. "We're having a little party for Randy at the station at six p.m. You're both invited."

"What did you get him?" Monk asked.

"Nothing yet."

"Everything you need is right here," Monk said. "You can use our employee discount."

"No, he can't," Arthur said.

"I intend to buy it myself and have the captain reimburse me," Monk said.

"You can't," Arthur said.

"Why not?"

"Because you're fired."

Arthur was being totally unfair and I wasn't going to stand for it. "This was inconvenient, and maybe cost you a little business, but he did a good deed. He saved a life. It was no different than if he performed CPR on somebody who collapsed in an aisle. Would you fire him for that?"

"No, I wouldn't. I'm firing him because he intentionally overcharged every customer he's had today, and, if that wasn't reason enough, he accused another of being a dishonest old coot."

"She was," Monk said.

"I can't believe she actually called you to complain," I said.

"She's my mother," Arthur said. "Complaining is her job."

At least there was somebody out there who still had one.

CHAPTER FIFTEEN:
MR. MONK GOES TO A PARTY

Getting fired after just one day on the job was a big blow to Monk, but he didn't hold a grudge. He still bought Disher's birthday present at Safeway. Stottlemeyer did, too, along with the cake and drinks, since he didn't know if he'd get another chance to leave headquarters without Disher before the party.

Arthur offered to let me stay on, but I wasn't willing to abandon Monk for a job, at least not yet, and certainly not for this one.

We collected our paychecks for our single day of work and left the grocery store. Monk walked to my car with his shoulders slumped and his head down, as if he was carrying fifty pounds of shame on his back.

"Do you think I'll still be welcome to come back and clean the store at night?"

"Why would you want to after how you've been treated?"

"I still help the police for free. They have no hard feelings."

"They don't," I said. "But *you* should."

"I don't see why."

"Because you have been treated unfairly. Don't you have any self-respect? You should stand up for yourself."

"That's why I have you."

"But what if you didn't have me?"

Monk stopped walking and faced me, his eyes wide. "Are you leaving me?"

"No, but I'm not with you all the time."

"You could be if you like. I'm not standing in your way."

"You're missing my point. If you don't value yourself, no one will."

"They don't anyway and I don't want to discourage the few who do by getting them angry."

"That's pitiful," I said.

"That's my life. Haven't you been paying attention all these years? The only time people respect me is when I'm solving a crime."

"That's because it's also the only time you respect yourself."

When Monk solved a crime, the world felt to him like it was in perfect balance and everything was in its place. In that moment, he was in complete control, confident, self-assured, and virtually free of the anxieties that plagued him.

Even if he hadn't told me that was how he felt, I knew it to be true because I could hear it in his voice and see it in his stature, even in the intensity of his gaze when he confronted a killer and summed up exactly how the murder was committed.

That was when Monk was as happy, and secure, as it was possible for Monk to ever be.

Monk looked at me glumly, as if reading my thoughts. "And now I've lost that, too."

Lieutenant Disher had been sent out of the station on some meaningless errand before we got there and when he came back everybody yelled "Surprise" and whooped and hollered, just the way Stottlemeyer had ordered them to. The captain figured that if we did that, then the office gathering would technically qualify as the surprise party that Disher was hoping for.

If Disher was disappointed, he didn't show it. He was all grins, high-fiving everyone and making a big show out of blowing out the candles on his Safeway cake and opening his presents. He didn't even complain that none of them came from his gift registry at Nordstrom.

Monk gave him Q-tips, Stottlemeyer gave him a $50 Best Buy gift card, and I got him a DVD of the first season of the old cop show *The Streets of San Francisco*.

"I love this show," Disher said, admiring the cover photo of Karl Malden and Michael Douglas against a backdrop of the San Francisco skyline.

"Because you're a cop in San Francisco," I said.

"People mistake me for Michael Douglas all the time and the captain is a dead ringer for Karl Malden, only without the crunched nose, the hair, the hat, or the overcoat."

Stottlemeyer frowned. "So what's left that makes me a dead ringer for him?"

"You're a grizzled old detective at the end of his career and I'm a brilliant young hotshot with an amazing future."

It was Disher's birthday, so Stottlemeyer let that comment slide with a forced smile, picked up his piece of cake, and went back to his office.

We stayed for another hour or so, long enough for me to get hit on by two detectives and for Monk to clean up after everyone and sweep the floor. On our way out, Stottlemeyer took us aside, out of Disher's earshot, and thanked us for coming.

"Randy is our friend," Monk said. "Why

191

wouldn't we come?"

"We would have been hurt not to have been invited," I added.

"I'm glad, and more than a little relieved, to hear you say that," Stottlemeyer said. "It's nice to know you aren't taking this job thing personally."

"It's not Randy's fault that you fired Mr. Monk," I said pointedly.

"I didn't fire him," Stottlemeyer said. "The city did."

"But the city is a big, amorphous, faceless thing," I said. "You are standing right in front of me."

"So you just want to take your anger out on somebody and it's me."

"Can you think of a better person?"

"William Hanna or Joseph Barbera," Monk declared. "Take your pick."

Stottlemeyer and I both looked at him.

"Who are they?" Stottlemeyer asked.

"The men responsible for Fred Flintstone and Barney Rubble, both of whom were drawn with only three toes on each foot and four fingers on each hand," Monk said. "Everybody knows that's inaccurate, even among Stone Age people. They perpetuated a fraud in a cartoon that misled countless numbers of children and they were never prosecuted for it."

"What does that have to do with you getting fired as a consultant to the police department?" I asked.

"Nothing," Monk said. "But they deserve your anger more than Captain Stottlemeyer does."

"I appreciate that, Monk," the captain said. "By the way, you were right about that lady at the supermarket. The tests came back positive for poisoning. She'll be in the hospital for a few days but her husband will be in jail for years."

"I'm right about Bob Sebes, too," Monk said.

"He's a crook. I agree with you on that," the captain said. "But he's not Haxby's killer. It's impossible."

"I could prove it if you'd let me," Monk said.

Stottlemeyer shook his head. "Sorry, Monk. You're just going to have to leave the police work to us from now on."

"But if you've ruled out Sebes because it was impossible for him to have committed the murder, then you'll never arrest him for it."

"That's true. We'll arrest the person who actually did it instead," Stottlemeyer said. "This may come as a shock to you, Monk, but we actually do solve murders without your help."

"Not the impossible ones," Monk said.

I dropped off Monk at his apartment on my way home. As I passed by Mama Petrocelli's Italian restaurant, I thought of Warren Horowitz, the proprietor, and what he'd asked me every time I went in to order a pizza.

I made a U-turn, parked illegally in front of the restaurant, and ran inside. As it happened, Warren was behind the maître d' stand, waiting to seat customers.

"Every time I come in for a pizza you offer me my old waitressing job back," I said. "Are you serious? Or are you just flirting with me?"

He seemed startled at first, but then his surprise quickly gave way to a big smile. "Both."

"I'll take the job on one condition," I said.

"I have to marry you," he said.

"You have to hire Adrian Monk, too."

"Done," he said.

"Don't you even want to know anything about him?"

He shook his head. "The only thing that matters to me is that I will get to see you every day and that my life will be brighter as a result."

"But you'll have to cut back on the flirting," I said. "Once I start working for you, it will be sexual harassment."

I was teasing him, and he knew it.

"There's nothing sexual about it," he said. "I don't want to sleep with you."

"You don't?" I said.

"At least not until we're married," he said. "Then we'll do it twice a day, three times on weekends."

"You've obviously never been married," I told him.

I brought home a Matzorella Pizza, courtesy of Warren Horowitz, and found Julie in the living room, rubbing her hands with moisturizing cream.

She'd gotten the job at the car wash and now her fingertips were raw and shriveled from holding wet towels all day. But she told me she was surprised by how much she actually enjoyed herself, despite how hard and occasionally demeaning the work was.

"What was demeaning about it?" I asked.

"Some kids from my school brought their car in and I had to wash it. They made me go over it five or six times, just because they could. How was your first day?"

"I got fired," I said, then corrected myself. "Actually, Monk got fired and I quit in solidarity."

I told her the whole story, and informed her about the new jobs as we ate our pizza.

I expected her to complain that all of her friends went to Mama Petrocelli's and that she would be humiliated if I ever waited on them. But she didn't raise a single objection. Either her experience at the car wash made whatever humiliation I might bring her seem inconsequential by comparison, or she realized that whining about it wouldn't get her anywhere.

Whatever her reasoning, it was nice not to have an argument over dinner for a change. But telling her about the job reminded me that I'd forgotten to notify Monk about our new employment, which would be starting the following day. So after we ate I gave him a call and filled him in.

He was thrilled. He only had one concern.

"Does he provide the compasses, T squares, and tape measures, or do we provide our own?"

"We're not engineers, Mr. Monk. We're making pizzas."

"How do you think they make each pie perfectly round and each piece a true triangle?"

I sighed. "You should probably bring your

own pizza measuring equipment."

"Gladly," he said.

Chapter Sixteen:
Mr. Monk Makes a Pizza

We came in before noon and Monk's first assignment was cleaning the kitchen and setting the tables — tasks he not only loved but tackled with genuine enthusiasm, immediately winning over his new boss.

"This man is amazing," Warren said to me. "The kitchen has never been so clean and the tables have never looked so good."

"He's just doing what he loves."

"Nobody loves cleaning and table setting. I did it to break his spirit and test his mettle from the get-go."

"Is that why you have me grating cheese, slicing pepperoni, and cutting onions?"

"No, I just like having you with me in the kitchen," he said.

"If you really want to make Mr. Monk happy, ask him to wash the dishes, scrub the floors, and clean the restrooms."

"You're kidding me."

"Honest," I said. "He'll thank you for it."

So Warren followed my advice and asked Monk to wash dishes during the lunchtime rush and clean the bathroom afterward. Monk thanked him and happily tackled both assignments. Warren was stunned.

Mama Petrocelli's has a big lunch crowd, so I was kept busy waiting on tables with one other waitress, Erin, a bubbly twenty-two-year-old aspiring hairstylist. Erin offered to cut my hair and Julie's for five bucks each if we stopped by her beauty college during her class. She needed people to practice on and offered each customer the same opportunity she'd given me.

Waitressing came back to me as if I'd never stopped doing it. And so did the sore feet.

Warren was mighty impressed with Monk. He must have thanked me fifty times for bringing him in. Monk also expressed his gratitude as we sat in one of the booths during our early afternoon lunch break.

"This is a fantastic job. Thank you so much for recommending me for it."

"My pleasure," I said.

"I think the boss is giving me preferential treatment. I'm getting all the plum assignments."

"Like cleaning the bathrooms."

"I hope you don't feel slighted."

"Not at all. You deserve it."

"It's true," Monk said. "I do seem to have a natural affinity for the restaurant business. Who knew?"

"See, Dr. Bell was right — you're discovering new things about yourself already." I gestured to the cheese pizza that we were supposed to be sharing but that he hadn't touched. "Aren't you hungry?"

He leaned toward me and whispered, "I can't eat that. It's deformed."

I nodded. "It's not a perfect circle."

"Warren is such a nice man and he's already given me so many opportunities. I don't know how to tell him that his pizzas are repulsive to look at."

"So don't do it. Volunteer to make pizzas, instead. That way, instead of raising a complaint and offending him, you can show him by example how to do it right."

"That's a great idea, Natalie. Besides, it's a chance to impress Warren by volunteering for one of the menial jobs without being asked."

"Ingratiating yourself with the boss never hurts. Speaking of which, I wouldn't mention that you consider making pizzas menial labor."

"Of course not," Monk said. "What kind

of person do you think I am? I'm not tactless."

So Monk volunteered for pizza-making duty. Warren was glad to grant the request and suggested that we both give it a try.

Warren showed us diagrams on the wall that illustrated with photos each step in the process of making every kind of pizza Petrocelli's offered. The dough was premade; all we had to do was flatten it. All the sauces, cheeses, and toppings were already prepared and kept in their own individual containers. Monk liked this very much. The process was orderly, clear, and uniform.

What Monk didn't like was the photos of the finished pizzas, which looked like, as he put it, "crime scenes on misshapen dough."

He used his disinfected compass, tape measure, and T square to make sure his pies were perfectly round. Then he applied an even coating of sauce and cheese.

So far, so good.

The problem came when he applied the toppings. He had to make sure that each slice had the same number of items in the same position. This made his pizzas look like targets in a shooting range, the meat and vegetables arranged in concentric circles, evenly spaced from one another, getting ever smaller as they reached the center.

This wasn't so bad on a one- or two-topping pizza, but it looked bizarre on the combination pies. We got a few of them out before Warren finally came back with one.

"This pizza looks like it was manufactured by a machine," Warren said.

Monk beamed with pride. "Thank you very much."

"You can't make a pizza like that," Warren said. "The toppings should be all mixed up."

"Why, in God's name, would you want to do that?" Monk asked.

"So you get a little of everything in each bite."

"You can't do that," Monk said.

"Why not?"

"It's unnatural, unbalanced, unethical, unhealthy, uncomfortable, unsanitary, unearthly, unspeakable, unappealing, untouchable, unstable, unforgiveable, unpleasant, unpatriotic — it's uneverything that humanity and a civilized society holds dear."

"It's just a pizza," Warren said, looking a bit stunned by Monk's passionate tirade.

"It's a messy pizza," Monk said.

"That's how we like them."

"I urge you to reconsider, Warren, in the strongest possible terms, or you will regret it for the rest of your life."

I spoke up before Warren could say anything. "What Mr. Monk means is that perhaps his talents and sense of order are put to better use in ways other than pizza-making."

"Definitely," Warren said. "Change of plans, Adrian. You can seat the customers tonight and I'll make the pizzas."

"You're the boss," Monk said, then motioned to his tools. "Would you like to use my compass, T square, and tape measure?"

Warren stared at Monk in bewilderment. "What for?"

I spoke up again. "I think Warren prefers to use his own tools."

"I understand completely," Monk said, gathering up his things. "Let me just clean and disinfect these and then I'll go out to the dining room."

As soon as Monk walked away, Warren turned to me. "Tools? I'm making pizzas, not building shelves."

"I know," I said.

"What is his problem?"

"He likes things clean and orderly."

"Even his pizzas?"

"*Everything.* But I think you can agree that it's an aspect of his personality that, if properly directed, can be very beneficial to a restaurant."

"I can see that," Warren said. "I can also

see how it could drive a person insane."

I went back to waiting tables with Erin while Warren and another cook worked in the kitchen and Monk acted as the new maître d'.

There was trouble from the start. A party of three, two men and a woman, came in and Monk told them they'd have to wait.

One of the men looked past Monk to the dining room. "But there are plenty of empty tables."

"Let me know when the rest of your party arrives," Monk said.

"We're all here," the woman said.

"You know what I mean," Monk said.

"No, we don't," she said.

"Then you'll have to wait until a woman comes in," Monk said.

"Why?" the man said.

"Your party is odd and unbalanced," Monk said. "You need to find one more woman."

"We are not going to sit with some strange woman," the man said.

"You should have thought of that before you came to dinner," Monk said.

I rushed up, grabbed three menus, and gave them a smile. "This way, please."

Monk grabbed me. "You can't seat them. They are short one woman."

"They have me," I said and led them to a table, glancing at the kitchen as I went to see if Warren had overheard any of the argument. Thankfully, he seemed preoccupied with something else in the kitchen.

But while my back was turned, another customer came in, a man in an untucked shirt and jeans, a magazine under his arm.

"Table for one," he said as he approached Monk.

"You'll have to button your shirt," Monk said.

"Why?"

"The top four buttons are undone, exposing your chest," Monk said. "It's unsanitary."

"What's unsanitary about it?"

"You can get chest hair in your food."

"I'll take that risk," the man said.

"The rest of us won't," Monk said. "We can't have your filthy chest hair flying all around the room."

The man turned and walked out before I could get back to Monk.

"Mr. Monk, you can't throw people out for having an open collar," I said.

Monk pointed to a sign by the door that read *No Shirt, No Shoes, No Service.*

"He was wearing a shirt," I said.

"Barely," Monk said.

I tried to keep my eye on Monk, and to mitigate problems before customers walked out, but things got so busy, I just wasn't able to do my job and his at the same time.

Things were fine when he was dealing with parties in multiples of two, but he made odd-numbered groups wait until a single person came in who was willing to join them. Or he suggested that the odd-numbered parties call another friend or family member to come join them.

That was bad enough, but he also refused service to people with crooked teeth, messy hair, and piercings on the grounds that they were "health code violations."

Luckily, all of that occurred without Warren noticing. But things got out of hand once people were seated and food began to be served.

Most of the customers ordered "messy" pizzas, and that was hard enough for him to ignore. But he simply couldn't abide people sharing pizzas and eating them with their hands. He ran from table to table, trying to stop people from doing it, but they just wouldn't listen.

"That's how E. coli spreads," Monk said to a family of four who were all sharing a pizza at their table. "And black death."

"Rats caused black death," the mother said.

"Rats who ate pizza that people touched with their dirt-and-slobber-soaked fingers," Monk said.

"You don't know what you're talking about," the woman said.

"I know that you're betraying your husband by having an extramarital sex affair."

"What?" the man said, nearly choking on his mouthful of pizza.

The preteen daughter was wide-eyed. "Mom is sleeping around?"

"I am not. Don't listen to this horrible man." She covered her daughter's ears with her hands and looked at her husband. "Fred, do something."

"Your adultery is obvious," Monk said. "Your husband is clean-shaven, but your lover, who trimmed his beard before your rendezvous, left tiny hairs on your neck and collar. And I saw you tear off the hotel valet ticket from your key ring and drop it in the trash as you came in."

"You're sleeping with *Tod?*" Fred stammered.

Her face turned bright red, which was as good as a confession.

"It's bad enough you betrayed your family with your infidelity," Monk said. "Now you're endangering their health with your slovenly eating habits. Have you no shame?"

I grabbed Monk and led him away. "What are you doing?"

"Saving lives," Monk said.

"People eat pizza with their hands. It's the custom."

"And look what it leads to," Monk said, motioning to the family that he'd just spoken to. They were leaving the restaurant, all four of them in tears. "An entire family torn apart."

"The way they eat their pizza has nothing to do with that," I said. "It was you exposing her adultery."

"She led an unhealthy lifestyle. It's indicative of moral decay."

"Everybody eats pizza with their hands. There's no harm in it."

"Think of all the things they've touched before grabbing a slice of pizza with their hands. They should wear gloves. Or use a knife and fork."

"It's their choice," I said. "Not yours."

"It's disgusting," Monk said. "It spreads disease, pestilence, and death."

At least it wasn't *wanton* pestilence. "I don't see anybody dropping dead in here."

"Not yet," Monk said.

"Please, Mr. Monk, be reasonable about this."

"It's not going to be easy," he said.

"I'm begging you, not just for myself, but on your behalf, too. We need these jobs."

Monk nodded. "Okay, that's what I'll do."

"Thank you," I said, turning my back to him to continue waiting tables.

That was when Monk clapped his hands and raised his voice, loud enough for everyone to hear.

"Could I have everyone's attention, please? I have a very important announcement. You need to stop talking, put down your food, and listen to me if you want to live."

Everyone stopped what they were doing and turned to look at him. And that included Warren, whom I could see in the kitchen, staring at Monk in disbelief.

I rushed up to Monk. "You said you were going to be reasonable."

"I am. It's unreasonable to turn a blind eye to this just because it might be embarrassing for Warren. I told you it wouldn't be easy."

"This is exactly what I didn't want you to do."

"Then you should have told me to be unreasonable."

"Do you want us to lose our jobs?"

"Of course not. That's why I am stopping this before the health department shuts the place down." Monk raised his voice again to address the diners. "You have to stop eating with your hands or you will all die."

I knew it was all over then. I resigned myself to the inevitable. A rumble of distressed chatter spread through the dining room. Warren bolted out of the kitchen, waving his hands to get everyone's attention.

"Ignore what this man is saying," Warren said. "He's just joking."

"Food poisoning and bubonic plague are no joke," Monk said.

"Food poisoning?" one of the customers said, spitting out his pizza. "What's wrong with my food?"

"Nothing is wrong with it," Warren said. "It's perfectly safe."

"It's your hands that aren't," Monk said and gestured to another customer, a man. "Especially his. He wiped his nose on the back of his hand before reaching for his slice of pizza. That whole table should be quarantined."

"Shut up, Adrian," Warren said and turned to everyone else. "Please forgive this rude interruption. Your food is fine. It's okay for you to eat with your hands. And dinner is on me tonight. And so is dessert."

Warren grabbed Monk by the arm and practically dragged him out the front door onto the street. I followed after them, untying my apron and leaving it behind. I knew I wouldn't need it again.

I stepped outside just in time to hear Warren say to Monk what I knew was coming.

"You're fired!"

"Why?" Monk asked, genuinely confused.

"Because you just terrorized my customers and cost me a night of business," Warren said. "I'll be lucky if the people in there ever come back."

"You don't want them back," Monk said. "They're savages."

Warren just shook his head and turned to me. "He's not welcome in my restaurant ever again. But you're welcome to stay on, Natalie. I know this isn't your fault."

I smiled. "I appreciate it, Warren. I really do. But we're a package set."

"Then you better get used to being out of work," he said and went back inside.

Monk glared at me. "Traitor."

I stepped toward him. "If that was true, I would have kept my job when he fired you. Instead, I gave it up."

"But not before kissing up to him first."

"What I did was thank him for his kindness, for not letting his anger with you damage our friendship."

"Exactly," Monk said. "Instead of supporting me for doing the right thing, you were more concerned about how he felt about you, the man who fired me so he wouldn't have to confront the public health crisis that's exploding right in his dining room. That's cowardly, Natalie, and shows a shocking lack of character."

I looked down at my feet, trying to hold back the anger that was making me shake. But I couldn't. I was too weak, too frustrated, and too scared about where my life was headed.

"The problem is *you*," I said, poking him in the chest with my finger, forcing him to take a step back. But I kept right on coming, poking him again. "I am sick and tired of supporting the fantasy that you're right and the rest of the world is wrong. And you know what? I don't have to anymore because I don't work for you. In fact, thanks to you, I don't work at all."

Every time I said *you,* or any derivation of the word, I poked him again with my finger to drive home my point, to make sure he not only heard me but felt what I was saying.

"It's time that you realized that you're living in an alternate universe that has no relation to the one we're all in. We don't have to learn to live the way you do — you have to adapt to the way *we* live. And here's a news flash: *we eat pizza with our hands.* We always have. We always will. Get used to it."

Monk couldn't have looked more shocked if I'd torn off all of my clothes and ran naked into the street singing songs from *The Sound of Music.*

He stared at me for a long moment as I caught my breath, my shaking wore off, and I became painfully self-conscious of what I'd said and what I'd done.

"Are you just going to stand there?" I asked. "Don't you have anything to say for yourself?"

He held out his hand. "Could I have a wipe, please?"

I reached into my purse and slapped one into his palm. He reached out, wiped my mouth roughly with it, and shoved it back in my purse before turning his back on me and walking away.

CHAPTER SEVENTEEN:
MR. MONK MOVES IN

I can't say I felt regret after the incident, because I meant every word that I'd said and I was right, but I did feel some guilt. Monk had a psychological disorder and, for the most part, couldn't help the way he behaved. Yelling at him and poking him wasn't going to change that. All I'd managed to do was hurt him and make myself feel better for a few fleeting seconds.

I chased after him as he marched down the street. "Where are you going?"

"Home."

"You're walking in the wrong direction," I said. He pivoted and started walking in the opposite direction. "It's also miles away from here."

"What do you care?"

"Don't be that way, Mr. Monk."

"Oh, so it's okay for you to tell me how to behave but it's wrong for me to do it."

"That's not what I said."

"You see the world one way and I see it another. Your way is right; my way is wrong. You've made that abundantly clear. What I don't understand is why you are still here."

"Because I care about you."

"I'm not paying you to care about me anymore, so you don't have to. You made that clear, too."

I grabbed him by the arm. "I did not say that, Mr. Monk. What I meant is that I could be more honest with you now than I was when you were my employer."

"Lucky me." He yanked his arm free and marched on.

I hurried after him again. "Friends are honest with each other, especially when they are hurting. Well, I'm hurting."

"You? What do you have to be hurt about? You haven't lost your job."

"Yes, I have."

"You aren't broke."

"Yes, I am."

"You aren't dying of thirst."

"You don't have a child to support."

"I have you *and* your child to support," Monk said. "And now I can't."

That struck me hard. I'd never thought of it that way before.

"You really think of us like that? As a family you have to support?"

"I know that it's mostly my paycheck that you're living on. I'm scared, Natalie, for all of us."

"So am I, Mr. Monk."

"No, no, you don't understand. I'm not talking about the never-ending, suffocating, oppressive fear I've had since the instant of my conception, but a truly new level of terror."

"Me, too."

"Really?" Monk asked.

"I'm a single parent with a teenager to raise and send to college, but I have no income, no savings, and no job prospects. If I don't find a way out of this, I could end up losing my house, one of the few things I have left that Mitch and I shared before he was killed."

"There's no hope," he said.

"That's a positive attitude."

"If you accept that there's no hope, and there isn't, then when everything inevitably gets much worse, and it will, there won't be crushing disappointment to go along with it, and that's a relief. Feel better now?"

"Not really."

"Good," he said. "Now you're prepared for what's to come."

"What a horrible way to go through life."

"That *is* life," he said. "One horror after

another, followed by despair."

We walked side by side to my car. He rubbed his chest where I'd poked him a few times.

"I think you broke my sternum."

"I don't think so, Mr. Monk." We reached the car and I unlocked the doors.

"We'll know for sure when my lungs collapse."

"If the dehydration doesn't kill you first."

I turned my back on him before he could see my smile and walked around the car to the driver's side.

We were good again.

I stopped my car at the curb outside of his apartment. He opened the door and looked over at me before he got out.

"Will I see you tomorrow?"

It was a good question. I wasn't working for him and we didn't have another job lined up yet. There was really no reason for me to be at his door first thing in the morning. In fact, there was no reason for me to see him at all.

Except that he needed me.

But I needed some space, some time to clear my head and figure out what I was going to do.

"Let's see how it goes," I said.

"What does that mean?"

"Let's see what happens."

He cocked his head. "I still don't understand."

"We may or may not see each other tomorrow. It depends on how events play out."

"What events?"

"I don't know. That's why we will have to wait to see how it goes and what happens."

"How do you know that there will be any events or happenings? And what events or happenings could there be that will determine whether I will see you or not?"

"That's what we'll find out."

"You're delirious," he said.

"I'll give you a call, Mr. Monk."

"When?"

"At some point," I said.

"I can't deal with all of this uncertainty."

"Neither can I. That's why I need some time to myself, to sort it all out and come up with some kind of plan."

"I have a plan," he said.

"What is it?"

"You come to my apartment tomorrow and we do business as usual."

"But we are out of business."

He shook his head. "I'm in business. All I am is business. I have lots of business I need to do. I have lists of business. I mean business."

"Then you will have plenty to keep you busy," I said. "Good night, Mr. Monk."

I reached over, closed his door, and drove off. I glanced in my rearview mirror and saw him standing at the curb, looking forlornly after me.

I had to resist the powerful, self-destructive urge to make a U-turn, pull up beside him, and promise to be at his door first thing in the morning.

I am proud to say that I marshaled all of my willpower and managed to resist the urge. I went straight home, sat down at the kitchen table with Julie, took a half gallon of ice cream out of the freezer, and we picked at it with spoons while I told her about my night.

We might have finished off the entire carton if there wasn't a knock at the front door.

I went to the door, peered into the peephole, and saw Monk standing on the porch, a taxi driving off behind him.

I groaned and leaned my head against the door.

"It's Mr. Monk, isn't it?" Julie said.

"How did you know?"

"You did the Monk groan," she said.

"I have a Monk groan?"

"Everybody who knows him does," she said.

I sighed and opened the door. "What are you doing here, Mr. Monk?"

"I need to stay with you," Monk said and walked past me into the house without waiting for an invitation.

"You really can't deal with uncertainty, can you?"

Monk went into the kitchen and stood beside Julie. "So I see you're eating ice cream directly out of the container with a spoon."

"It's how we like to eat it," she said.

"Both of you at once?"

"That way we only have to rinse two spoons instead of washing two bowls."

He stared at her.

"You can't stay, Mr. Monk," I said.

"Why bother with spoons? You could just use your fingers and not have to wash anything at all. You could lick your fingers clean. Then again, why even do that?"

"You're not listening to me, Mr. Monk."

"Why bother with clothes? Or a house? Why not go all the way and live in a tree and eat bananas? No wonder you see nothing wrong with pizza."

"What's wrong with pizza?" Julie asked.

"You poor girl," Monk said. "It's like you've been raised in the wild."

"Mr. Monk," I said, "I'm taking you home."

"I don't have one anymore," Monk said. "But maybe that's my new mission in life, to move in here and save you both from yourselves before it's too late."

"Oh, God, no," Julie said.

I hushed her with a look and turned to Monk. "You can't live with us just because you're out of work and you don't know for certain exactly when you're going to see me again."

"That's not why I'm here," he said.

"Then what is the reason?"

"I don't have a home."

"What does that mean?"

"It means he's lonely and he misses you," Julie said. "He just can't say it."

"It's only been thirty minutes," I said.

"The landlord changed all of the locks on my apartment and taped an eviction order to my door." Monk reached into his jacket and handed me an envelope. "See for yourself."

I opened the envelope and scanned the letter. It was from his landlord's lawyer and written in all kinds of legalese. Basically, it said that Monk's rent hadn't been paid in ninety days, violating his rental agreement, and that he wouldn't be allowed back into his home until his overdue rent was paid.

"Let me guess," I said. "Bob Sebes paid your rent. Or at least he was supposed to."

Monk nodded. "Sebes obviously ignored the warning notices from my landlord."

"Why didn't your landlord come to you directly?" Julie asked.

"I've kind of barred him from talking to me or setting foot in my apartment."

"Kind of?" Julie said.

"He's missing a tooth. I can't stand to look at him. As soon as he replaces it, we can talk."

"Couldn't he have called you?" Julie asked.

Monk shook his head. "He's barred from that, too."

"Why?" Julie asked.

"Because the tooth is still missing. I would see it in my mind and hear the air moving through the monstrous gap in his face."

"Okay, why couldn't he write you a personal note?" Julie asked.

"I couldn't read a note from somebody who is missing a tooth," Monk said. "There's bound to be words missing important letters."

"So he hates you now," I said. "And this

was his opportunity to finally get rid of you."

"It would be easier just to get a tooth," Monk said. "Now I have to move in with you. But it's a sacrifice I'm willing to make to civilize you both. It may not be too late."

Julie shot me a desperate look. But she didn't have to. I didn't want Monk moving in, either.

"I know you're in trouble, and you can't afford a hotel, but you can't stay here."

"Why not? I have before."

That was exactly why not. He'd stayed with us briefly a few years back, when his apartment was being fumigated, and it was a living hell. I was under enough pressure as it was without having Monk under my roof, too.

"Because Julie and I drink milk out of the carton and eat food with our hands," I said.

"Only more reason why you need me here," Monk said.

"I'm having my period," Julie said.

"Me, too," I said.

"So is my hamster," Julie added for good measure. Her hamster had died years ago, but Monk didn't know that.

He winced and took a step back from both of us, as if menstruation was contagious.

"What am I going to do?" he said. "Where am I going to go?"

"What about staying with your brother, Ambrose?" I said.

"No way," he said. "The last thing I need right now is to live under the same roof with a crazy person."

I knew how Monk felt. We were in an awful mess and running out of options. And then I thought about why we were in this lousy situation and then I knew where Monk could stay.

"Don't worry, Mr. Monk," I said, picking up my purse and car keys. "I have a solution."

It was too late to buy Monk a change of clothes from his favorite men's shop, but not too late to pick up a toothbrush, some toiletries, Lysol, Windex, bleach, disinfectant wipes, Wonder Bread, and other survival essentials from my local grocery store.

We bought some bottled water, because even Monk knew he had to drink something (and tap water was absolutely out of the question). But he intended to take extensive measures to purify the water first and to drink as little as possible to cut down on his chances of getting sick.

We arrived outside of the bland, charmless, four-story condo complex just before midnight. It was a late 1990s stucco box in a gentrified corner of the Mission District, more or less midway between the Civic Center and police headquarters.

I parked in a red zone and we got out, each of us carrying a grocery bag, and went to the lobby door. I leaned on the buzzer and announced myself without mentioning that I had a guest. I figured otherwise we might never get inside the building. All I said was that it was an urgent matter.

We were buzzed through and we took the two flights of stairs to the second floor.

When we got to the apartment, Captain Stottlemeyer was standing in his open doorway, wearing sweatpants, a T-shirt, and a terry-cloth robe tied loosely at the waist. He'd obviously been in bed when I rang.

"You didn't tell me Monk was with you," Stottlemeyer said.

"Oops," I said. "Is that a problem?"

Stottlemeyer glanced at Monk, then back at me. "Of course not, I was just making an observation. What's the emergency?"

"I'm a homeless transient bum," Monk said.

"Come on in," Stottlemeyer said, stepping aside and ushering us into his apartment.

I'd never shown up at his place unannounced before. In fact, it was only the third time I'd been to his place since he'd bought

225

it a few years ago, shortly after his divorce. He'd selected the condo primarily because his then girlfriend was a Realtor and she'd liked it. All he really cared about was that it was close to work, was within his price range, and had an extra room for his boys to stay in on weekends and holidays.

The condo was barely decorated and all the furnishings were very masculine. The front door opened onto the small living room, which was dominated by a faux-leather couch, a faux-recliner, and a massive TV with a Wii, a PlayStation, and a DVD player.

The kitchen was separated from the living room by a counter, where we placed our grocery bags.

"You brought refreshments?" he said.

"Provisions," Monk said and began to unpack the bags.

"For what?" Stottlemeyer asked.

"The duration," Monk said.

"Of what?"

"His stay," I said.

"How long are you expecting this conversation to take?"

"Only a few minutes," I said. "But then I'm going home and he's moving in with you."

"The hell he is," Stottlemeyer said.

We both watched Monk as he took a pot from one of Stottlemeyer's kitchen cabinets, set it on the stove, and began pouring bottled water into it, turning his face away as if it was raw sewage.

"He's been evicted because Bob Sebes didn't pay his rent," I said. "He needs a place to stay while he works things out."

"Why can't he stay with you?"

"Because they are hemorrhaging," Monk said.

"Excuse me?" Stottlemeyer said.

"The women and the hamster," Monk said. "It's not safe."

Monk took the bottle of bleach, opened it, and squeezed a couple of drops into the pot of water.

"What about your brother? He's got a big house with plenty of room."

"A house he hasn't left in nearly thirty years," Monk said. "You know why?"

"He's agoraphobic," Stottlemeyer said.

"Which is a fancy way of saying that he is cuckoo for Cocoa Puffs. How would you like to be cooped up with a nut?"

Stottlemeyer gave me a look. "I wouldn't like it at all."

"You said you'd be here for Mr. Monk if he needed you, Captain. Now he needs you."

Monk turned up the flame under the pot of water.

"What are you doing?" Stottlemeyer asked him.

"It was too late to buy water purification tablets, so I am cleaning the water myself. It should be reasonably safe to rinse with it, and perhaps drink a few sips, after I bring it to a boil for five minutes, let it cool down, and then strain it through a coffee filter."

Stottlemeyer glanced at me. "Monk is cleaning bottled water."

"I can see that," I said.

"He's only been here two minutes and that is what he's doing."

"Which proves that I'm not going to be any trouble at all," Monk said. "I can take care of myself."

Stottlemeyer rubbed his forehead and sighed. "Okay, here's the deal. You can stay with me for a couple of days until you get your life sorted out."

"Thank you, Leland."

"But — and this is a big *but* — I am not going to make any changes to my home or to my lifestyle to accommodate you. Do you understand?"

"No," Monk said.

"My home, my rules," Stottlemeyer said.

"May I see a copy?"

"A copy of what?"

"Your rules," Monk said.

"I don't have them written down."

"Then how do you expect people to follow them?"

"There really is only one rule. It's my way or the highway. Don't try to change anything about me or my home. I am who I am and I don't want my place Monked."

"What does that mean?" Monk looked at me, baffled.

I shrugged like I was baffled, too, but I wasn't. I knew exactly what Stottlemeyer was talking about. That's why I didn't want Monk staying with me ever again.

"What I'm saying is that I don't want you to make yourself comfortable," Stottlemeyer explained.

"You want me to be uncomfortable."

"That's right, because if you are, then I'll know for sure that you haven't Monked anything." Stottlemeyer led us down the short hall to the guest room, where there were two single beds and a bureau. "This is where my boys stay when they're here. You can have whichever bed you want."

"Do you have fresh sheets?"

"Those are fresh."

"They've never been slept on?"

"Not since they've been washed."

Monk nodded. "Do you have any fresh sheets?"

"If you're asking me if I have any brand-new, unopened, vacuum-sealed bedding in its original packaging, then the answer is no, I do not."

Monk nodded again. "So where am I going to sleep?"

"You have your choice of those beds, the couch, the recliner, the floor, or the sidewalk."

Monk turned to me and whispered: "Help."

I patted him on the back. "Everything is going to be fine, Mr. Monk. Good night."

I went to the door. Both Monk and Stottlemeyer hurried after me.

"What time are you coming back tomorrow?" Monk said.

"I'm not sure that I will be." I opened the door and stepped out into the hallway.

The captain chased after me. "What does that mean?"

"We'll see how things go."

"What things?"

I'd already had this conversation once that night and I wasn't going to have it again. Monk and Stottlemeyer could both live without me for a while.

"Sweet dreams," I said, gave him a little wave, and took off down the stairwell.

CHAPTER EIGHTEEN: MR. MONK AND THE NEVER-ENDING NIGHTMARE

The next morning I slept in, made myself a bagel and cream cheese, and read the newspaper. Julie met some friends for coffee before she went to work. I wished that she could have found something more stimulating for a summer job than washing cars but I knew how tight the job market was lately. I was worried that I might have to grab a towel and join her.

Instead of looking forward to a day of solitude and relaxation, I felt my anxiety rising, a trembling sensation in my midsection that jacked up my pulse and made my throat dry.

Where would I find us another job? I was fresh out of luck and inspiration. I'd have to search want ads and job-hunting Web sites just like the tens of thousands of other people in the Bay Area who were unemployed.

But first, I'd start by applying for unemployment benefits. That couple of hundred dollars a week could mean the difference between keeping our house and losing it. At least I had that — what was Monk going to do?

As if on cue, someone knocked at my front door. I flung the door open, certain that I was going to find Monk standing on my porch. But it wasn't him.

It was Stottlemeyer.

"You have got to find Monk another place to stay," he said.

There were dark circles under his eyes and his hair was a mess. He looked like he'd rolled right out of bed and into his clothes without bothering to shower or shave.

"Why do I have to do anything?" I asked, stepping aside to let him in.

"Because you're his assistant."

"Not anymore. You should know that better than anybody."

"Okay. Then *we* have to find him somewhere else to go, because if he stays with me, I'll kill him, and that could really hurt my career as a homicide detective."

"How did it go last night?"

"How do you think it went?" He paced in front of my couch, his hands shoved in the pockets of his wrinkled slacks.

"I don't know. You laid down some pretty

strict ground rules that didn't leave much wiggle room for him to cause trouble."

"I thought so, too. After you left, he wanted to talk with me about the Haxby murder, so I said good night and went right back to bed."

"That was nice of you."

"What was I supposed to do?"

"You could have talked with Mr. Monk about his troubles and offered him some sympathy and advice. The man just lost everything he has except you and me. He's feeling very scared and vulnerable right now."

"We're men. We don't sit around whining. We take action."

"Like running into your room, closing the door, and hiding under your sheets, hoping the problem goes away."

"I had a long day and I was tired."

I sat down on the couch. "So far it doesn't sound to me like you had such an awful night."

"Hell began at daybreak," he said.

"That could be the title of a western."

"More like a disaster movie," he said, and then he told me his story.

Stottlemeyer woke up at dawn because he had to go to the bathroom. Still half asleep and not accustomed to having guests, he'd completely forgotten that Monk was in his apartment.

He went into the bathroom, stood in front of the toilet, and began to pee when someone screamed.

Stottlemeyer yelped and staggered back, stunned to discover Monk lying in the bathtub, fully dressed.

"What are you doing in there?" Stottlemeyer demanded, turning back to the toilet and continuing to empty his bladder.

"Stop," Monk screamed. "For God's sake, *stop.*"

It took Stottlemeyer a moment to remember why Monk was at his apartment, but it still didn't explain why Monk was in the bathtub, curled into the fetal position, and hiding his face in his hands.

"I pee, you pee, everybody pees, especially in their own bathroom toilets."

"Not in front of other people!"

"Men pee in front of other men all the time."

"And those men are in lunatic asylums where they belong. It's barbaric! Inhuman! Disgusting!"

Stottlemeyer pulled up his sweats and flushed the toilet. "Haven't you ever been in a men's room and seen the row of urinals?"

"Once," Monk said.

"Haven't you ever used one?"

"Never," Monk said.

"But you are familiar with what urinals are and how they are used."

"I am also familiar with cannibalism but that doesn't mean I engage in the practice."

"What happened here is your own fault for hiding in my bathtub."

"I was sleeping," Monk said. "Or at least trying to."

"Why in my bathtub?"

"Because it is a contained area, comprised of tile and fiberglass, with a curtain for privacy. I was able to thoroughly clean the tub with a minimum of effort. I didn't think some insane barbarian would come running in and urinate all over the place."

"You startled me," Stottlemeyer said. "Besides, what did you think the toilet was for? Decoration?"

"You should have knocked first!"

"The bathroom door was open."

"It makes no difference! Before you relieve yourself you are required to take every possible precaution so that innocent bystanders aren't placed in physical danger or traumatized for life."

"It's my bathroom," Stottlemeyer said.

"And now it's my never-ending night-mare."

My laughter interrupted Stottlemeyer's story. He stopped pacing and glowered at me.

"It's not funny, Natalie."

"It is hilarious," I said.

"Not if it's happening to you."

It took me a moment to catch my breath. "That's the beauty of it. I'm always the one it's happening to. I never get to be the one who hears about it from a safe distance."

Stottlemeyer nodded and sat down next to me. "You have a point."

"So, where did you leave it with him?"

"I'm letting Monk clean my entire apartment, but I told him he couldn't throw out anything without my approval first," he said. "We have to get him back into his place."

"How do you suggest we do that? Mr. Monk is broke and owes three months of back rent."

"Hire a lawyer. What the landlord is doing can't be legal."

"Mr. Monk can't afford a lawyer," I said. "If you're so sure the landlord is breaking the law, arrest him."

"I can't."

"But he probably doesn't know that. Maybe you can convince him to at least let you in to get Mr. Monk some water, sheets, and fresh clothes."

Stottlemeyer glanced at me. "You might have better luck with that."

"You're big and brawny and have a badge."

"You have a pretty face and cleavage. You might even get dinner and a date out of it."

"He's missing a tooth," I said.

"So?"

"Would *you* date a woman who is missing teeth?"

"It depends on how many," he said.

"You're that desperate?"

Stottlemeyer sighed and got to his feet. "Sadly, yes."

"I'll go see the landlord, but I'm doing it just because I feel sorry for you."

"Thanks," the captain said.

"But if it doesn't work, it's your turn."

"You have a deal." Stottlemeyer went to the door. "While you're doing that, I'll call around and see if I can find some legal aid agency that will take on Monk's case."

I got up and went to the door with him. "You'd do that for him?"

"I'd take a bullet for Monk," Stottlemeyer said and walked out.

And I knew, regardless of how casually he tried to say it, that he meant it.

■ ■ ■ ■

I went to Monk's apartment and met with the landlord, Phoef Sutton, who must have lost the tooth when somebody slugged him. I don't know that for sure, but since I wanted to slug him, I figured others before me had experienced the urge, too.

Phoef was in his midthirties, wore tortoiseshell-framed glasses, a vintage bowling shirt, cargo pants, and canvas tennis shoes. He had carefully maintained stubble on his pale cheeks and seemed quite taken with himself, which also made me want to smack him.

We met in his apartment, which was decorated in prints and movie posters from the 1970s and furnished with reproduction sofas, lamps, and tables from the same era.

He refused to let me into Monk's apartment to get any of his things, despite my winning smile and the extra button I'd opened on my blouse.

"Depriving that crazy man of access to his possessions is an incentive to get him to pay his overdue rent," Phoef said. "Without that leverage, I doubt that the cheapskate will ever pay."

"He's been a good tenant," I said. "He's

quiet, clean, and courteous."

"One day, he stripped all the odd numbers off of the apartment doors, and when I confronted him about it, he said it was no different than rescuing people from a burning building."

"That was an isolated incident."

"He circulated a petition to have the tenant in the apartment above his evicted because one of his legs was amputated."

"Perhaps Mr. Monk has made a few mistakes, but you have no right to lock him out of his apartment and deprive him of his possessions," I said. "He'll sue you."

Phoef laughed in my face. "If he had the money for lawyers, he would have paid his rent. I'll unlock his doors the day the back rent is paid and the moving trucks show up. Otherwise, I'll auction off his belongings to settle his debts."

I didn't punch him.

Instead, I acted in a reasonable and thoughtful manner. I waited until dark, broke into Monk's apartment, and stole a set of sheets, a change of clothes, and as many bottles of water as I could carry.

I dropped them off that same night at Stottlemeyer's apartment. The captain wasn't back from work yet and Monk was very happy to see me. He was wearing an apron and gloves and holding a mop when I arrived. I could see all of the furniture was pushed up against the wall alongside dozens of moving boxes, each securely taped shut.

"What is all that?" I asked, gesturing to the boxes.

"Garbage," Monk said. "The captain wouldn't let me throw anything out without his approval first."

"It looks like you've packed up everything he owns."

"There was a toxic spill this morning. Nothing could be saved. You don't want to know."

I didn't tell him that I already did, nor that he was right about it being knowledge that I didn't want to have. I gave him the stuff that I'd stolen from his apartment but I told him that I'd talked Phoef into giving it to me.

Monk nodded. "Here's what happened. You covered the kitchen window of my apartment with a towel to protect your hand and muffle the sound while you broke the glass with your fist. You unlocked the latch and climbed in, took only what you could grab in two minutes and hold in both hands, and ran out the back door."

I stared at him. "How did you know that?"

"It's obvious. The evid —"

"Never mind," I interrupted. "It was a dumb thing to ask you."

"Don't you want to hear my summation?"

"There's no need. You got me. I confess."

"But you don't know how I knew how you did it."

"I don't care," I said. "Are you going to call the police?"

"A conviction for breaking and entering could lead to imprisonment and ruin your chances of finding future employment, plus you were mentally and emotionally incapacitated by your female troubles, so I won't press charges . . ."

"That's a relief," I said.

". . . on the condition that you let me do my summation."

"There's nobody here to be impressed by it."

"There's you," he said.

So I let him do his summation. He gleefully, and I thought rather smugly, pointed out all of the dumb mistakes that I'd made committing what I thought was the perfect crime. But there's no reason you have to know about them — I'm embarrassed enough as it is.

I learned something, though, from the experience. Now I know what it feels like to be unmasked by the greatest detective on earth.

It's humiliating.

And makes you want to murder somebody.

Him.

CHAPTER NINETEEN:
MR. MONK WORKS FOR FREE

I forgot to mention to you that after I left Phoef Sutton's place, and before I broke into Monk's apartment, I spent the day at my kitchen table polishing my résumé and Monk's.

I'd had so many jobs before becoming Monk's assistant that I could pretty much slant my résumé to fit whatever open position I applied for. But Monk's résumé took some creative writing talent. I stressed his skills, his attention to detail, his dependability, and his dedication to cleanliness, rather than his experience as a police officer and Homicide consultant.

If you're applying for sales, clerical, secretarial, and service positions, the people doing the hiring don't really care about how many homicides you've solved. But they do value cleanliness, education, reliability, and intelligence, and Monk had all those attributes.

After I left Stottlemeyer's condo, I went back home and logged on to every job-hunting site on the Web and submitted myself and Monk for every opening in San Francisco that didn't require degrees, certifications, licenses, or extensive experience in a particular field or profession.

That didn't leave a lot of great opportunities. For instance, there was an opening for a dishwasher at a Fisherman's Wharf restaurant. I thought Monk had a pretty good shot at that one if he could just get in for an interview and demonstrate his talents.

I also knew it would have been a tragedy if Monk got the job. Sure, he would be ridiculously content washing dishes, but the pay would be crap and it would be a waste of his talent and abilities.

It just wasn't right.

I found myself hoping some brilliant serial killer would strike, murdering a ton of people and terrifying the public, so that the police would have to hire Monk again out of sheer desperation.

That was how bad I was feeling. I was actually wishing for a massacre just so I could have my job back and not have to worry about losing my house.

Maybe Monk's worldview wasn't so wrong after all.

I gave up on applying for lousy jobs around midnight, turned off the laptop, and dragged myself to bed, depressed and scared. I was sure that I was so anxious that I'd never get to sleep, but I was unconscious in about sixty seconds.

My phone rang at 3:33 in the morning. If Monk saw those numbers flashing on his clock radio, he'd assume he was having a waking nightmare, hide his head under his pillow, and wait until 4:44 to peek at the clock again.

I foolishly answered the phone instead. It was Captain Stottlemeyer.

"There's been a murder in San Mateo," Stottlemeyer said. "You need to meet us there."

"Us?"

"Me and Monk," the captain said. "He says he can't do his thing without you."

"Have you rehired him as a consultant?"

"No," he replied.

"Too bad. Tell Mr. Monk that if he wants to tag along with you to look at some putrid corpse in the middle of a cold, dark night, that's his stupid, self-destructive decision, not mine. I don't work for him anymore. And you can remind him that I don't work for him because he can't pay me, and he can't pay me because you — the man he is now consulting with for free — fired him. Have fun."

I hung up the phone and put my face back into the warm spot on my pillow. I was beginning to slip back into sleep when the phone rang again. I grabbed the receiver.

"San Mateo is out of your jurisdiction," I said, turning my head but keeping my face in the warm sunken spot in my pillow.

"Yes, it is," Stottlemeyer said.

"So what makes this murder so special that you're schlepping all the way out there and you're letting Monk come with you?"

"The victim is Lincoln Clovis," the captain said. "He was Bob Sebes' accountant and was responsible for auditing the Reinier Investment Fund."

I'd read about him. He'd been charged with a ton of stuff, including securities fraud, and was facing a hundred years in prison if convicted on all the counts against him.

Bob Sebes had victimized both the wealthy and the poor, individual investors as well as pension funds and charities. It was a crime that outraged the public, not just in San Francisco but across the country. There was enormous pressure on law enforcement agencies to win a conviction. But that wouldn't be easy to do with coconspirators and potential prosecution witnesses getting killed left and right.

Whoever murdered Haxby and Clovis — and I assumed it was one guy — wasn't a serial killer, at least not the kind that terrifies the general public. Even so, I realized that this could be the case I was hoping for.

The pressure on the police to solve these murders, and to do it quickly, had to be intense.

The police department wasn't paying Monk yet, but they soon could become desperate enough to cave in, especially if he started to make headway in the case and then abruptly stopped working for free (even if it meant I had to tie him up and lock him in my attic to do it).

We'd have a gun to their head. They'd have to hire him again.

So I didn't hang up the phone this time. Instead, I asked for the address and told Stottlemeyer that I would be right there.

San Mateo is a southern suburb of San Francisco and was once part of a massive Spanish land grant known as Rancho de las Pulgas, which in English means "Ranch of Fleas." I could have torpedoed Monk's presence at the crime scene and his involvement in the investigation just by letting him know that little historical fact.

But I am not that spiteful.

Lincoln Clovis lived in a two-story Cape Cod–style house with blue-shingle siding and a wraparound deck overlooking the lagoon that snaked through the Mariner's Island and Seal Slough neighborhoods of San Mateo. The street was clogged with the usual official vehicles. The house was cordoned off with yellow crime scene tape and was illuminated with portable floodlights like a movie set.

I identified myself to the uniformed police officer stationed on the street and he led me to the back of the house, where the lawn sloped down to the water and a small boat dock.

Monk and Stottlemeyer were standing beside a woman who looked to be about my age and had the slender toned body of a runner or a ballet dancer. She wore casual clothes, a T-shirt and jeans, but there was nothing casual about the gun and badge clipped to her belt.

The three of them were looking up at the back of the house. I followed their gaze and saw a man hanging from a noose tied to a thick wooden railing post on the second-story deck. His face was bloated and dark red, his eyes bulging, and his tongue was sticking out of his gaping mouth.

Aside from the fact that he was dead, Clovis seemed physically fit and well off. He was dressed in slacks, a shirt with a buttoned-down collar, and a V-neck cashmere sweater. The Rolex on his wrist glimmered in the glow from portable floodlights.

"You must be Natalie Teeger," the female cop said, offering her hand to me. "I'm Captain Erin Cahill, San Mateo Homicide. Thanks for coming out."

She made the comment without a trace of sarcasm, as if my presence was an honor and I actually had some professional expertise to offer the investigation.

"I'm afraid I'm not going to be of much help to you," I said, shaking her hand.

Cahill tipped her head toward Monk. "He seems to think you will be. He wouldn't let us tell him anything about the case until you got here."

"I like Natalie to know what I know," Monk said. "Sometimes I miss things."

"You never miss anything," Stottlemeyer said. "You just like having someone to run interference for you."

"What sort of interference are you concerned about?" Cahill asked Monk, but Stottlemeyer answered for him.

"There's a list," Stottlemeyer said. "It's in

several volumes and comes with an index. He gave me a copy one year for Christmas."

"That reminds me," Monk said. "I didn't see it in your apartment."

"My wife got it in the divorce," Stottlemeyer said. "She cherishes it. Can we focus on the murder now?"

The mention of divorce seemed to catch Cahill's interest. She gave Stottlemeyer a long, appraising look that he missed entirely. Men are so stupid.

"How do you know it's a murder and not a suicide?" I asked. "He's got plenty of motivation for killing himself."

"Like what?" Monk asked.

Cahill turned to him. "Don't you know who Lincoln Clovis is?"

"I know he was Bob Sebes' accountant," Monk said. "But that's all I let Captain Stottlemeyer tell me until Natalie got here."

"I know who he is," I said.

"How?" Monk asked.

"Because I'm an engaged member of our society. I keep up on the news so that I am well informed on matters that might impact my life or enrich my understanding of myself and others."

"It sounds exhausting," Monk said.

Cahill cleared her throat and spoke up. "Clovis ran a one-man accounting business in a strip mall here in San Mateo. Before Sebes found him, Clovis made his living doing simple income tax returns for walk-in customers."

"I don't know how Sebes found him," Stottlemeyer said. "But he bought Clovis some fancy stationery and paid him two hundred thousand dollars a year to falsely certify that he'd audited the books and reviewed the securities."

"Did Clovis know it was a Ponzi scheme?" Monk asked.

"I don't think Clovis ever opened the books," Stottlemeyer said. "But if he did, he obviously didn't understand what he was looking at."

Monk cocked his head. "Why do you say that?"

"Because Clovis invested most of the money Sebes paid him into the fund and even convinced his family and friends to invest in it, too."

"He was supposed to be an independent auditor," Cahill said. "So the investment and his soliciting other investments in the fund were also violations of the law."

"The guy was an imbecile," Stottlemeyer said.

"So Clovis not only lost everything," I said, "but he was looking at a hundred years behind bars for aiding and abetting the scheme that swindled him. Is it any surprise that the dope hung himself?"

"He didn't," Monk said.

"How can you tell?" Cahill asked. "The medical examiner hasn't arrived yet and the crime scene unit hasn't finished collecting their forensic evidence."

"If he killed himself, he would have stood on the rail and jumped," Monk said. "But there are splinters in his cheek and on his sweater, indicating that he was rolled face-down over the railing."

She took a step closer to the body and squinted up at it. "I'll be damned. You're right. Maybe the rope will give us some leads."

"It won't," Monk said. "It came from his boat."

"How do you know that?" she asked.

"It's exactly the length you'd need to tie a boat to those cleats on the dock," Monk said, gesturing to the water. "And his boat is gone."

"I've been with you since you got here. You haven't measured the rope or the distance between the cleats. How can you possibly know it's the right size?"

"I'm not blind," Monk said.

"I can guarantee you that his eyeball

measurements will be correct," Stottlemeyer said. "Within an eighth of an inch."

"I wouldn't be that far off," Monk said. "Have a little faith in me."

Cahill waved over an officer. "Send a patrol boat down the lagoon. I want his boat found, secured, and examined by a forensics unit."

The officer nodded and went off. Cahill stared at Monk as if he was some kind of extraterrestrial. I turned to Stottlemeyer.

"When you called me, you said that Clovis was murdered. But Mr. Monk didn't prove it until just now. So why did you jump to that conclusion before you had any evidence?"

"Clovis agreed yesterday to a reduced sentence in exchange for his testimony against Sebes. He would have done ten years in a minimum-security prison. And he's the second indicted conspirator to the Sebes scheme to die this week. I don't think it's a coincidence."

"Neither do I," said Cahill. "I'd love to take this homicide off my desk and put it on yours."

"Gee, thanks," Stottlemeyer said.

"It's not that I don't care about the death of one of our citizens, but our budget has been slashed to the bone and our limited resources are already stretched to the max."

"I know the feeling," he said.

"Maybe we could commiserate," she said.

Stottlemeyer seemed startled by the suggestion. He stuck his hands in his pockets and found something to look at on the water.

"I haven't commiserated in a while," he said. "There hasn't been much opportunity."

"We could commiserate about that, too."

He was smiling when he turned back to her. "I'd like that, Captain."

"Call me Erin," she said.

Standing in front of a bloated corpse at a quarter to five in the morning, and surrounded by crime scene techs and police officers, seemed like an odd and inappropriate time and place to be arranging a hookup. But perhaps it was precisely that circumstance, and the many like it, that filled their days and nights, that made it hard for them to find somebody to commiserate with. They practiced a lonely profession. Come to think of it, it had become mine and it had been a long time since I'd commiserated with someone, too.

But all of this was lost on Monk. He walked around the yard, framing the scene between his hands, looking for incongruities, yet missing the congruence that Stottlemeyer and Cahill were attempting to establish with each other.

"Did Clovis live here alone?" Monk asked.

"Yes," Cahill said.

"I'd like to see inside the house."

Cahill led us up the path to the front yard. A question occurred to me as we approached the front door.

"If he lives alone, how was the body discovered?"

"By patrol officers," she said. "His neighbors called to complain about a barking dog that was keeping them up."

We went inside the house, which was decorated like an upscale seafood restaurant with lots of nautical and fishing-related paraphernalia on the walls. Monk stopped to examine the alarm console on the wall beside the front door.

"Was this activated?"

"Nope," Cahill said. "And the door was unlocked when the officers arrived."

"So Clovis knew his killer and didn't feel threatened by him," Stottlemeyer said. "He invited him in."

"One last, dumb mistake," Cahill said.

The entry hall led into an open kitchen and large living room that faced picture windows and the wraparound deck. There was a shag carpet and a large stone fireplace with a swordfish mounted over it. Monk froze and let out a little terrified squeal.

The source of his anxiety was a large Dalmatian sitting docilely on the white couch beside a young police officer, who was petting the dog and holding its leash.

"It's all right," Cahill said. "The dog is tame. She was on the deck barking when the officers arrived. But she ran up and licked them when they came in."

"How are they doing?" Monk asked.

"Who?"

"The officers," Monk said.

"One of them is sitting there on the couch," Cahill said. The cop on the couch waved. He didn't look old enough to drink alcohol. I thought about offering to commiserate with him.

"Why isn't he on his way to the hospital?" Monk asked.

"Because he hasn't been hurt," Cahill replied.

"He was licked by a wild animal," Monk said. "The officer may look fine now, but in a few days, when he's foaming at the mouth and shooting civilians, you'll wish you'd listened to me."

Monk lifted his hands and started scanning the room, but he made a point of never turning his back on the dog.

"You'd better go get yourself checked out," I said to the officer. "I'll handle the dog."

The officer shot a look at Cahill, who nodded her approval.

"Yes, ma'am." The officer got up and left. I sat down next to the dog and held her leash.

"Interference," Stottlemeyer whispered to Cahill.

"You have an observation?" Monk asked Stottlemeyer.

"I was just saying to Captain Cahill that there are no signs of a struggle. Nothing seems to have been disturbed at all."

"There's a huge disturbance." Monk squatted by the fireplace and examined the wrought-iron tools, which were hanging individually from hooks on a special stand.

"Where?" Cahill asked.

"On the couch," Monk said. "The animal will have to be euthanized."

"Why?" Cahill asked.

"Look at it," Monk said. "It's in agony."

"She looks fine to me," Cahill said.

"How can you say that?" Monk replied, continuing to move around the room, hands out in front of him, one wary eye cast at the dog. "She's a mess, neither black nor white, wearing a coat of schizophrenia. Imagine how she feels."

"She'll feel worse being killed," I said.

"I sincerely doubt it," Monk said.

Cahill looked aghast. "You can't put down a dog for having irregular spots."

"It's an act of mercy to end its suffering."

"You're suffering," Stottlemeyer said to Monk. "The dog's not."

Monk suddenly froze, as if he'd stepped on a land mine. "Nobody move."

"What's wrong?" Cahill asked, her hand instinctively going to the butt of her gun.

"I've got dog on me," Monk said. "You probably all do, too. The important thing now is not to panic."

I glanced at Monk's pants and saw barblike strands of black and white dog hair sticking to his pants. Stottlemeyer looked at his own legs and brushed the hair off.

"Stop!" Monk yelled. "Are you insane? Do you want us all to die?"

"What's the problem?" Stottlemeyer asked innocently.

"Now the hair and dog particles are in the air."

"Dog particles?" Cahill said.

"It's like asbestos," Monk said, "with added dog."

"Added dog?" Cahill said.

"Just stand very still until help arrives," Monk said. "Try not to breathe."

We were all silent and very still for a moment.

"Isn't somebody going to call for help?" Monk asked.

"Not until you tell us what happened to Lincoln Clovis," Stottlemeyer said.

"Talking requires breathing," Monk said.

"Cover your nose and mouth with your hand," Stottlemeyer said.

Everyone covered their noses and mouths except for Stottlemeyer.

"Here's what happened," Monk said, his voice muffled by his hand. "Bob Sebes hit Clovis on the back of his head with an ash shovel and dragged him out onto the deck. Sebes tied the rope around the railing post, slipped the noose over Clovis' head, lifted him onto the rail, and rolled him off. You're not covering your nose and mouth, Captain."

"I have a mustache," Stottlemeyer said. "It filters dog particles."

"How do you know it was Bob Sebes?" Cahill asked.

"He doesn't," Stottlemeyer said. "Sebes is under constant observation and electronic monitoring. The man hasn't left his house."

"It was Sebes," Monk said.

"The GPS strapped to his ankle is tamper-proof, Monk, and there are a dozen officers and a hundred reporters camped outside his door. It wasn't Sebes."

"It was him," Monk said.

"How do you know Clovis was smacked with the ash shovel?" Stottlemeyer asked, abruptly changing the subject. "I don't see any blood on it."

"Or dust," Monk said.

"What does dust have to do with it?" Cahill asked.

"Clovis hasn't made a fire in ages," Monk replied. "There's a fine layer of dust on top of the firewood in the basket and on top of all the fireplace tools — except the shovel."

"I'll be damned," Cahill said.

"Will you call for help now?" Monk whined. "Please?"

CHAPTER TWENTY:
MR. MONK
SHARES THE MOMENT

Monk's rescue was reluctantly accomplished by two crime scene investigators armed with lint brushes, which they used to remove the dog hair from his pants, and a roll of plastic sheeting, which they unfurled on the carpet to give us a safe path to the door.

Monk insisted on accompanying Stottlemeyer back to the police station to personally examine the readings from Bob Sebes' GPS ankle bracelet. So the captain called ahead to rouse the police tech expert from his bed to come down to the station and walk us through the data.

By the time we got to the station, a surprisingly perky and alert Disher was there to meet us, along with Ingo Koenig, a bleary-eyed, scrappy-haired man with a neck that seemed too short and narrow to support his massive head. He was like Charlie Brown come to life, only without the shirt with the zigzag stripe.

They were at Disher's desk, huddled over a laptop computer. There were several windows open on the monitor. One window showed a map of Pacific Heights, another showed a multicolored graph that looked like a flatline EKG, another had raw stats that meant nothing to me, and yet another seemed to be a timeline of some kind.

Stottlemeyer made the introductions, then asked Ingo to tell us about the GPS monitoring unit and bracelet that Sebes was wearing around his ankle.

"The judge would probably have locked Sebes up if his lawyer hadn't convinced him that the Triax XG7 8210, out of all the brands out there, is the ultimate in constant, tamperproof monitoring technology," Ingo said.

"Nothing is tamperproof," Monk said.

"I suppose you could wrap the unit in aluminum foil or lead to block the unique wireless signal from being emitted. Or you could use a bolt cutter, or a blowtorch, or even the actual key to remove the bracelet."

"So how can you say it's tamperproof?" Monk said.

"Because the beauty of the Triax XG7 8210 is that any attempt to tamper with it will be instantly detected. There's an infrared beam between the unit and your leg. If you try to slip anything between the bracelet and the skin, or to move the unit away from your body beyond its preset range, we are alerted. If the strap is broken, cut, or unlocked, we are alerted. Any time the transmission of your unique signal is broken, for any reason, we are alerted. But that's only a fraction of the XG7 8210's ingenious monitoring features. . . ."

Ingo then explained the XG7 8210's other features with a passion that approached reverence. We learned that the unit utilized GPS technology to not only track the offender's movements but also to enforce individual inclusion and exclusion zones.

For instance, if the person is a stalker or sex offender and is not allowed within two thousand feet of schools, or a particular home or place of business, the unit will alert authorities the instant he breaks those boundaries or is in the vicinity. Sebes was under house arrest; therefore his unit would alert authorities the moment he stepped outside of his property line or, as Ingo called it, his inclusion zone.

The unit could also analyze changes in the skin and sweat to detect any drug or alcohol use.

"Some people buy these units by mail order to keep tabs on their troublesome kids or their philandering spouses," he said.

I could understand the temptation. I'd worry a lot less about Julie if she had an XG7 8210 strapped to her ankle.

"So you'd know if Sebes ever tampered with the unit or left his house?" Stottlemeyer asked.

"Me and the half dozen other law enforcement agencies that are constantly monitoring his unit," Ingo said. "Even if we weren't watching twenty-four-seven, the system is designed to call my house if there is any breach of the established protocols."

"Have you received any alerts?" the captain asked. "Has Sebes tampered with his device in any way?"

"We've detected no irregularities of any kind." Ingo pointed to the readouts on his laptop screen to prove it.

The captain nodded. "Has Sebes left his house in the last twenty-four hours?"

"No, he hasn't. In fact, I can even tell you which rooms of the house he's been in."

Stottlemeyer turned to Monk with a look of smug satisfaction.

"See, Monk? There's no possible way the killer could be Bob Sebes. So you can stop fixating on him and open your mind to other possible suspects."

Monk cocked his head from side to side

and then pointed to the screen and a spike on an otherwise flat line on a graph.

"What is this blip," he asked, "around ten forty-five last night?"

"Sebes had a drink or two," Ingo said. "We forgot to deactivate the alcohol-monitoring function on his unit."

"What kind of drink?" Monk asked.

"I would say a strong martini or several glasses of wine, judging by the traces of ethanol the unit detected."

I felt a tingle of realization at the base of my neck, as if someone was standing right behind me, breathing on my skin.

"What difference does it make what Sebes was drinking?" Disher asked. "He's not under arrest for being a drunk."

Monk smiled. And everyone in the room but Ingo knew what that smile meant. Me, most of all, because I'd miraculously made the same connection, at the same moment, that Monk did.

"Because it proves Sebes wasn't in the house," Monk said. "And that he killed Lincoln Clovis."

Stottlemeyer would have liked for the five of us to visit Bob Sebes without attracting the attention of all the reporters who were staked out in front of the house. But Monk made that impossible.

Monk refused to go inside the house, which he referred to as "a hotbed of virulent *tinea pedis*," without wearing a crime scene technician's white jumpsuit, goggles, gloves, and booties to protect himself. So Monk borrowed a suit from the crime lab and was wearing it when we walked up to the front door.

Anna Sebes was on her way out, but changed her plans when we arrived and she saw how Monk was dressed. It conveys a very negative message when a group of somber-faced detectives show up at the door with someone outfitted for the collection of forensic evidence. And she clearly didn't appreciate the sudden attention our arrival sparked among the press, who were yelling out questions and jostling for position outside the gate for the best shot with their cameras.

"Is that outfit really necessary?" she said to Monk. "You're creating the impression that a crime has taken place."

"One has," Monk said.

"My husband is innocent," she said. "He's not a swindler or a killer."

"Your husband is a plague," Monk said. "If you were smart, you'd be wearing one of these, too."

She reluctantly led Stottlemeyer, Disher, Ingo, Monk, and me into her home.

Bob was sitting on the couch in his den, his bare feet up on the coffee table, watching *Deal or No Deal* on a massive flat-screen TV. His den was lined with sports memorabilia and vintage movie posters, which Ingo strolled around admiring as if he was in a museum. There was a snack bar along one wall that included a popcorn machine, soft drink dispenser, and glass display case filled with candy. Whoever said crime doesn't pay obviously had never met Bob Sebes.

"I hope you don't eat off that table," Monk said, holding his hand up in front of him, warding away the image of Bob's bare, blistered, scaly feet.

Bob switched off the TV with his remote but didn't bother to get up. "What can I do for you gentlemen today?"

"We're here about the murder of Lincoln Clovis," Stottlemeyer said.

"I heard about that on the morning news," Bob said. "Someone desperately wants me to go to jail."

Monk raised his hand. "That would be me."

"I'm talking about whoever is killing the people who actually committed the crime that I am accused of," Bob said. "This is all about covering up their tracks and tightening up their frame on me."

"You killed Russell Haxby and Lincoln Clovis," Monk said.

"Haxby was murdered up in Marin County, Clovis was down in San Mateo, and I'm stuck here under house arrest," Bob said. "How could I have killed either one of them?"

"You weren't here last night," Monk said.

"I never left. But you don't have to take my word for it. Ask him." Bob gestured to Ingo, who was scrutinizing a framed baseball mitt, his back to us.

Stottlemeyer smacked Ingo on the shoulder to get his attention. Ingo whirled around.

"Sorry. I was just admiring your collection. Did that mitt really belong to Willie Mays?"

"Forget about the mitt," Stottlemeyer said. "Check out his ankle bracelet."

Ingo started toward Bob's feet when Monk let out a cry.

"Halt!"

Ingo froze. "What?"

"Do you have a death wish?" Monk said. "You can't get near those without protection. I'm wearing protection and I still wouldn't touch them."

Ingo sighed. "Actually, I can see the Triax XG7 8210 just fine from where I'm standing. It obviously hasn't been tampered with. But I knew that before we left headquarters. I'm still not sure what we're doing here."

"We're arresting a murderer," Monk said.

"He just told you that I didn't leave," Bob said.

"Actually, he said your ankle bracelet wasn't tampered with," Monk said. "It's not the same thing."

"Actually, it is," Ingo said.

"I know you weren't here last night," Monk said. "Because you're here right now."

Stottlemeyer scratched his head. "You're not making a hell of a lot of sense, Monk."

"I am so glad to hear you say that, Captain," Disher said. "I thought it was just me."

"I understand what Monk is saying," I said.

"You do?" Stottlemeyer said.

"I do," I said. "It's simple. Bob Sebes couldn't have been here last night and that monitoring unit proves it."

"You just contradicted yourself," Disher said.

"No, I didn't," I said. "Tell them, Mr. Monk."

And then Monk did something extraordinary. He shook his head and smiled at me.

"You tell them, Natalie."

"But it's your moment," I said.

"It's our moment. You understand what I'm thinking. Do you know how long I've wanted someone to understand where I'm coming from? Until now, it's only happened once in my life and I thought it would never happen for me again."

I was afraid he'd tell me that he loved me. And he probably did, but not in the same way he'd loved Trudy. Or that I loved Mitch.

But I knew what he meant. I was also thrilled that for once things had clicked for me at the same time they did for Monk. That had never happened for me or for anybody else before, at least not since his wife, Trudy, was killed. We all were always at a loss to understand how Monk had figured things out until he told us.

"Please, Natalie," he said. "Share with everyone what we are both thinking."

"Oh, for God's sake," Anna said. "Nobody cares what you're thinking."

"I do," Stottlemeyer said and regarded me with a strange expression on his face. I think it might have been envy.

I looked at Anna Sebes. "Did you know that the XG7 8210 on your husband's ankle not only detects where he is but how much alcohol he drinks?"

"Why should I care?" she said, but she obviously did. And I knew why.

"Because Bob was drinking last night, and since he's seriously allergic to alcohol, that should concern you very much. One drink and he could go into anaphylactic shock, just like he did on that cruise with you a few years ago."

"You should be dead," Monk said to Bob. "But since you're not, and no paramedics came rushing in here last night to save your life, you obviously weren't the one drinking."

"Time out," Disher said. "You're saying that he somehow got the XG7 8210 off of his ankle, put it on somebody else and snuck out of the house, got past all of the cops and reporters outside, murdered Lincoln Clovis, and then snuck back in?"

"I'm saying Bob Sebes wasn't here last night or he'd be dead," Monk said. "I don't know how he disabled the monitoring unit or got in and out of the house undetected."

"He didn't," Ingo said, shaking his head, refusing to accept the notion. "He couldn't have."

"Maybe he has a secret tunnel under the house," Disher said.

272

"There is no secret tunnel," Stottlemeyer said.

"How do you know? The entrance could be hidden behind a secret panel in the wall activated by adjusting a picture, pulling a book off a shelf, or pressing just the right spot." Disher began walking around the room, testing his theory by knocking, pulling, pressing, and adjusting things.

"We would have detected any attempt to tamper with the XG7 8210 before he even got it off his ankle," Ingo said, still shaking his head. I thought he might start stomping his feet, too. "He could not have removed the unit and attached it to someone else. It's impossible. So the secret tunnel is irrelevant."

"I'd still like to find it," Disher said.

What struck me during all of this back-and-forth was that Bob Sebes didn't look like a man who'd just been exposed as a murderer. He was distracted, like his thoughts were somewhere else entirely.

Something was very, very wrong with how this was unfolding.

"It's so pitiful, Adrian, that it's almost funny," Bob said. "You are so eager to arrest me for two murders that I didn't commit that you are missing the simplest, most shameful explanation for what happened."

"What's that?" Monk asked.

"I was here last night and I was drinking."

"So why aren't you dead?" I asked.

"I wanted to be," he said dolefully. "But Anna saved me."

"Your wife wasn't here," Disher said, knocking on the wall. "She left yesterday afternoon and didn't get back until after midnight."

Sebes nodded. "After she left, I started thinking about all the mistakes that I've made, about how my ego and inattention to the business gave Haxby, Clovis, and others the opportunity to mount a massive fraud right under my nose. My life and reputation are ruined and I will lose everything. But the worst part of it all is the hell that Anna, an innocent bystander, the love of my life, is going through. I decided that the least I could do was end this ordeal for her and leave her with what little I still had that the prosecutors couldn't take — my life insurance. If everything had worked out, I would have been long dead by the time she got home and this nightmare would have been over for me."

Anna joined her husband on the couch and took his hand. "And my nightmare would have just begun. I don't blame you for any of this and I certainly don't want to lose you, Bob. We're in this together, no matter what happens."

"Your explanation is that your drinking was a suicide attempt," Monk said.

He stated the obvious, but I believe he was simply thinking out loud, making the declaration so he could hear it, study it, and see if it was the missing piece that would solve the mystery and restore order.

Tears began to stream down Anna's cheeks. "I went to the movies last night. Two stupid comedies, just to take my mind off of things. If only I'd known what Bob was thinking. When I got home, I found him lying on the floor, his face swollen, the empty martini glasses on the table. I was terrified. Thank God I always carry EpiPens with me now in my purse, just in case some fool puts wine sauce on Bob's steak or something. So I injected him with all the pens I had until he came around."

I knew about EpiPens. A friend of mine was allergic to bee stings and carried some EpiPens around with her. They were pre-measured doses of epinephrine in spring-loaded, auto-injecting syringes that she could jam into her thigh, even through her jeans.

"Why didn't you call 911 and get him to a hospital after that?" I asked. "He could have died."

"The last thing we need on top of everything else is the world ridiculing Bob for attempting suicide," she said. "The media would twist it into an admission of guilt."

"I do feel guilty," Bob said. "But not for stealing two billion dollars or killing anybody. I didn't do that. My crime was hubris and stupidity."

Monk rolled his shoulders, then cocked his head from side to side. "Nope, you're still the guy."

I believed it, too, even if I couldn't prove it.

"His explanation makes a lot more sense than yours," Ingo said.

"That's enough," Stottlemeyer said to Ingo.

"But he cast aspersions on the Triax XG7 8210," Ingo said. "That can't go unchallenged. It's —"

"Get out of here," Stottlemeyer said, cutting him off. "And don't say a word to anyone, especially the reporters outside, about what has occurred here today. Do I make myself clear?"

Ingo nodded and marched out.

Stottlemeyer turned to Disher. "You can stop knocking on the walls now."

"But I haven't found the secret door,"

276

Disher said.

"There isn't one," he said.

"Maybe it's on the floor," Disher said, and started stomping around.

Stottlemeyer grabbed him by the arm. "Stop. Stand still. Take your notebook and the pencil out of your pocket and make notes."

Disher did as he was told.

Stottlemeyer took a deep breath and turned to Bob and Anna Sebes. "Do you know anybody who might have wanted Lincoln Clovis dead?"

"Him," Monk said, pointing at Bob.

Stottlemeyer sighed. "I wasn't talking to you, Monk. In fact, it's time for you to go."

"But we're not done here," Monk said.

"You are," Stottlemeyer said. "I'll see you back at the station."

Monk didn't argue. He turned and walked out of the room. I hung back for a moment, making sure to catch Stottlemeyer's eye with my angriest look. I did, but he didn't wither under it. If anybody withered, it was me.

Chapter Twenty-One:
Mr. Monk Is Unappreciated

We waited over an hour in Stottlemeyer's office for him to return. Monk occupied himself by sweeping the floor, dusting the shelves, and organizing everything.

There was a time when I would have wondered how Monk could humiliate himself by cleaning Stottlemeyer's office after the captain had just treated him so rudely.

But now I was familiar enough with Monk to understand that he wasn't cleaning the office for Stottlemeyer, he was doing it for himself. It was a way to relax, to clear his mind, and to create an oasis of order amidst all the disorder around him.

I didn't have any handy rituals or activities to relieve myself of all my anxiety, frustration, anger, and fear. So I sat on that horrible vinyl couch, stewing in it all.

Aside from my money woes and uncertain future, I was upset that Sebes was getting away with murder. I knew that Monk was right, and that Sebes was lying about his suicide attempt. But I had no idea how Sebes had outsmarted the sophisticated monitoring device strapped to his ankle, or how he got past all the reporters and cops outside his house. And judging by how intensely Monk was cleaning, he didn't know the answers, either.

I was also sure that the murder wasn't the only thing on Monk's mind. He was broke, unemployed, and homeless. And it was unlikely that Stottlemeyer would let Monk stay at his place much longer.

I had no answers, and going over all the questions only made me more anxious, frustrated, and scared. But I couldn't stop myself from doing it anyway. I guess that's what Monk felt, on a much bigger scale, every minute of every day about everything.

Maybe we were on the same wavelength, as he put it, in more ways than I cared to admit.

When Stottlemeyer and Disher finally returned, the captain regarded his clean, orderly, shining office as if it had been ransacked instead.

"This is my private space, Monk," Stottlemeyer said.

"It was a messy private space."

"Did I ask you to clean it?"

"I did it as a courtesy," Monk said.

"The courteous thing to do would have been to leave my things alone," he said. "That goes for my office and my home."

"Oh, spare me." I'd had enough. I got up off the couch. "We didn't sit here for an hour so we could listen to more of your whining."

Stottlemeyer turned to me. "What did you say?"

"You heard me. You told us to wait here and you know Mr. Monk. If you didn't expect him to do you this courtesy, then you're a lousy judge of character and you have no one to blame but yourself. So let's move on, shall we?"

Monk couldn't have looked more astonished if I'd taken out a gun and shot the captain.

Disher whistled, or at least he tried to. It came out sounding more like he was blowing his nose. "Wow, someone got up on the wrong side of the bed this morning."

"I certainly did. I was summoned at three thirty in the morning to a crime scene by someone I don't work for and who I don't owe a damn thing," I said. "But like a fool, I went anyway."

"She's menstruating," Monk said.

All three men nodded knowingly, as if that

explained everything, which only made me angrier, because it was sexist, patronizing, and not true.

"That has nothing to do with it, Mr. Monk. I don't appreciate being treated like crap and you shouldn't, either."

"Please don't use the c-word," Monk said, and then, by way of apologizing to the others, he added: "She's menstruating."

They nodded again.

"Stop that," I said. "You have no idea how insulting that is, and if you do, and you continue anyway, then you're pigs."

"I'm sorry if I was abrupt with you and Monk when we were questioning Sebes," Stottlemeyer said. "But I couldn't have Monk distracting us any longer with his dead end."

"He's the guy," Monk said.

"That's exactly what I'm talking about, Monk. He is not the guy — he can't possibly be the guy. You're wrong."

"He's never wrong about murder," I said.

"He is this time," Stottlemeyer said. "Unless Monk can tell me how Bob Sebes managed to get that monitoring unit off without activating all those alarms, put it on somebody else, and sneak out of the house. And how he snuck somebody else in, whoever the hell that somebody is, to wear the monitor and have a few drinks, and snuck the guy out again."

"The secret tunnel could explain the in-and-out stuff," Disher said with authority. "But not the monitor thing."

"There is no secret tunnel," Stottlemeyer said.

"We don't know that," Disher said. "Because it's still secret until we find it."

"The only person to leave that house was Anna Sebes," Stottlemeyer said. "And she went in and out the front door."

"Maybe she killed them," Disher said. "She was out when Haxby was killed, too."

Monk shook his head. "With her arthritis, she couldn't have tied the rope into a noose or lifted Clovis up onto the railing. And it still doesn't explain Bob's drinking."

"Bob explained it, Monk," Stottlemeyer said. "Pretty convincingly, too."

"He didn't convince me," Monk said.

"And that's why I had to throw you out," Stottlemeyer said. "You've become a hindrance to this investigation. There are other suspects."

"Like who?" I asked.

"Clovis talked his family and friends into investing with Sebes and they lost everything," Stottlemeyer said. "How do you think they felt when they discovered Clovis was part of the scheme?"

"Hanging him from the deck also could have been meant as a message to others involved in the scheme," Disher said.

"How so?" Stottlemeyer asked.

"In 1982, an executive with a private Italian bank, a guy known as 'God's banker' because of his dealings with the Vatican, was hung from a bridge over the Thames in London. The bank was one billion dollars in debt and was supposedly owned by the mob. It was a huge scandal. The theory was that the banker was killed by the mob to prevent him from talking and as a warning to others to keep their mouths shut. Both that banker and Clovis were involved in financial scandals and hung near waterways. The symbolic similarities between the two killings may be a coincidence or maybe they're not."

Stottlemeyer looked thoughtfully at Disher for a long moment. "How did you know that story about the Italian banker?"

"It happened when I was a kid and it was something I never forgot."

"That's really good, out-of-the-box thinking. You may be on to something there."

"Really?"

"Yeah, of course," Stottlemeyer said. "Let's put some men on it and see where it leads us."

"How about the secret door?" Disher asked.

"Don't push your luck," Stottlemeyer said.

Disher hurried out and Stottlemeyer directed his attention back to the two of us. Frankly, I don't know why we were still standing there. Stottlemeyer had made his point clear. Maybe the reason we hadn't moved was inertia, exhaustion, or the knowledge that we had nowhere else we had to be.

"Sometimes Randy surprises me," Stottlemeyer said.

"Mr. Monk does, too," I said. "This is not the first time you've told him that the person he's accused of murder couldn't possibly be guilty."

"I know, I know, I know," Stottlemeyer said and sighed wearily. "This is where you bring up the astronaut again, whose alibi was that he was in outer space at the time of his girlfriend's murder."

"I could mention a lot of cases."

"So now you're going to remind me that I didn't believe Monk when he said the killer was a guy who was in a coma at the time of the murders."

"No, I'm going to tell you about the killer whose alibi was that he was in his house, wearing a tamperproof monitoring bracelet, and under constant surveillance by the media and the police, at the time of the murders."

Stottlemeyer went behind his desk and sat down heavily in his chair, as if he weighed ten thousand pounds. "I don't know why I am discussing this with you. You're not part of this investigation."

"You thought we should be included at three thirty this morning," I said.

"I couldn't leave Monk alone in my apartment," Stottlemeyer said.

"Why not?" Monk asked.

"You know why not," Stottlemeyer said. "You wanted to throw out everything I own. I brought you along to San Mateo to keep you out of trouble and to do you a favor."

"If you wanted to do me a favor you would have let me throw out all of the contaminated trash in your condo," Monk said.

"I knew you were personally interested in anything that might be potentially connected to the Sebes case," Stottlemeyer said. "That was the favor I was doing by bringing you with me."

"You were taking advantage of him," I said. "Again."

"We're done discussing this. I have work

to do." Stottlemeyer reached into his pocket, took out a set of keys, and tossed them to Monk. "Go home, get some rest, and put everything of mine back where it was."

Monk tossed the keys back to the captain. "I can't stay in your home another night."

"Is it because of this Sebes thing?"

"It's because of the way you live," Monk said. "No offense, but I can understand why your wife left you and your girlfriend became a psychopathic killer."

"Where are you going to stay?"

Monk shrugged. "There are plenty of overpasses in this city. There must be space for another homeless, transient, hobo bum like me under one of them."

He walked out and I followed him. We were almost at the stairs when Disher came running up to us and asked us to wait.

"I heard about the trouble you're in," Disher said. "I think I can help. I've got a job for you."

"You're going to bring us on as your consultants," Monk said.

"I'm afraid not." Disher reached into his pocket and handed me a piece of paper. "But here's another offer. Fashion Frisson is a clothing store in the Bayview Mall. The manager owes me a favor and I happen to know that she needs two new salespeople."

"How do you know that?" I asked.

"Because I arrested them," Disher said. "They had hidden cameras in the dressing rooms and got their jollies taking videos of the naked customers. I managed to keep their arrest quiet so the media never found out about it. Her business would have been ruined because of those two sickos and it wasn't her fault."

"You did a good deed," Monk said.

"And now you're doing another," I said. "Thank you, Randy."

"What are friends for?" he said. "It's all worked out. You start tomorrow at ten."

At least I had one less thing to worry about, even if it was barely more than a minimum wage job. But there was still the question of where Monk was going to stay. I asked him about that when we got into my car.

"Do you have a particular overpass in mind?"

"I wasn't serious about that," Monk replied.

"That's a shocker," I said. "You really had me going. So what's your plan?"

"Take me to hell," Monk said.

"An all-you-can-eat buffet?"

"Take me home," he said.

"You can't get into your apartment," I

287

said. "Not unless you want to break in."

"I didn't mean that home," he said. "I meant home."

CHAPTER TWENTY-TWO:
MR. MONK GOES HOME

The Victorian house in Tewksbury, just over the Golden Gate Bridge in Marin County, was unchanged since the time Monk grew up there with his older brother, Ambrose. The Monks don't like change.

Ambrose was every bit as brilliant as Monk and just as messed up. He made his living writing instruction manuals, encyclopedias, and textbooks and could recite them entirely from memory in a dozen different languages (including Dratch, which is only spoken by elephant-nosed aliens on a cult sci-fi TV series). That made him a self-proclaimed expert on just about everything, something he was glad to demonstrate given the slightest opportunity.

He was also a fair handyman, able to do his own electrical, plumbing, and carpentry work and repair household appliances (it didn't hurt that he'd written the owner's manuals for most of them). I'd schlepped out to Tewksbury a dozen times just to have him fix my broken blenders, hair dryers, toasters, and answering machines.

Ambrose developed those skills out of necessity because he was afraid to leave the house. He's only stepped outside twice in thirty years. That isolation meant he had little face-to-face exposure with people. Hardly anybody ever came to see him. Most of his interactions were conducted over the phone or the computer. So he was awkward and inexperienced in even the most basic of social interactions, especially with women.

But he was a sweet, exceedingly polite guy, and, despite his awkwardness, I liked him a lot. In many ways he was more self-sufficient than his younger brother, whom he admired as an outgoing, risk-taking, thrill-seeking rebel.

Yeah, I know, it's hard to believe.

Ambrose must have heard us drive up, because his front door was open and he was standing several steps back from it in the shadows of the entry hall, as if he might inadvertently get sucked out into the street otherwise.

He had on his customary long-sleeve flannel shirt, buttoned at the collar and cuffs, an argyle sweater-vest over it, corduroy pants, and a pair of shiny Hush Puppies shoes tied with neat, perfect bows.

"Natalie, what a delightful surprise. Do come in," Ambrose said, standing as stiffly as a soldier at attention. "You can come in, too, Adrian."

"Thank you, Ambrose," Monk said as we stepped inside.

Monk looked into the living room and scowled. It was lined with filing cabinets and crammed full with about forty years' worth of newspapers and magazines, neatly stacked and laid out in perfect rows.

I knew that the cabinets contained every piece of mail that had ever been delivered to the house as well as the notes for Ambrose's various books.

"You're always welcome, Adrian. This is your house, too, though you'd never know considering how rarely you come to visit."

"It's not my house anymore," Monk said. "It's yours."

"It's *ours,*" Ambrose said. "It was left to both of us in Mom's will."

"But you live here."

"I don't have a choice."

"Of course you do," Monk said. "The door is right there. All you have to do is step outside."

"Not everyone is as fearless as you," Ambrose said and nudged the front door closed

291

with his foot. As soon as the door was shut, his whole body seemed to loosen up, as if he'd been released from suspended animation. "Can I offer you a marshmallow?"

"No, thank you," I said.

"Are you sure? In 2000 BC, they were a pleasure reserved solely for the enjoyment of the pharaohs. Now everybody can have them whenever they want. But I save them for special occasions."

"This isn't a special occasion," Monk said.

"It is for me. It's not often that I have such beguiling guests." Ambrose smiled at me, then glanced at his brother. "And you, too."

"Maybe you'd have more visitors if you got rid of all this garbage." Monk gestured to the newspapers and file cabinets.

"That's probably what Julius Caesar said before he burned the Library of Alexandria. I suppose if you had your way we'd gut the Smithsonian as well." Ambrose turned his back on Monk and devoted his attention to me. "How about a refreshing glass of chilled water?"

"You have water?" Monk said.

"Of course I do," he said, still refusing to face his brother. "I can't survive without it. Nobody can."

"Oh my God, you haven't heard," Monk said. "I was afraid of that."

"What are you talking about?" Ambrose asked, turning now to Monk again.

Monk took a deep breath. "There's no easy way to say this. The news I am about to share is shocking and will change your life, so prepare yourself. There's no more Summit Creek. It's gone. We're going to die."

Ambrose looked at his brother for a long moment.

"*That's* why you came all the way over here, to tell me that? I knew that Summit Creek was going under months before it happened."

"You did?" Monk said. "How?"

"I'm living in a house, Adrian, not a cave."

Ambrose turned his back on his brother again and walked into the kitchen. Monk rushed after him.

"You knew and you didn't tell me?"

"You're a man of the world," Ambrose said. "I figured you knew."

"I didn't," Monk said. "It came as a horrible surprise."

Ambrose took three glasses from a cabinet, set two of them on the kitchen table and one on the counter beside him. "Don't you watch TV, read the newspapers, or surf the Web?"

"I don't have as much idle time as you do."

"So if you didn't come here to warn me about the water, what brought you?"

Monk sat down at the table and laid his hands, palm down, on top of it. I sat down beside him.

"I've lost my water, my job, my life savings, and my home. It turns out I am not a man of great expectations after all. I have been bred to no calling and I am fit for nothing. So I have returned to whence I came, to my common little home on the marshes, for want of a clean bed to sleep in and a roof over my head."

It was true that he'd suffered a tragedy of Dickensian proportions, but I still thought Monk was laying it on a little thick.

"Now you know why I don't leave the house," Ambrose said. "You definitely need a drink."

He opened the refrigerator and took out three bottles of Fiji water and gave one to each of us. He remained standing. I'm not sure whether he stood as a courtesy to Monk or if he was just as phobic about symmetry and even numbers as his brother was and felt three people at a table for four would topple the balance of the universe.

Monk examined the bottled water. "What is this?"

"Rain that fell through the virgin skies of emerald blue on the pristine mountains of Viti Levu island in 1515 and percolated slowly through layers of silica, basalt, and sandstone into a subterranean chamber," Ambrose said, "where it remained sealed and pure until it was drawn out and captured in the bottle you now hold in your hands."

Monk held the bottle up to the light and licked his lips. "It looks good."

"Have as much as you want." Ambrose opened his bottle and poured it into a glass. "I've got a ten-year supply."

I filled my glass and took a sip. "It's delicious. I think it's even better than Summit Creek."

Truthfully, it tasted like tap water to me. But maybe that was five hundred years old, too.

"I spent weeks researching the best alternative to Summit Creek and this is what I found," Ambrose said.

Monk unscrewed the cap on his bottle, closed his eyes, and took a tentative sniff of the water. "The fragrance reminds me of Mom."

Ambrose nodded. "Me, too. That's when I

knew it was right."

I sniffed my water but I couldn't detect any fragrance at all.

Monk poured a little of the water into the glass. He swirled the liquid around a bit, held the glass up to the light, scrutinizing it for any impurities, then he took a tiny sip.

He rolled it around in his mouth and then swallowed it hard, like it was a golf ball instead of a teaspoon worth of water.

Monk waited a moment, as if expecting some sort of immediate, adverse physical reaction. When none came, he took another, larger sip and smiled at his brother.

"You've saved me, Ambrose," Monk said, his eyes tearing up. He turned to me and pointed to his eyes. "That's Fiji water."

We spent the next few hours drinking five-hundred-year-old water and eating marshmallows as if we were the pharaohs of Marin County.

The more water Monk drank, the more relaxed and talkative he became. He told Ambrose all about the murders of Russell Haxby and Lincoln Clovis.

As I listened, I became absolutely convinced that Sebes was guilty and disheartened that there was no way we could prove it, especially since we were no longer even remotely associated with the investigation. And if we tried to nose around, we were sure to get slapped down hard by Captain Stottlemeyer.

Monk finished his story by declaring emphatically that Bob Sebes was the killer and that the alcohol reading on the Triax XG7 8210 proved it.

Ambrose nodded thoughtfully and sipped his water.

"There's a major flaw in your theory, Adrian."

"What's that?" Monk asked.

"Bob Sebes couldn't have committed the murders," Ambrose replied.

Monk dismissed the argument with a wave of his hand. "You're just saying that because he's wearing a GPS monitoring unit and his house is surrounded by reporters and police officers."

"There might be a way out of the house," Ambrose said, "but there's no way to beat the XG7 8210."

"How would you know?"

"Because I wrote the book on it. Well, the technical manual anyway. I've got one of the units upstairs."

"So you could write about it?" I asked.

He nodded. "And because I like to wear it from time to time."

At first I thought he might be joking, but the expression on his face was dead serious.

"Why would you want to wear it?" Monk said. "Is it so people will think that there's a sane reason why you can't leave the house?"

"I wear it as a precaution in case I ever wander out."

"How would that happen?" Monk asked.

"What if I became a sleepwalker one night, wandered out the front door, and woke up hours later" — Ambrose glanced at the window and shuddered — "out there?"

"Is that something you dream about?" I asked.

"It's something I have nightmares about." Ambrose knocked back some water as if it was whiskey.

Monk shook his head. "That's just silly. Who is going to come get you if your XG7 8210 sends out an alarm that you've left the house?"

Ambrose smiled at me. "I have it set to call Natalie."

"Why me?" I asked.

"Because I know that I can depend on you."

"Why not me?" Monk asked.

Ambrose looked at his brother. "Are you going to get in an automobile, find me wherever I am, and bring me home safely?"

"Of course I would," Monk said. "I'd call Natalie, she'd pick me up, and we'd be right over."

"I'm not family," I said. "What makes you so sure you can depend on me?"

"Because Adrian does," he said.

"I don't depend on her," Monk said. "I employ her. There's a difference."

"Are you employing her now?" Ambrose asked.

Monk shifted in his seat. "Yes and no."

"Yes and no?" Ambrose said. "How does that work?"

"I can't wait to hear this," I said.

"She's still working for me," Monk said, "but I am not paying her for it."

"Then why do you suppose she's doing it if she's not getting paid for it?" Ambrose asked.

"Because it's a higher calling."

Ambrose shook his head. "That's not why, Adrian."

Maybe I'd underestimated Ambrose. Perhaps he understood people and relationships more than I thought he did. He certainly understood them better than his younger brother.

Ambrose looked at me, but when I caught his eye, he immediately shifted his gaze, suddenly self-conscious.

"There have been times when I've imagined what it would be like if I sleepwalked out of the house and you rescued me."

"Is that one of your nightmares, too?" I asked.

Ambrose shrugged. "That one might qualify as a dream."

Chapter Twenty-Three:
Mr. Monk Has Style

I wanted to break our record of always being fired after just one day on the job, so I tried to anticipate all the things Monk might do that could offend, infuriate, or horrify our new employer.

On our drive downtown to the Bayview Mall the next morning, I ordered Monk not to round up or down any charges on the register, not to rearrange the clothing in the store to fit his own sense of order, and not to criticize the fashion choices of any of his customers.

"Your job is to make the customer happy," I said, "not yourself."

"That's easy," Monk said. "I'm never happy."

"Glad to hear it," I said.

"If people want to make foolish decisions, what do I care? I'm hydrated."

"Did you spend all night drinking?"

Monk nodded. "We partied like I was back

in college. It was unhooked."

"Unhooked?"

"The Monk brothers aren't as buttoned-down as you think we are."

Monk's shirt was buttoned to the collar, his sleeves were buttoned at the cuffs, and he was wiping down my dashboard with a disinfectant wipe. He couldn't have been more buttoned-up, literally or figuratively, if he'd tried.

"You are two wild and crazy guys," I said.

"We went through an entire box of Cap'n Crunch," Monk said. "With Crunch Berries, which are a synthetic fruit."

"That's edgy."

"Don't ever tell anyone that we've recreationally indulged in synthetic fruits. I wouldn't want people to get the wrong idea about us. I'm sure you've got your vices."

"One or two," I said.

I found a spot on the second floor of the parking structure and we went into the mall, which was designed to look like an idealized version of an iconic San Francisco street. All the interior storefronts had bay windows and Victorian architectural flourishes. A cable car even ran through the mall on a winding track that ended up in a food court made to look like Fisherman's Wharf, only without the panhandlers, the crapping seagulls, the souvenir shops, the gum on the sidewalks, or the smell of the bay, a heady mix of salt water and outboard motor exhaust.

Monk loved the fake streets, of course. They were exactly the way he wanted the world to be — unnaturally clean, free of nature, sanitized and climate-controlled.

But I wondered why anyone but Monk would trade the experience of walking down the real San Francisco streets outside for the fake ones in the mall. You might as well be in Owensboro, Kentucky, or Walla Walla, Washington.

Fashion Frisson was a long, narrow clothing store tucked between a RadioShack and a jeweler. The store featured contemporary, brightly colored fashions with a slightly retro, '70s feel.

The layout of the store was straightforward, with women's clothing on one side and men's on the other. That even division appealed to Monk's sense of order, symmetry, and separation of the sexes.

Fashion Frisson's proprietor was Kiana Claire, an energetic, overaccessorized brunette with a squeaky voice that made me wonder if she inhaled helium whenever our backs were turned.

I'd brought our résumés along but she

wasn't interested in seeing them.

"Randy's recommendation is enough for me," she said. "He's a fantastic judge of character. Plus it saves me from having to run background checks on you both, which is going to be standard procedure for me from now on."

Not every crook and pervert has been arrested before, but I wasn't going to tell her that. Nor was I going to admit that I actually had a criminal record, though not for anything major, mostly for civil disobedience. Monk was falsely arrested and convicted of murder once, but I wasn't going to mention that, either.

"How do you know Randy?" I asked.

"He's a longtime customer," she said. "Have you ever heard him sing?"

Unfortunately, I had. He'd only written and performed one song, at least as far as I knew.

"Oh, yes," I said. "It was unlike anything I've ever heard before."

"It's a catchy tune," Monk said. "But it's no '867-5309.' "

Monk liked the Tommy Tutone 1982 hit song, also known as "Jenny," because the numbers added up to thirty-eight.

"He's got Bob Dylan's depth and Pitbull's party-hearty, raw sexuality," Kiana said.

"Randy has got a cult following in France, you know."

I did. The cult was a dozen French women with cop fixations. I'd seen them for myself and it was something I tried hard to forget.

Monk raised his hand. "Excuse me, but I have a confession to make."

"No, you don't," I said. Whatever it was, it couldn't be good.

"I have no fashion sense," he said, ignoring my protests.

"Of course you do," Kiana said.

"I do?"

"Look at how you've dressed. It's fresh and original. It defines your character and reveals a powerful awareness of how fashion can express personal identity. I'm blown away by it. You have style, Adrian."

Monk smiled at me. "I have style."

"What about me?" I asked her. "How's my fashion sense?"

She hesitated. "We'll work on it."

Kiana proceeded to explain our duties to us. They weren't too complicated. We would help customers with their purchases, manage the dressing rooms, keep the place orderly, and ring up purchases at the register. She would be in the back office most of the day, taking care of the invoices and other paperwork that had piled up since she'd

305

fired her salespeople two weeks ago.

"I was afraid to hire anyone after what happened," she said. "But I have complete faith in you. This job is ninety-eight percent people skills and I can see that you're people persons."

Monk started to raise his hand again to make another confession, but I slapped it down, and held it down, until she was in the back room.

The morning was slow, which gave Monk a chance to make sure that all the hangers were facing in the same direction, to wash the windows and vacuum the floors, and to arrange the clothes by size, while I handled the few customers who came in. It worked out nicely for both of us. It was certainly less stressful than going to crime scenes and questioning suspects. I didn't miss seeing corpses every day, though I hadn't had much of a break from that.

"I love this job," Monk said.

"You haven't waited on any customers yet."

"I hope it stays that way," he said.

I did, too, because it reduced the odds that Monk would do something that would get us fired. But business picked up around lunchtime. Luckily, most of the customers were women, who preferred to have me wait on them while Monk manned the register. I didn't know anything about fashion but I knew how to kiss up. Mostly I told the women how nice they looked in whatever garment they tried on and how it made them look slimmer and yet curvier.

My customers bought everything they tried on, which was a good thing, not only because it racked up sales but because, as I only realized in hindsight, it postponed a disaster.

Monk cleaned and disinfected the dressing rooms after each customer used them, which should have been my first hint of the trouble to come. He didn't offend any of the customers with what he was doing because he didn't start sanitizing their dressing rooms until they were at the register, paying for their purchases, their backs to him.

The trouble started with the first customer who didn't buy the clothes that she had tried on. Unfortunately, she was also Monk's first customer of the day. She was a short, stout woman who dressed too young for her age, probably to the embarrassment of her children. (No sooner did I think that thought than I wondered if I was projecting just a little.) She handed three blouses to him with a dismissive frown.

"You can take these back," she said.

"You're not buying them?"

"These make me look fat."

"You should have thought of that before you wore them," Monk said, dropping them into a trash can.

"Excuse me?"

"You can't just put on clothes and not buy them."

"There's no obligation to buy when you try clothes on," she said.

"Of course there is," Monk said.

"How else can you see if they fit?"

"Use your imagination," Monk said. "We can't sell these now. They're contaminated."

"They're *what?*"

I quickly excused myself from my customer and rushed over to the dressing rooms, forcing a laugh.

"Don't mind him. He's got a strange sense of humor," I said and gave Monk a playful punch on the shoulder. "Just because there are curtains here doesn't mean it's your stage."

"These clothes will have to be incinerated," Monk said.

The woman laughed. "For a moment there I thought you were nuts."

"Would you like to try on something else?" I asked.

"I'm thinking about that V-neck sweater," she said, pointing to a display on the other side of the store.

"Mr. Monk will be glad to get you one in your size."

"When was the last time you bathed?" Monk asked.

She laughed again. "He's actually pretty funny."

"He's a riot." I faked a laugh of my own, then shoved Monk. "Get the lady her sweater, Leno."

Monk went off. I excused myself again, and returned to the customer I'd abandoned.

Before Monk returned to the dressing rooms, I intercepted him.

"Do not say another word to that woman except *thank you* or *good-bye*," I whispered.

"I totally agree. She's a psycho," Monk whispered. "Who knows what she might do next?"

Thankfully, the stout woman ended up buying the sweater. She was leaving the store when Kiana emerged from the back room to ask us how everything was going.

"It was going great until she came in," Monk said, gesturing to the customer.

"Why? What happened?" Kiana asked.

"Nothing," I said. "She bought a V-neck

sweater."

"And soiled three blouses that she wore without buying," Monk said.

"Soiled?" Kiana said.

Monk nodded grimly. "Where's your incinerator?"

"Why would I have an incinerator in a clothing store?"

"He is just joking with you," I said.

"There's nothing humorous about the black death," Monk said. "Who knows how many germs are swimming in the sweat that those blouses are drenched in?"

"The black death didn't come from people trying on clothes," I said. "It was rats."

"Who lived in nests of soiled clothing and ate pizzas."

Kiana laughed and clapped Monk on the arm. "Stylish and funny, too. No wonder you and Randy are such good friends. Why don't you two take off for lunch? I recommend the food court. Mall employees get a twenty percent discount."

"Sounds great to me," I said. "Thank you for the tip."

We walked out, Monk rubbing his shoulder. "Why do women keep hitting me?"

"Because you don't think before you speak," I said.

"Maybe I should get shoulder pads."
"Maybe you should take a vow of silence."

CHAPTER TWENTY-FOUR:
MR. MONK RETURNS A FAVOR

The food court had the usual mix of franchised eateries, along with mall versions of local San Francisco restaurants offering a few of their signature dishes over the counter. The mall's Chinese food place was an outlet of a Chinatown institution rather than yet another Panda Express. I had to give the mall credit for trying to add some genuine local flavor. It also meant that we actually had lots of good choices for lunch.

"Which is the best place for toast?" Monk said.

"That's all you're going to have for lunch? Look around, Mr. Monk. There are so many choices."

"Too many," he said.

"How about a hot dog on a stick?"

"Mmm. That sounds so appetizing. Deep-fried, stuffed intestines impaled on a piece of wood. Maybe for dessert I could have some grilled donkey testicles served on a rock. Do I look like a Neanderthal to you?"

"I don't think cavemen ate corn dogs."

"I'm a civilized man. I don't eat things with sticks. I use utensils."

"Technically, the stick is a utensil," I said, just to be argumentative.

"It is as if you are a savage living in a cave, a mud hut, or Captain Stottlemeyer's apartment. Modern men use knives, forks, and spoons. You and Julie might want to try them. I could teach you how they are used."

"Maybe you could show us how to make fire, too."

I led him over to Yang Chow, where two young Chinese women stood at the counter with bright smiles on their faces, offering people samples on toothpicks. Monk scowled with disapproval.

"How about a bowl of white rice and a teriyaki chicken breast?" I said. "All the grains of rice are the same shape and color and you can ask them to chop the chicken breast into a square."

"That actually doesn't sound bad."

"And look," I said. "They even serve bottled Fiji water."

That sealed the deal for him. Any place that sold Fiji water had to be good.

"Just don't go overboard on the water," I warned him. "We still have half a day of work left."

While he ordered his meal, I went over to the Boudin Bakery outlet and got myself a turkey sandwich with havarti cheese on fresh San Francisco sourdough.

Monk found us a two-seat table that was bathed in filtered sunshine from an enormous skylight and that overlooked the first-floor shops below. It gave us the illusion of being out in the open.

The economic downturn had hit the mall as hard as everywhere else. The jewelry store below us was offering a 40 percent off sale on selected rings. Its neighbor on one side, a children's clothing store, was offering a half-off sale, while the business on the other side was gone, the storefront boarded up, the wood flats covered with an advertisement promising "exciting changes ahead that will make your shopping experience more fun than ever."

The only change that would have improved my shopping experience was either winning the lottery or getting a better-paying job, neither of which seemed very likely for me.

In front of those stores, in the center of the wide faux street, was a kiosk selling colorful umbrellas. It was one of many kiosks throughout the mall that sold things like personalized T-shirts, stuffed animals, cell phones, and popcorn.

A security guard sauntered up to the umbrella kiosk, had some words with the young salesgirl, gestured to the stores around her, and then helped her wheel the kiosk a few feet away from where it had been.

I guess the umbrella kiosk was impeding foot traffic, or was too close to a neighboring kiosk, or was blocking a storefront. I didn't know nor did I care, but for some reason Monk seemed very interested in what was going on.

"The security guard has dirty pants," he said.

"We should report him to the mall management right away."

"I agree," Monk said and started to get up.

I grabbed his arm. "I was joking. Sit down. It's none of our business if the security guards have dirty uniforms."

"It reflects poorly on law enforcement."

"They aren't cops and neither are we."

He sat down and I figured that was the end of the matter. But I was wrong. After lunch, we took a stroll through the mall, and he stopped, stared up at one of the mall security cameras, and pointed at it, waving his finger as if admonishing a misbehaving child.

"What, exactly, do you think that is going to accomplish?" I asked him.

"I am putting them on notice that I am watching."

"I'm sure that will mean a lot to them."

We went down to the first floor and walked back toward our end of the mall. I did some window shopping and stopped to look at the big colorful umbrellas at that little kiosk. They seemed more decorative than practical to me. Either way, I couldn't imagine anybody spending $39.99 on one of them in this economy.

Monk peered around the kiosk at the security camera on the second floor and wagged his finger at that one, too.

We returned to Fashion Frisson, Kiana went back to her office, and we worked the floor. There was a steady stream of customers throughout the afternoon and, for the most part, Monk kept himself in check.

Almost all of our customers were women. The few men who came in browsed but didn't buy. I think they were creeped out by Monk, who followed closely behind them and immediately refolded everything that they picked up and put them back on the shelves.

A very hairy man wearing a tank top and shorts came in and admired some of the short-sleeved shirts. He picked one up and turned to Monk, who was stalking him.

"Is there somewhere I can try this on?"

"No," Monk said.

"Why not?"

"Our dressing rooms are closed."

"They look open to me."

"They're for women only," Monk said.

"No problem," the man said. "I can try it on over this."

The man lifted his arms up to pull the shirt over his head and showed off more hair under his armpits than I had on my head.

Monk went wide-eyed and snatched the shirt from him. "You can't."

"Why not?"

"It's a health code violation. We could lose our business license if we let people try on clothes outside of the dressing rooms."

"When did they start doing that?"

"Today," Monk said.

"Today?"

"Every clothing store is following the new law, so whatever you do, don't go anywhere else and try on any clothes on the sales floor."

"Just in San Francisco?"

"The whole world," Monk said. "And the

international space station."

The man shrugged and walked out. Monk sighed with relief, then looked over at me expectantly.

"What?" I said.

"I'm waiting for you to criticize me for not letting the ape man try on this shirt."

"You did the right thing," I said.

"That hasn't stopped you before."

We might have debated the point for hours on end if not for a mall security guard and a customer coming into the store at the same time.

The security guard wasn't the same guy we'd seen at lunch. This guy was younger, in better shape, and had a mischievous grin that made my heart flutter. He was so buff, with pecs Superman would envy, that for a moment I was worried that he might actually be a stripper sent to surprise me with a public striptease. Or maybe that was just wishful thinking on my part. My birthday was still months away.

"You're new here," the security guard said, offering me his hand. "My name is Mike."

I shook it. His hand was dry and rough. I thought about how nice it would be to rub some moisturizing lotion on his hands, which I knew was a pretty bizarre thing to be thinking about. But it had been a long time since I'd had a date and my imagination was filling the void.

"I'm Natalie. Do you keep track of all the saleswomen who come and go in the mall?"

"It's my job to keep my eye on things."

Monk came over to us. "If that was true, you'd have noticed there's dirt on your knees. Do you do a lot of crawling in your job?"

"A woman lost her keys under her car," Mike said. "I retrieved them for her."

"That must happen a lot here judging by how filthy the guards are," Monk said.

"Women often have their hands full with kids and shopping bags," Mike said. "And I like to be helpful."

"Don't you have a customer, Mr. Monk?" I motioned toward a man sorting through some women's blouses.

Monk went over to help him and I turned my attention back to the guard.

"So have you worked your way through all the other women in the mall?"

He laughed. "Not exactly. I just wanted to let you know that I'm here if you ever need security or someone to escort you to your car after work."

I looked past Mike to see Monk approach the customer: a man in his twenties with close-cropped hair, heavy eyeliner, earrings, and a floral scarf around his neck. He was holding a pink blouse against himself and looking at his reflection in the mirror.

"You're in the wrong department," Monk said. "Menswear is on the other side."

"I'm exactly where I want to be."

"Are you shopping for a friend?"

"I'm shopping for myself, sweetie. How does this look on me?"

"Wrong," Monk said.

"Pink isn't my color?"

"That's a blouse, which is a shirt that women wear. You are a man. We have shirts for men in the men's department" — he gestured to the other side of the store — "which is where men shop for shirts that men wear."

I could see big trouble brewing between Monk and his customer, so I had to cut the flirtation with Mike short.

"How do I reach you if I need you?" I asked him.

"Dial 0336 from your store phone," Mike said, then handed me a card from his breast pocket. "Or call this number to reach my cell anytime."

"I will," I said.

"I prefer to shop in the women's department," the customer said. "The men's shirts are too butch for me."

"Only women are allowed to wear women's clothing," Monk said.

"Where did you get that silly idea? This is San Francisco. Half the men in this city are wearing bras and panties."

Mike headed out, walking past Monk and his customer, who gave him a thorough once-over.

"Don't I get a card?" he asked Mike. "I might need help."

The security guard smiled politely at the man. "You look like you can take care of yourself, sir."

"I can take care of you, too, honey. Just give me a chance."

Mike kept on going, pretending he didn't hear him. The customer watched Mike go and caught me doing the same thing.

"I'm definitely tossing my keys under my car," he said to me. "How about you, girl?"

I decided to let that comment pass. "May I help you pick out something?"

"He's in the wrong department," Monk said adamantly.

The customer put a hand on his hip, striking a judgmental pose, and wagged his finger at Monk. "Are you some kind of homophobe?"

Monk shook his head. "I'm a totalphobe."

■ ■ ■ ■

We broke our record. We got through the day without getting fired. I felt like celebrating.

I was tempted to call Mike so he could escort me to my car and protect me from rapists, robbers, and malcontents and then maybe take me to dinner. But with Monk tagging along, asking Mike to escort me would have seemed even more like the ridiculous excuse to see him than it was.

I thought I might have to toss my keys under my car after all. Monk certainly wouldn't crawl under the car to get them for me, nor would he question me for calling someone else to do it for us.

I was mulling over that possibility as we walked past the umbrella kiosk.

A custodian parked a large trash cart behind the kiosk and began emptying nearby trash cans into it.

"He's dirty," Monk said.

"He's a custodian," I said. "If anybody is going to be dirty, it's him. He spends his days cleaning up messes."

"He's been crawling around on his knees."

"I'd think you'd admire the man for being thorough," I said.

Monk rolled his shoulders and peered around the kiosk up at the security camera on the second floor. "You should call Randy."

"That's a great idea, Mr. Monk. I'm sure Randy will appreciate us letting him know how well our first day on the job went. We owe him a lot for doing us this favor."

"And we're going to pay him back for it tonight."

"How?"

"We're going to give him a major arrest."

"Oh my God." I stopped and faced him. "You've figured out how Bob Sebes got away with murder."

"Sadly, no," Monk said. "But I'm working on it."

"Then what are you talking about?"

"The big jewelry heist, of course."

"What big jewelry heist?"

"Tonight Mike and his fellow security guards are going to break into that store," Monk said, tipping his head toward the jewelry store that we'd just walked by.

I looked back at the store, and then at Monk. I was truly dumbfounded. "What makes you think that?"

"I don't think it. I *know* it. Didn't you see their pants?"

"Not everybody with dirty pants is going

323

to commit a crime."

"Filthy on the outside usually means filthy on the inside. Besides, both guards had dirty knees and dry hands."

"You noticed Mike's dry hands?"

"And the custodian's knees and hands, too."

"I don't understand how that all adds up to a jewelry heist."

"Mike and his cohorts have the mall all to themselves at night and have been digging a tunnel into the jewelry store from the vacant storefront next door. The tunnel is just large enough for them to crawl through on their hands and knees, hence the dirty pants and dry hands."

"How do you know the robbery will be tonight?"

"Because the security guard we saw at lunch moved the umbrella kiosk over a few feet to be sure that it blocked the security camera view of the unoccupied store. The guard wouldn't have cared unless the robbery is going to go down tonight."

Monk laid out the rest of their plan for me. The guards would rob the jewelry store during the night, taking turns so that each of them would be seen on security cameras elsewhere in the mall walking their usual shift, though most of the time their faces would be obscured by their hats or other carefully placed obstructions, like potted plants and kiosks.

When a guard, his face obscured, walked past the blocked camera in front of the boarded-up storefront, he would duck into the unoccupied store and switch places with one of the other guards, who would then continue the patrol, creating the illusion that all the guards were constantly on duty.

"That still leaves one guard stuck in the empty storefront," I said. "How would he get out without being seen?"

"He'd slip out of the storefront, his exit blocked from view by the kiosk and umbrellas, and hide in the trash cart the custodian has just parked here. The custodian will come along later and push it away with his cohort hidden inside."

"That's a lot of cohorts," I said.

"It's a major heist," Monk said. "When the robbery is discovered tomorrow by the jeweler, the evidence will lead the police to assume that the robbers hid in the vacant store until morning, unnoticed by the security guards on patrol, and then escaped by slipping into the crowd when the mall opened."

"But won't the old security tapes show the guards going in and out of the unoccupied store over the last few weeks?"

"They've undoubtedly been reusing old security camera footage, feeding it into the system and putting a new date stamp on it. I'm sure if we study the tapes we will find some tiny inconsistencies that they missed."

He might, but I doubted that anybody else would unless they were told what to look for.

"You figured all that out from dirty pants, dry hands, and a guy moving an umbrella kiosk a couple of feet?"

"It was like a confession," Monk said. "If Randy stakes out the mall tonight, he can catch them in the act."

I took Mike's card out of my pocket, tore it in half, and dropped it into the trash cart.

I had lousy taste in men.

CHAPTER TWENTY-FIVE: MR. MONK HAS A BREAKTHROUGH

I called Disher but he was too busy to talk to me. He was at the scene of a murder in Golden Gate Park, so naturally Monk suggested that we stop by to deliver our favor in person.

It was almost dark when we got there. I parked under a wildly overgrown tree and we walked down the long jogging path toward a dense grove that was roped off with yellow crime scene tape. Forensic techs moved carefully through the brush, looking for clues, while others were setting up klieg lights to illuminate the scene in the creeping gloom.

People jogged, biked, and drove past the taped-off area without even stopping for a peek. I guess with three *CSI* shows, three *Law & Order* shows, and two *NCIS* series on TV, they were jaded. They'd seen plenty of crime scenes and with much better lighting and wardrobe than this one.

We went up to the police line and waited to be noticed. Stottlemeyer, Disher, and the medical examiner were huddled around the body of a man in a bright blue jogging suit who was lying in the weeds beside the path.

They seemed very intent on their work and I was in a hurry. I'd rescheduled Monk's regular appointment with Dr. Bell to early that evening and I didn't want him to miss it. So I stuck my fingers in my mouth and whistled as loudly as I could. It sounded like a bird being disemboweled.

Stottlemeyer's face crunched into a particularly nasty scowl and he marched over to us in a fury.

"I told you that you're off the Sebes case and I meant it," Stottlemeyer said.

"This murder has something to do with Bob Sebes?" Monk said.

Disher caught up with Stottlemeyer. "This is my fault."

He glowered at Randy. "You called Monk?"

"No, I didn't. Natalie called me. I told her that I couldn't talk to her now because I was busy at a crime scene in Golden Gate Park. I didn't tell her it was Duncan Dern."

I knew the name. I'd read all about him in the *Chronicle.* It was no wonder that Stottlemeyer was upset to see us there.

"Duncan Dern is dead?"

"Try saying that three times fast," Disher said. "Someone tackled him on his morning jog, strangled him with their gloved hands, and dragged his body into the brush."

"Why are you telling these civilians about the case?" Stottlemeyer said, rubbing his temples. "It is none of their business."

"Sorry," Disher said. "Force of habit."

"Who was Duncan Dern?" Monk asked.

"He ran the largest feeder fund that brought new investors into Sebes' Ponzi scheme," I said. "He earned millions in fees and all his clients lost everything."

Monk cocked his head to one side. "Why was he strangled?"

"Maybe because somebody wanted to kill him," Disher said. "That's a wild guess on my part."

"But why not shoot him or stab him or beat him to death with a blunt object, like a rock, a baseball bat, or a crowbar? Strangulation seems like an awfully time-consuming and personal method of killing."

"We are not having this conversation, Monk," the captain said. "If Dern wasn't what brought you down here, what did? We're kind of busy right now."

"We just wanted to thank Randy personally for getting us great jobs," I said. "And to tell him how well our first day went."

Stottlemeyer raised his eyebrows and faced Disher. "You got them jobs?"

Disher shrugged. "It's no big deal."

"It is to us," I said.

Stottlemeyer nodded in agreement. "It was a hell of a nice thing you did, Randy. What kind of jobs are you doing?"

"We're in the fashion industry," I said.

"I have style," Monk said.

"You certainly do, Monk," Stottlemeyer said. "Sorry about hauling off on you like that. I didn't know about the new jobs. Congratulations."

"That's okay, Captain," Monk said. "You're under a lot of pressure at work and your home life is a living hell."

"Actually, things are a lot better at home now. I'll let you have a minute with Randy." The captain leaned close to Disher. "Do not say another word to them about this case."

The captain went back to the body.

"We didn't mean to get you in trouble," I said.

"Don't worry. I thrive under pressure. How did it go at Fashion Frisson?"

"Really well," I said.

"Except for the man with all the body hair," Monk said. "And the man who bought

330

a blouse for himself."

"Isn't Kiana great?" Disher said. "She has incredible taste in music."

I let that comment pass unmolested as a courtesy to Disher. "We came down here because Mr. Monk wanted to return the favor you did for us by giving you a present."

"That's really thoughtful," Disher said. "But I have enough Q-tips to last me for a lifetime."

"You can never have too many Q-tips," Monk said. "But this is something different. It's a jewelry heist."

And then Monk told him everything. Disher couldn't take the notes down fast enough in his little notebook.

"This is huge," Disher said. "Thank you so much."

Monk shrugged. "It was nothing."

"Maybe for you, Monk, but nobody else would have seen those details and put them together the way you did. And nobody else would have given the bust to me."

"I'm not a police officer," Monk said. "You are."

"This is so much better than the birthday present that you got me that I'm going to say that *this* is the birthday present instead."

"What was wrong with Q-tips?"

"They're fabulous," Disher said. "But this

arrest could get me a promotion."

"I hope so," I said. "Then you can hire us."

We walked away. We hadn't gone two feet before Monk whispered to me.

"Sebes is the guy."

"I know, Mr. Monk. I just hope you can prove it before anybody else gets killed."

I regretted the words the instant I'd said them.

"So now I'm responsible for everyone he kills until I solve the case. Just what I needed, added pressure and a healthy dose of guilt. Thanks a lot, Natalie. I wasn't nearly frustrated and miserable enough."

"I'm sorry, Mr. Monk. I didn't mean it that way. I know you are doing your best."

I immediately regretted saying that, too.

"That's just it. I'm not. Instead of investigating these murders, I'm making pizzas and selling clothes."

I decided to keep my mouth shut because everything I said was coming out wrong. I wanted to tell him that it wasn't his fault — it was the economy that was the big obstacle. If he was still a police consultant, he'd have access to the crime scenes, the evidence, and the suspects and have a real shot at proving how Sebes committed three murders while under house arrest and constant surveillance.

But now, broke and homeless, working odd jobs, and completely shut out of the case, it was nearly impossible for Monk to prove the impossible was possible.

That wasn't going to stop him from trying. Monk couldn't stop if he wanted to. I knew his mind was still churning over the details of every crime scene, of everything he'd seen and heard and that most of us probably missed.

Monk stopped a few feet away from my car, which was stained with bird crap and some kind of berries from the overgrown tree I'd parked under.

"You go on ahead," he said. "I'll get a taxi to Dr. Bell's office."

"You can't afford a taxi. Get in the car."

"I can't. I'll walk."

"Dr. Bell's office is on the other side of the city. It will take you hours to walk there. You'll miss your appointment."

"Okay, I'll wait here while you buy a new car."

"I can't afford a new car. The car may be dirty on the outside but it's clean on the inside."

"There's no such thing. I can't get into that car. It would be suicide."

I took out my cell phone and called

Randy, even though he was only a few yards away. I didn't want to provoke Stottlemeyer but I needed a favor from Randy. I apprised him of the situation and reminded him of the big favor Monk had just done for him. Randy agreed to have a patrolman drive Monk to Dr. Bell's office for me.

While Monk waited for his ride, I went to a quickie drive-thru gas station and car wash and then headed to the McDonald's near Dr. Bell's office for a cup of Mc-Cheapo McCoffee.

I was just about to walk into the Mc-Donald's when my cell phone rang. It was Dr. Bell, asking me to come to his office right away.

My first reaction was that Monk had suffered a complete mental breakdown and that Dr. Bell needed my help dealing with him. But when I walked into Dr. Bell's office, I found them both sitting in their leather easy chairs, looking relaxed and contented.

Dr. Bell motioned to the couch opposite them. "Please, have a seat, Natalie."

I felt like I'd been called into the principal's office for disciplinary action.

"What's wrong?"

"Nothing at all," Dr. Bell said.

"If you don't count getting fired, losing

my life savings, being evicted from my home, and nearly dying of thirst," Monk said.

"That's true, Adrian, but now look at all the good that has come out of those setbacks, losses, and challenges."

"I don't see the good. Only the no-good."

"I'm with Mr. Monk on this one," I said.

"That's exactly what I wanted to talk about," Dr. Bell said. "Adrian told me how you were both on the same wavelength about the mistake Bob Sebes made. That's a great success."

"Bob Sebes is still a free man," Monk said.

"But what happened between you and Natalie represents a major breakthrough, not only in your relationship with her but potentially with other people. You experienced a powerful, intimate connection."

"I have never had intimate connections with Natalie," Monk said. "And never will."

"I second that," I said.

"Perhaps *intimate* was the wrong choice of words, but you both know that something special happened between you two. Natalie knew what you were thinking and you knew that she did. You told me yourself, Adrian, that you haven't experienced a connection like that with anyone since Trudy was killed."

Monk had told me the same thing at the time but we'd both consciously avoided talking about it. Dr. Bell wasn't letting us get away with it.

"What do you think about men who dress in women's clothing?" Monk asked him. "It's wrong, isn't it?"

"Don't try to change the subject," Dr. Bell replied. "Unless you're telling me that you've started wearing women's clothing."

"Of course I haven't."

"Then let's focus, shall we? You can't let this moment slip past you without appreciating its significance and how you can build upon it."

"You're making too much out of it. Let's talk about why anyone in their right mind would eat pizza with their hands. Or let their feet be devoured by raging pestilence."

"I know you're uncomfortable dealing with intimacy, but I'm not going to let you run away from this. You've opened yourself up to another person, and she's opened herself up to you, so now it's possible for you to think like each other, to empathize with each other, to connect on a deeper level. That connection not only strengthens a relationship but gives you invaluable emotional support and comfort in times of extreme stress and uncertainty, like what you two are going through right now. It's nice to be on the same wavelength with someone, isn't it?"

Monk shifted in his seat, unable to get comfortable. "It cuts down on the explaining that I have to do."

"You enjoy the explaining," I said.

"I enjoy being understood," he said, shifting some more. "There's a difference."

"Ah, now we're getting somewhere." Dr. Bell rubbed his hands together. "So what does it feel like to have someone who understands you, Adrian?"

"Like I'm not so alone."

"But you aren't alone," I said. "You have me, Captain Stottlemeyer, Lieutenant Disher, your brother, Ambrose."

"You could have a lot more people in your life, too, if you use what you've learned from this experience," Dr. Bell said. "Friendships are built on mutual interest and shared intimacy."

Monk did a full-body cringe.

"You're misunderstanding me, Adrian," Dr. Bell continued. "I'm not talking about physical intimacy, I mean sharing personal information about yourself — your history, your hopes, and your fears."

"My fears are available to anybody who is interested. They are detailed in ten volumes, not including the index. I give all my friends copies."

"That's one way of doing it. I'm suggesting a more personal approach. If you allow yourself to be as open with others as you have been with Natalie, I'm sure that you will discover that she isn't the only person who can be on the same wavelength as you."

Monk jerked as if zapped by an electrical shock. He cocked his head from side to side, rolled his shoulders, and sat up straight in his seat, staring at nothing and at everything.

I looked at Dr. Bell. "What do you make of that?"

"It's a strong reaction to something, but I don't know what it means."

"I do." I knew that it meant that everything was about to change for the better.

"There you go, Adrian. Another example of shared intimacy." Dr. Bell smiled, obviously pleased with how events were unfolding. "So, Natalie, what is his body language telling you?"

"Mr. Monk just figured out how Bob Sebes got out of the house and murdered Russell Haxby, Lincoln Clovis, and Duncan Dern."

Dr. Bell looked at Monk. "Is she right?"

Monk nodded. "He's the guy and I can prove it."

"Well," Dr. Bell said, clapping his hands, "I think that counts as another break-through. What a marvelous session this has been."

"If you enjoyed it so much, it hardly seems right that I should pay you for it," Monk said. "This should be a freebie."

"How do you figure that?" Dr. Bell asked.

"For what I'm paying you, if anyone is having any fun, it should be me and I'm not."

CHAPTER TWENTY-SIX:
MR. MONK MAKES A DEAL

What Dr. Bell said wasn't entirely true. I was able to read Monk's expression but I wasn't on the same wavelength as him this time. I didn't know how Sebes had managed to sneak out of his house and murder those people without setting off the tracking device or being spotted by the reporters and cops on the street.

And Monk wasn't giving me any hints.

"What's the harm in telling me?" I asked him once we were in my car. "It's just the two of us."

"I have a system and part of it is not revealing what happened until the decisive moment with the suspects present. I don't deviate from my system. Besides, I still have a few things to double-check. Can you take me back home?"

As I drove him back to Ambrose's house, I realized it might be a very good thing he hadn't told me how he'd solved the case.

"Promise me you won't call Captain Stottlemeyer or Lieutenant Disher and tell them anything about the case without clearing it with me first."

"Why not?"

"Because sometimes you are your own worst enemy and I don't want you to squander this opportunity."

"What opportunity is that?"

"To save yourself," I said.

The first thing Monk did when he walked into the house was to ask Ambrose if he could see the last few months of the *San Francisco Chronicle.*

"Of course you can," Ambrose said. "It's the last two stacks at the end of aisle eight. But don't mess up the order."

Monk headed for the living room. "When have I ever messed up the order of anything?"

Ambrose followed after him. "I find it rather ironic that just yesterday you were suggesting that I throw them all out and now you want them."

"I'll see you tomorrow morning at eight, Mr. Monk," I yelled. "Don't call or contact anyone until then."

I slipped out and made a little detour on my way to my car. I stopped at the junction box outside the kitchen window and disconnected the phone lines. It's no harder than unplugging a light. You might ask how I knew how to do that. A word to the wise: sometimes it pays to watch what the repairmen do when they come to your house.

I called Captain Stottlemeyer from the car on my way back over the Golden Gate Bridge from Marin County into the city.

"Are you still in Golden Gate Park?"

"I'm back at the station. Why?"

"I need you to take a break and meet me for coffee at the Starbucks by my house."

"I'm very busy right now, Natalie. You might not have noticed, but I am in the middle of investigating three murders and I've got the mayor riding me like a donkey."

"That's what I wanted to talk with you about."

He sighed wearily. "There's nothing to talk about. We're in a financial crisis. We can't afford Monk and we don't want his help. I don't know how many different ways I've told you that."

"Mr. Monk has solved the three murders and Bob Sebes was the killer. He knows how Sebes was able to leave the house undetected and he can prove it. If you're interested, it will cost you a White Chocolate Mocha Frappuccino and a brownie to hear our terms."

"Your *what?*"

I hung up and headed for Starbucks.

Stottlemeyer must have used his light and siren, because he got to the Starbucks at the same time I did. But he didn't look thrilled to see me. His surly mood only made me happier. I had leverage and I intended to use it.

"I don't appreciate being dragged out of my office so you and Monk can play games."

"I dragged you out of the office because I can't afford Starbucks anymore and I'm tired of McCheapo coffee. The games haven't started yet but I think they'll be less painful if you're sipping a nice cup of coffee."

We ordered our coffees and brownies and didn't speak to each other again until we got our order and settled down in two wing-backed Queen Anne chairs in the only corner of the room that wasn't lit by the glow of Mac PowerBooks.

He took a sip of his coffee, frosting his mustache with crème. It was hard to take him too seriously like that.

"Has Monk really solved the murders?"

"He has."

"Like he solved them yesterday?"

I shook my head. "I told you, he knows how Sebes fooled the tracking device and slipped out of the house without being seen. He's got him nailed."

"So why are we here having coffee and not in Bob Sebes' house hearing Monk's long-winded summation?"

"Because, as you so gruffly pointed out, Mr. Monk doesn't work for you anymore. You also made it clear that it was impossible for Sebes to be the killer and that Mr. Monk's input on the case was no longer welcome."

"I'll be sure to apologize to Monk, and thank him for his help, as I'm putting the handcuffs on Sebes." Stottlemeyer wiped his mustache with a napkin and ate half his brownie in one bite.

"Oh, you will, but that's not going to happen until our conditions are met."

"Conditions? You've got to be kidding me."

"We want a written agreement, signed by the mayor and the chief of police, guaranteeing Mr. Monk a three-year pay-or-play consulting agreement under the previous payment terms. Upon receipt of that agreement, Mr. Monk will disclose how Bob Sebes pulled off the murders. The agreement will be void if the disclosure doesn't lead to Sebes being arrested and charged with murder on the basis of the evidence gathered on Mr. Monk's information. Oh, and we want the district attorney's office to investigate Mr. Monk's landlord for illegal eviction of a tenant."

Stottlemeyer laughed. "Is Starbucks putting liquor in the coffee now? There's no way the mayor or the chief will agree to those demands."

I casually sipped my coffee. "I think they will."

"That shows how little you know about politics. The city is broke. Giving Monk a three-year pay-or-play consultancy agreement would cause a huge uproar, not just within the police union but with the public. It would also send the message that the police are incapable of solving the murders on their own."

"Which is true," I said.

"We'll nail the killer. We're still in the very early stages of the investigation."

"Let's be honest here, Captain. You're completely and utterly lost. You have no suspects, no evidence, and no case. And while you dither around in all the wrong directions, the witnesses you need to put Sebes in jail and recover the billions of dollars that he swindled are getting killed, one by one. When he walks out of court a free man, what message is *that* going to send?"

Stottlemeyer finished his coffee. "Nice try, Natalie. As Monk's friend, I appreciate what you're trying to do for him. He's damn lucky to have you. But I'm not going to take your deal upstairs. They would laugh at it and maybe even demote me for being dumb enough to take it to them."

"Mr. Monk can give you Bob Sebes, not just for the murders but for the financial swindle, too."

"You're going way, way over the top now." Stottlemeyer finished off the other half of his brownie.

"Am I? With a triple-murder charge hanging over his head, Sebes will tell you what he did with every swindled penny if it will keep him from the gas chamber. That would be a public relations bonanza for the city, far overshadowing whatever minor brouhaha giving Mr. Monk a consultancy agreement for his heroic efforts might raise."

"I'm not convinced that Monk has solved the case," Stottlemeyer said. "The tracking unit is tamperproof and there's no way Sebes could walk out of that house without the mob of reporters seeing him. I also know that Monk has taken a lot of hits in the last week or so that have seriously affected his judgment."

"I understand. If you don't like the deal, that's no problem. I came to you first as a courtesy. I'll go to the feds next and ask for a percentage of the recovered funds as Mr. Monk's fee. It might even be more lucrative for him than the consultancy agreement."

I worked on my coffee and brownie for a few moments while Stottlemeyer narrowed his eyes at me and mulled over what I'd said. I tried to appear confident, relaxed, and a little smug, like all my problems had been solved.

"There's a big flaw in your scheme," Stottlemeyer said. "If Monk has really solved the crime, he won't be able to keep the solution to himself. He'll tell me everything for nothing."

I shook my head and gave Stottlemeyer my best poker face. "Not this time. He's lost too much and he is too hurt by your lack of confidence in him."

"He's the best detective I've ever known, but even he's got to be wrong sometime."

"This isn't that time."

"Let's say you're right. We both know that Monk desperately wants to nail Sebes. I don't need to do anything. He won't keep quiet waiting for a deal and risk the guy killing someone else in the meantime. He couldn't live with that on his conscience."

"That's true. That's why this deal has an expiration date of noon tomorrow. If we don't hear from you by then, the feds get the arrest and you, the chief, and the mayor get egg on your faces." I got up and wiped the brownie crumbs off my pants. "Mr. Monk has never been wrong about murder before. You should think about that. So should your bosses. Thanks for the coffee, Captain."

I walked out. There was nothing more to talk about, plus I wasn't sure how long I could maintain my poker face under the glare of an experienced interrogator.

This was more than just a homicide investigation now. It was my house, food on the table, my daughter's college education, and Monk's financial future that were at stake here.

Our salvation depended on Monk proving the impossible was possible, and on the chief, the mayor, and the captain being desperate and frightened enough to believe that he could.

I hoped that wasn't asking too much.

CHAPTER TWENTY-SEVEN:
MR. MONK GETS WET

I hardly slept that night. I was too keyed up thinking about the endgame that I knew would play out the next morning. No matter what happened, Sebes would end up behind bars. The big question mark was whether Monk and I would be able to leverage the situation to save ourselves.

It all depended on what Monk did or didn't do.

Could I convince Monk to keep his mouth shut until it could do us the most good?

I wasn't sure that I could.

Monk's eagerness to nail Sebes, and announce the solution to the mystery, might trump his self-interest . . . and mine.

The news about Duncan Dern's murder was all over the front page of the *San Francisco Chronicle*. One of the articles focused on the impact the murder would have on prosecuting Sebes for his Ponzi scheme. Several pundits opined that the case against Sebes could fall apart before it ever got to the courtroom.

I was pleased by the news, not because I wanted Sebes to get away with his crimes but because it put even more pressure on law enforcement to accept my offer before things got even worse.

On my way out to Tewksbury, I called Kiana at Fashion Frisson and let her know that we wouldn't be coming in for personal reasons and that I wouldn't blame her if she fired us for letting her down. But she took the news with giddy nonchalance.

"No worries," she said. "The mall is closed anyway and I don't know when the police are going to let them open it up."

"What happened?" I asked innocently.

"Our own security guards tried to rob a jewelry store last night and Randy caught them. There was a shoot-out and everything."

"Is Randy okay?"

"He's wonderful. He's like an action hero."

"I'm sure he'd love to hear that."

"Oh, he knows. He's the one who told me."

I was glad that things had worked out so well for Disher and that we still had a job to go back to if my plan didn't work out.

I arrived at Ambrose's house a few minutes before eight and crept up to the junction box. I was reconnecting the phone lines when I sensed someone watching me. I stepped back and saw Ambrose looking at me disapprovingly from the kitchen window.

This wasn't good.

The front door was open, and he was waiting for me in the entryway as I walked up.

"Why did you disconnect my phone?"

"I wanted to be sure that Mr. Monk couldn't call Captain Stottlemeyer."

"You could have discussed it with me first."

"It didn't occur to me to disconnect the phones until I was walking to my car. After that, it would have been awkward to come back and explain myself to you."

"But it wasn't awkward for you to vandalize my home."

"I'm sorry, Ambrose. It was wrong. I shouldn't have done it. But the phone is fixed."

"You violated my home and my trust. You haven't fixed that yet."

"I did it for Mr. Monk. I'm trying to get him his job back."

"And yours, too," Ambrose said.

"Yes."

"So you really vandalized my home for

351

yourself."

"For Mr. Monk, myself, and for Julie. But I think calling what I did *vandalizing* is a little harsh. It was more of a prank."

"For forty years, people have been pulling pranks on me. Egging my house, toilet-papering my plants, leaving dog excrement on my porch. They know I can't do anything about it. They think it's funny and harmless to harass the strange man who never leaves his house. I didn't think you were one of those nasty people."

"I'm not and you know it. What I did wasn't a prank, it wasn't vandalizing, it wasn't meant as an insult, and no harm was done."

"Really? What if Adrian slipped on the stairs and broke his back? How would I have called for help?"

"You could have yelled out the window."

"My house could be burning down and my neighbors wouldn't help. You know that."

It was true. His house was once on fire and his neighbors did nothing. Of course, it was one of his neighbors who started the blaze, but that's another story.

"You're right, Ambrose, and I'm wrong. I'm so sorry. What can I do to make it up to you?"

Ambrose shrugged.

"How about if I come over next Saturday, make you waffles, and then we can watch *Home Alone* together?"

Ambrose smiled. "That's a start."

Monk came down from upstairs carrying a stack of newspapers. "I thought you'd never get here. You need to call Captain Stottlemeyer and tell him that I've solved the case."

"I already have," I said.

"Is he going to meet us at Sebes' house?"

"Eventually."

"What does that mean?"

"I'll explain on the way," I said.

Monk came outside. Ambrose called out after him.

"I need those newspapers back, Adrian. In pristine condition."

Monk stopped and gave Ambrose a withering look. "Have you forgotten who you are talking to? I'm the one who taught you how to iron a newspaper."

"I don't like it when my belongings leave the house. What if they don't come back?"

"They will," Monk said. "Even Dad came back."

"I don't want to wait thirty years for those newspapers."

"I'll bring them back before that."

We got into the car, and on our way back into the city, in stop-and-go rush-hour traffic, I explained to Monk the offer that I'd made to Stottlemeyer.

Monk listened without interruption, and when I was finished, he nodded.

"So is the captain going to meet us at Sebes' house?"

"You already asked me that. The captain hasn't accepted our conditions yet. My guess is that he will, but he has until noon today to make his move. If he doesn't, then we go to the feds."

Monk squirmed in his seat. "I'm not comfortable with this."

"You aren't comfortable with anything."

"We have to go to Sebes' house now."

"He's not going to let us in, and even if he did, it won't do you any good to confront him without the police."

"I could make a citizen's arrest."

"All you'd be doing is tipping him off that you're on to him and giving him a chance to cover his tracks. You have the leverage now to get the city to give you your consulting job back. Do you really want to work at Fashion Frisson and live with your brother?"

"I can't take the chance that Sebes might kill somebody else while we're waiting for the mayor and the chief of police to mull over your demands."

"So we make sure that he doesn't," I said, even though I didn't know how we could keep Sebes under any closer surveillance than the police and the media already were.

Monk nodded. "Okay. That's what we'll do."

I found us a primo parking spot in a red zone behind the row of police vehicles, news vans, and satellite trucks across the street and half a block down from Sebes' house. We could see part of Sebes' house and front gate from our car, and that seemed fine to Monk, though he was very uncomfortable with us "flagrantly breaking the law" to do it.

I assured Monk that we weren't parking if we remained in the car. We were idling. Parking meant stopping and leaving your unoccupied car behind.

Monk wasn't convinced. I told him that I'd never been ticketed by a cop for idling in a red zone. Once or twice I'd been asked to move on, so I drove around the block until the cop left and then parked in the red zone again.

I wasn't sure what we were waiting in the red zone to see anyway. If Sebes walked out of the house, the reporters would see him before we did. I noticed a manhole cover in the street near our car and wondered if maybe Disher was on the right track about the secret tunnel after all.

I glanced at the newspapers that Monk had brought along. They all had pictures of Sebes, or his wife, or both of them on the front page. I wondered if he was going to use the newspapers as prosecution exhibits to make his case and, if so, why.

I could have asked Monk all of those questions but I knew that he wouldn't answer them, not without the killer in front of us.

Monk lived for his summations, it was the one moment in his life when he was in absolute control and the entire universe felt balanced. He wasn't going to diminish that experience for me.

He suddenly straightened up in his seat. "Start the car."

I followed his gaze and saw Sebes' gate open and his black Mercedes glide out. Since the reporters weren't mobbing the car, I figured Anna Sebes was on her own.

"But it's just his wife," I said.

The car passed us and Monk started nudging me.

"Hurry up. She's getting away!"

I made a U-turn and followed her. "I thought you said that Sebes was the killer."

"He is."

"Then why are we following his wife?"

Monk didn't answer. He just leaned forward, his hands on the dash, keeping her under close scrutiny. I kept a car or two between us so she wouldn't notice that she was being tailed.

She headed north on Pierce and made a right onto a long, flat stretch of Lombard, which took us past motels, bars, hardware stores, and garages. It wasn't San Francisco's most picturesque street.

A Saab and a Miata were between her car and ours, but I could see her just fine. She made it easy by staying in the right lane and being very conscientious about using her turn signals, giving me plenty of notice about her intentions.

"Oh my God," Monk said.

"What's wrong?"

He pointed a little ways ahead of us. "I think she's going to that gas station with the drive-thru car wash."

"What's wrong with that?"

"Her car is filthy!"

"So you think she should be getting a more thorough cleaning."

"We can't let her clean that car!"

I gave him a look. "Are you sick? Since when have you ever objected to anything being cleaned?"

"That filth is evidence," he said. "Her car is covered in bird excrement."

I saw some bird crap and berry stains on the trunk when she'd first passed us, but I didn't think her car was any dirtier than mine had been last night.

In Golden Gate Park . . .

. . . at the scene of Duncan Dern's murder.

The Saab in front of us came to a sudden stop and I was so distracted by my thoughts that I had to slam on my brakes to avoid rear-ending him. The driver stopped to wait for someone to pull out of a parking space on the street. Half a block ahead, I could see Anna Sebes' car turning into the gas station.

I tried to go around the car in front of me but nobody in the left lane would let me in. We were stuck.

Monk squealed in frustration and jumped out of the car. While I waited for an opening, Monk ran to the gas station and I lost sight of him.

After what seemed like an eternity, I found an opening and cut into it, nearly clipping the front of a Volvo in the process. I sped around the Saab and into the gas station just in time to see Anna Sebes' car going into the car wash as Monk banged on her window.

But she didn't stop. Anna drove right into the center of the automated car wash.

Monk leapt up onto her hood and spread his body protectively across it just as the automated cleaning apparatus moved on a track over the car. He held on tight and pressed his face against the windshield as the high-powered jets blasted the car with water and nearly whipped off his clothes.

I drove my car around to the rear of the car wash and blocked the exit. Then all I could do was get out and watch as the cleaning machine moved back and forth along its track, first soaking the car and Monk with detergent foam and then whipping them with hundreds of strips of cloth on giant rotating cylindrical scrubbers. That had to hurt.

My cell phone rang. It was Stottlemeyer.

"Okay," he said. "You've got a deal. We'll meet you at Sebes' place."

The washing equipment was going into its next cycle, power-rinsing the soap off of Monk and the car. Monk was holding on tight and I could see Anna Sebes through the suds on the windshield staring at him in horror while talking animatedly to someone on her cell phone.

"That's great, Captain. But there's a slight

change of plans. Could you meet us at Sav-Mor Gas and Wash on Lombard? And bring a forensic team along and something dry for Monk to wear."

I hung up before Stottlemeyer could ask any questions.

Anna Sebes floored her Mercedes and burst out of the car wash the instant the dry cycle was over.

She was heading right for me.

I dove out of the way and she slammed into my car, plowing it into a telephone pole.

The impact sent Monk flying, landing hard on his back on the hood of my crumpled car. She backed up and was about to drive around my car when a black-and-white police car screeched up from Lombard and blocked her. She wasn't going anywhere.

I got up off the ground and hurried over to Monk. He was soaking wet and groaning. The front of his clothes was stained with berries and poop, but there was still plenty of the mess on her hood.

"Are you okay, Mr. Monk?"

He propped himself up on his elbows and spit out a mouthful of soap. "Somebody kill me and put me out of my misery."

"I may be mistaken, but I think that's

what Anna Sebes just tried to do."

"Could you ask her to please try again?"

CHAPTER TWENTY-EIGHT:
MR. MONK BREAKS
THE PERFECT ALIBI

Captain Stottlemeyer looked like he was in pain. He was grimacing and rubbing his forehead.

The car wash was closed off, police officers were taking reports from witnesses, and the forensic techs who'd taken Monk's clothes were now going over Anna Sebes' Mercedes and what was left of my Buick Lucerne, which was now shaped like bow-tie pasta.

Monk was wearing a gray SFPD sweat suit, which he had refused to put on until Stottlemeyer assured him that it was brand-new and that just because it was called a sweat suit, that didn't mean any sweat was added to the garment in the manufacturing process. He eventually changed clothes in the sterile environment of the forensics van.

Disher was talking to Anna Sebes, scribbling furiously in his notebook to keep up with her rapid speech and vivid profanity.

"Why isn't she in handcuffs?" Monk asked.

"Because I'm not entirely sure who is at fault here," Stottlemeyer said.

"She tried to kill us," I said.

"It was self-defense," Anna snapped and marched over to us. Disher rushed to keep up.

"Oh, give me a break," I said. "You weren't in any danger."

"The hell I wasn't," Anna said, pointing a gnarled, white-gloved finger at Monk. "That crazy man followed me here from my house. The moment I stopped my car, he ran up to my door, pounded his fists on my window, and demanded that I get out. So I drove into the car wash to get away and that psycho threw himself on the hood, staring at me the whole time with the twisted, insane look on his face that serial killers have."

"I know that look," Disher said. "It's sort of like this."

He furrowed his brow, flared his nostrils, and snarled. It looked to me like an expression of severe constipation rather than inherent evil.

"When his enabler blocked the exit with her car" — Anna gestured to me — "I was certain it was an ambush and that my life was in danger. So I called the police."

"A very clever move to throw suspicion off of you," Monk said. "But it failed."

"Suspicion of what?" she asked.

"Do you deny that you came here to wash the dirt off your car?"

"Of course I don't. I came to the car wash to wash my car. Isn't that what car washes are for, to wash your car? I wasn't aware that was a crime."

"It is when the dirt is evidence. The forensic experts will confirm that the bird doo-doo and berry stains on your car are a day old and came from Golden Gate Park, where Duncan Dern was strangled yesterday. This proves that you were there."

"As I often am, along with thousands of other San Franciscans, but I didn't kill Duncan Dern." She took off her gloves and showed us her arthritic hands. "If I was capable of strangling anybody, which sadly I am not, I would strangle you right now."

Stottlemeyer looked like he was tempted, too. "Is that true, Monk? Did you follow her here, pound on her window, and jump on the hood of her car?"

"Yes."

"Why?"

"To protect the filth," Monk said.

Stottlemeyer stared at him in disbelief.

"Did I hear you right? Did you just say 'to protect the filth'?"

"That filth puts this car in Golden Gate Park yesterday. You'll also find Dalmatian hairs and pine needles in the car, proving that she's also been to Lincoln Clovis' home and Russell Haxby's backyard."

"Of course I have, you lunatic. Both of those men worked with Bob for years and were dear friends. Or at least we thought they were until they swindled all of Bob's clients and framed him for their crimes."

Stottlemeyer took a deep breath and turned to me with an expression not unlike the one Disher demonstrated earlier.

"Can I speak to you for a moment in private?"

It wasn't a request as much as it was an order. I followed Stottlemeyer over to the car wash, out of earshot of Monk, Disher, and Anna Sebes.

"Adrian Monk threw himself on a dirty car to stop it from being cleaned," Stottlemeyer said. "If that doesn't scream out to you that he's completely lost his mind, nothing will."

"Mr. Monk knows what he's doing. It's all part of his cunning plan."

"You're forgetting who you're talking to, Natalie. I've known Monk a lot longer than you have. You have no idea what he's doing and he doesn't either."

"He's building his case."

"There is no case. The deal is off."

"You can't do that," I said. "He's solved the murders."

"I can't support him after this. Any reasonable person who found themselves in Anna Sebes' shoes today would have done the same thing that she did."

"Mr. Monk told you why he jumped on her car."

"And it's insane," Stottlemeyer said. "She's right. The crap on her car and the dog hair inside of it prove absolutely nothing. He's just lost whatever credibility he had left with us or with the feds."

"So forget the deal. You've still got to take Mr. Monk back to confront Bob Sebes and make his case."

"Why would I want to do that?"

"Because if Mr. Monk is right, Bob Sebes murdered three people and is damn close to getting away with it. But if Mr. Monk is wrong, you can cut him out of the investigation and any future police work without feeling any lingering doubt or guilt about it."

"What makes you think that's what I'd feel?"

"Because you know that solving crimes is what Mr. Monk was born to do and that he's never been wrong about murder before. I know he sounds crazy today, but in the end, it always makes sense."

"This might be the one time that it doesn't."

"It might be," I said. "But we won't know until it's over. Can you live with not knowing?"

Once again, Monk insisted on wearing a crime scene jumpsuit, gloves, and booties before entering Bob Sebes' house. He also brought along his stack of newspapers, but only after he'd carefully picked off the bits of shattered glass from the car crash.

Stottlemeyer drove me and Monk to the house while Disher drove Anna, who refused to be in the same car with us, which was fine with me. I didn't want to be near her, either. The fact that she'd trashed my car, and what that was going to cost me, was just beginning to sink in.

We all walked up to the front door of the Sebes house together, causing a flurry of interest from the press photographers.

Bob met us at the door in a polo shirt, shorts, and leather flip-flops, his Triax XG7 8210 ankle bracelet prominently displayed for the media. He and his wife dramatically embraced, as if they'd both survived a harrowing experience and a long separation. It was a wonderful performance.

We went into the house and Sebes slammed the front door shut, immediately confronting Stottlemeyer.

"How can you bring Monk into my house after he brutally assaulted my wife? She barely escaped with her life. Why isn't he behind bars where he belongs?"

"Why aren't you?" I asked.

"I demand an explanation," Bob said, ignoring my remark.

Stottlemeyer glanced at Monk. "That's your cue."

"You killed Russell Haxby, Lincoln Clovis, and Duncan Dern," Monk said. "And I can prove it."

"Oh God, not this insanity again. I am under house arrest. I've got a GPS tracking unit bolted to my leg, and my house is surrounded day and night by a pack of reporters. Why are you still listening to this madman's rantings?"

Bob turned his back to us and stomped into the living room with its spectacular view of the bay. I was sure the drapes on the window were open for the benefit of the photographers outside. He was going to do everything he could to use the incident at the car wash to his advantage in the media, to portray himself and his wife as victims.

"You're right, except for the ranting-madman part," Monk said as we followed Bob into the living room. "The tracking unit is absolutely tamperproof and you couldn't walk outside that door without being seen."

"So you're saying that his wife is the killer and she did it for him," Disher said.

Monk shook his head. "No, I'm not. The way they were killed rules her out. Anna couldn't have killed them, not with her arthritic hands. Bob is the murderer."

"So how did I do it, Monk?" Bob said. "Teleportation? Astral projection? Or maybe I simply willed them to die and they did."

"For me, the key to figuring out how you did it was to accept two facts — the tracking device on your ankle is tamperproof and your wife is physically incapable of being the killer. And that explains everything."

"It does?" Disher said.

"Why do you think Bob is always wearing shorts and modeling his tracking unit in front of this picture window?"

Disher shrugged.

"To remind everybody that he's wearing a tamperproof tracking unit," Monk said. "Why do you think Lincoln Clovis was hung and Duncan Dern strangled when there were so many other, more efficient ways to kill them?"

Disher shrugged again.

"To clear his wife as a suspect in the murders," Monk said. "But that arrogance is his undoing."

"You're babbling incoherently," Bob said, "but I suppose that's to be expected from a lunatic."

Anna went to her husband's side and put her arm around him. "Do we really have to be subjected to any more of this senseless drivel?"

"There's no harm in hearing him out," the captain said. "But it would be nice if you'd just get to the point, Monk."

"Here's what happened . . ."

As soon as Monk said those magic words, my heart raced and I couldn't help smiling. He said it with such confidence and contentment that I had no doubt that everything was going to fit, that balance would be restored, and that our troubles would be over.

Monk explained that Sebes knew his Ponzi scheme was on the verge of collapse and inevitable discovery days, perhaps weeks, before it happened because so many people were withdrawing money and he didn't have the cash to cover it all. Sebes also knew that he would be doomed if Haxby, Clovis, and Dern ever became government witnesses. His only hope for freedom, or lesser charges, was to keep them from talking, and he couldn't do that from a jail cell.

"So you had your lawyer fight for house arrest instead of imprisonment before trial. He persuaded the judge that you weren't a flight risk and that with the Triax XG7 8210, the most secure tracking device on Earth, strapped to your ankle, you couldn't go anywhere," Monk said. "The judge agreed, and was so convinced by your lawyer's argument that she specifically ordered that the police use the Triax XG7 8210 on you. What she didn't know was that the reason your lawyer argued so passionately for that particular model was because you'd already purchased one for yourself weeks earlier."

"What good would that do him?" Stottlemeyer asked. "We supplied the unit and placed it on his ankle. There was no way he could have swapped it out with his own tampered unit without being detected."

"The extra unit wasn't for him," Monk said. "It was for his wife. He calibrated her device so it was emitting the same unique signal as the one around his ankle."

Now I knew why everything fell into place for Monk during his session with Dr. Bell.

"They were on the same wavelength," I said.

"Exactly. Whenever he wanted to slip out of the house, she would strap the device to her ankle and activate it. That way, he could block the signal on his device without the breach being detected by the police."

"So it was Anna who was home drinking while her husband was out murdering Lincoln Clovis," I said. "They didn't realize the Triax XG7 8210 also measured alcohol consumption. That mistake almost torpedoed everything."

"It did," Monk said. "It just took me longer than I would have liked to figure it all out."

I looked at the Sebeses. Bob and Anna were clutching each other even tighter now and they both looked a little pale. I would, too, if I was facing the death penalty. It probably made a possible hundred-year prison sentence for financial crimes look attractive by comparison.

"That doesn't explain how Bob was able to get in and out of the house without being seen," Disher said. "Have you found the secret tunnel?"

"Bob didn't need a tunnel," Monk said. "He just walked right out the front door."

"He would have been seen," Stottlemeyer said.

"He was," Monk said, and held up one of his newspapers, which showed a picture of Anna Sebes leaving the house wearing an enormous hat, big sunglasses, and gloves. "Bob walked out dressed as his wife."

The reason Anna left the house every single day, Monk explained, was so it would become routine and mundane, the press would get used to it, and nobody would question her coming and going anymore or bother to follow her.

"Those blisters on his pestilent feet aren't from his raging case of *tinea pedis* but from wearing women's shoes," Monk said. "Either he was wearing his wife's or she bought an identical, slightly larger pair for him."

"You can't prove any of that," Bob said.

"You are slightly taller than Anna, but when you wear heels, that difference in height is substantially greater." Monk laid several newspapers down on the coffee table. "Each of these pictures appears to show Anna Sebes leaving the house at different times. In all three of these pictures, she is wearing the same shoes, but only in two of them is she the same height relative to windows she is passing." Monk pointed to one of the photos. "In this one, she's markedly higher. How is that possible if she's wearing the same shoes?"

"It's obviously an optical illusion created by the camera angle," Anna said.

"That may be an illusion, but the search warrant I'm going to get certainly won't be," Stottlemeyer said. "And I'm sure the additional Triax XG7 8210 and the extra pair of women's shoes that we're going to find won't be illusions, either."

Monk took a step toward Sebes and looked him right in the eye. "You're finished, Bob. The only upside to your tragic downfall is the warning it will send to others for generations to come: This is what can happen if you don't practice good foot hygiene."

While Disher placed Bob and Anna Sebes under arrest and read them their rights, Stottlemeyer called a judge for a search warrant, explained the situation, and immediately got the authorization he needed to proceed.

Hearing that, Bob and Anna demanded to see their lawyer. They knew they were finished. I'm sure Bob was already considering the pros and cons of the fungal-foot brain defense. There wasn't much else he could try.

The captain called in a forensics unit to handle the search, took another call, then waved the two of us over to him.

"We've got Sebes on those three murders and he knows it," Stottlemeyer said. "I think it'll go down just like Natalie predicted it would. He'll plead guilty to the Ponzi scheme and trade us all the money that he's hidden away in exchange for taking the death penalty off the table for him and showing some mercy to his wife."

"I certainly hope so," Monk said. "I desperately need whatever I can get back from my life savings."

"I think I can ease some of your financial worries." Stottlemeyer took a folded sheet of paper from his coat pocket and handed it to him. "There's your agreement, Monk, signed by the mayor and the chief of police."

"You're going to honor it after all?" I said.

"Monk held up his end of the bargain and we're going to hold up ours. That's a three-year pay-or-play consulting agreement, effective immediately and retroactive to the day we let him go. In addition, the city attorney will harass and intimidate Monk's landlord into revoking his eviction. And I'm even gonna throw in a police report on the car wash incident that you can give your insurance company so you won't be liable for the damage to your car."

"Wow. That's wonderful," I said. "Thank you, Captain."

"It's the least I can do." Stottlemeyer offered Monk his hand. "I'm sorry about everything. I hope you can forgive me."

They shook hands.

"You have nothing to apologize for, Captain. You were doing your job."

"I could have shown a lot more faith in you," he said. "The way Natalie did."

"She has to," Monk said. "She works for me."

"I'm your friend, Monk. And friends stick up for one another, through thick or thin, no matter what."

"You have."

Stottlemeyer shook his head. "I jerked you around and didn't give you the support you needed. I put the job in front of our friendship and that wasn't right."

"After Trudy was killed, I had a total meltdown. I was thrown off the force. Nobody wanted to have anything to do with me. But you didn't walk away. You never gave up on me. You cashed in every IOU you had and fought to get me hired as a police consultant. You saved me, Leland."

"I didn't this time."

Monk shrugged. "You will next time."

"That's a promise," Stottlemeyer said and started to walk away, when something seemed to occur to him. "By the way, that call I got was from the DA. The jury came back with their verdict in the Moggridge trial."

"Already?" I said.

"They only deliberated for thirty minutes, not counting the hour they took to eat one last lunch on the city's dime. The jury found the greedy SOB guilty on every count. So it's a winning day for the Good Guys all around."

"Yes, it is," I said.

"It bodes well for the future," he said.

"The future never bodes well," Monk said. "You can always be certain that you're facing disappointment and misery."

"I'm glad to see you're back to your old cheerful self again." The captain clapped Monk on the back and went to confer with Disher.

"I'm proud of you, Mr. Monk."

"For what?" he asked.

"For being so kind and forgiving to Captain Stottlemeyer. That couldn't have been easy after everything you've been through this week."

"He's my boss. It's called kissing up," Monk said. "You ought to try it sometime." I smiled at him. "What do you think I'm doing right now?"

ABOUT THE AUTHOR

Lee Goldberg has written episodes for the USA Network television series *Monk,* as well as many other programs. He is a two-time Edgar® Award nominee and the author of the acclaimed *Diagnosis Murder* novels, based on the TV series for which he was a writer and executive producer. His previous *Monk* novels are available in paperback, including *Mr. Monk and the Two Assistants,* which won the Scribe Award for Best Novel from the International Association of Media Tie-In Writers.

We hope you have enjoyed this Large Print book. Other Thorndike, Wheeler, Kennebec, and Chivers Press Large Print books are available at your library or directly from the publishers.

For information about current and upcoming titles, please call or write, without obligation, to:

Publisher
Thorndike Press
295 Kennedy Memorial Drive
Waterville, ME 04901
Tel. (800) 223-1244

or visit our Web site at:

http://gale.cengage.com/thorndike

OR

Chivers Large Print
published by AudioGO Ltd
St James House, The Square
Lower Bristol Road
Bath BA2 3BH
England
Tel. +44(0) 800 136919
email: info@audiogo.co.uk
www.audiogo.co.uk

All our Large Print titles are designed for easy reading, and all our books are made to last.